HELP
Among Us

GINIA FALCÓN

Copyright © 2024 Ginia Falcón
All rights reserved
First Edition

Fulton Books
Meadville, PA

Published by Fulton Books 2024

ISBN 979-8-88731-479-2 (paperback)
ISBN 979-8-88731-480-8 (digital)

Printed in the United States of America

To all the people who have inspired me in my faith in Jesus and who believed in me as a writer. Special mention goes to my parents and my sister, Kat, who helped shape my faith. Mostly, I want to thank my children, Christopher and Juliana, and especially my husband, Chuck (the love of my life), for believing in me and pushing me to keep going. I love you all so much!

Prologue

If only certain days came with a warning label—especially for those that would change everything. Pulling out of the school parking lot on a cold Saturday morning in February, the family smiles and waves back at their child now standing next to the gym entrance, waiting for his basketball practice to begin. As always, there is a brief pang of sadness followed by the paternal pride of accomplishment. Everything was going to be okay. They would be reunited in a few hours; this was just a normal, short separation.

Navigating their way through the heavy traffic, they turn onto the highway entrance ramp and begin the necessary acceleration to find a place in the endless blur of fast-moving missiles. After settling into the flow, they turn on the radio and start singing with the music. For a brief moment, life is as it is meant to be.

Cocooned in their private world, they have no idea what is happening just ahead of them. There is no time for their brains to process the vision of the eighteen-wheeler, engulfed in flames, that has just bounced-flipped over the grassy median onto their side of the highway and is now rolling end over end toward them. The screeching of forty tons of metal scraping the highway at sixty-five miles an hour was blending with the music playing on their car radio. How strange, they thought, the second before impact, that they are still toasty warm from their car heater.

In a single instant, life changed for them—forever.

Chapter 1

"Hey, honey, Maria? Where are you?" Paul shouted in a panic. "Lexy, sweetie, are you there? Please answer Daddy!" Paul was trying with all of his might to control his fear. He knew that they crashed. My god! Of course they crashed. He remembered the loud and brutal impact of crashing into the truck, but he had no idea what happened after that. Looking around, he struggled to see through a blanket of thick fog and intermittent bright lights. He turned and started making his way toward what looked like a stone wall. After stumbling over a large tree root that was arching through the ground, he saw something move. "Maria? Lexy? Please answer me!" he shouted in desperation. Where were his wife and daughter? Where, in fact, was he? Where were the highway, their car, and especially the massive truck that should now be a blazing inferno?

"Paul? Paul, is that you?" Maria called out. "Thank goodness you are all right! We are over here on the bench."

Never had a voice sounded so sweet to him. Paul almost fainted with relief. He was still having trouble seeing when his foot slid on something slippery. The next thing he knew, he was flat on his back with a wave of water rushing over him.

"Oh, Paul, watch out for the fishpond over here," Maria called out.

"Thanks for the warning," gurgled Paul, now sitting up in the pond, wiping water off of his face and pulling bits of seaweed from his head. "I'll make sure that I go around it," he mumbled sarcastically. In his wet surroundings, Paul took a moment to look around. Through the thinner patches of fog, he could see that they were no longer near the highway. In fact, it looked like they were in some kind of park or lush garden.

"Do you have any idea where we are?" he asked. "And have you ever seen light that particular color before?" In all of his days, he had never seen light the color of pure gold before. Holding out his hand, he watched the shimmering gold dance on his skin and reflect back up to the sky. Looking up, the light changed and appeared to be moving, mixing in dazzling shades of pink, sky blue, and dark purple. All brilliant, all beautiful. It was like a stained-glass window, yet it was everywhere, mixing in with the fog. He stood up, and a wash of water dripped down from his clothes.

"Daddy, look here! I have never seen fish these colors before! Come look!" Lexy, his eight-year-old daughter, had come toward the fishpond and was pointing in the water. He made his way, sloshing through the water, and then stopped in amazement as he looked where she was indicating. While he had seen his share of beautiful carp before, he had never seen fish shimmering like bars of gold and silver swimming around. They were dazzling and seemed to be generating the brilliance of their light, not merely reflecting it—kind of glowing from within.

Next, a fish that sparkled like a giant diamond swam right up to him. It circled him a couple of times and then rose to the surface of the water. Being out of the water intensified the sparkling, reflecting back the golden light beams from the sky in all directions. It radiated so brightly that Paul had to shield his eyes. The fish stared right at him for a minute, perplexed. "If you want to swim, why not change into fish form?" the fish asked. "Or perhaps this is an experiment you are engaging in?"

Paul was rendered speechless, in shock, and started babbling a bit. "I, uhm…I, ahh…Lexy?" Paul asked his daughter, "Did you hear the fish say something?" Either he was dreaming all of this or he was becoming delusional after the crash.

"Sure, Dad," Lexy responded. "He wants to know why you haven't changed into a fish." Lexy was clearly mesmerized by the fish, squinting hard to still look at him in the blinding light. "Wow! He is the most beautiful fish I've ever seen!"

"Why, thank you," the fish said. "I've worked hard to perfect this particular fish form."

"Worked hard?" asked Lexy. "So you don't always look like this?"

"Oh no!" laughed the fish. "The white diamond shell took many tries to perfect. But never give up, that's my motto!" The fish stopped laughing and then began to observe them both for a moment. Growing serious, he looked back and forth at each of them, staring into their eyes and around their heads. "Wait a moment, what is going on here? Who are you?" The fish swam quickly to the edge of the pond and then, in a flash, transformed into a short old man with a gray sweatshirt, navy-blue swim trunks, and neon-green swim fins. "How did you two get here?" he asked them.

"Wow!" screamed Lexy, clapping in appreciation.

Paul, not quite as appreciative as his daughter, felt his knees give way and nearly sank back down into the pond. He didn't think he could take any more bizarre occurrences today. Calling on all of his self-control, he answered, "We aren't sure ourselves. Truthfully, I am not even sure where 'here' is. The last thing I remember is that we were in our car, colliding hard into an eighteen-wheeler on the highway. Then, the next moment"—he gestured widely around him—"we find ourselves here, wherever this place is."

"Paul…Paul, I can't get any service on my cell here," Maria said, walking up to all of them while looking down at her phone. "Ha! Now I know one place in the United States that Verizon doesn't cover! Oh, hello!" She looked up finally. "Who are you?" she said to the old man.

"He's a fish," answered Lexy, gleaming up at her mom.

"Well, not exactly," answered the fish-man, smiling at Lexy.

"A fish? Uhm, am I missing something?" Maria asked Paul.

"Hang on a minute, hun. The, uh, fish-gentleman was about to tell us where we are," answered Paul.

"You are in the Garden Region, of course," answered the fish-man. "And it appears that this is a rather unexpected visit for you," he added. "I am Jonah, one of the many caretakers of this area."

"So," interrupted Lexy, pointing to the pond, "are all of the fish in there people too?"

"No," Jonah laughed. "Other than your father, I'm the only 'person' swimming in the pond right now."

"Nice to meet you, Jonah," Paul answered, turning back to the conversation. "Sorry to appear ignorant, but what is the 'Garden Region'? And how can we get back to Chicago?"

"Chicago, is it?" Jonah answered with a smile. "Very interesting place. I haven't been there in a while. Tell me, have the Cubs won the World Series yet? I have been immersed in my duties here and haven't heard any news."

Paul closed his eyes and mentally counted to ten in an effort to control his exasperation and rapidly building panic. "Jonah, under normal circumstances I would love to discuss sports with you. However, I am trying to figure out how we got here, to this 'Garden Region' after somehow surviving a deadly car crash. We need to get back to Chicago and find our son. He should be done with his basketball practice soon, and we need to pick him up." Paul inhaled and then slowly released his breath. "Please, Jonah, tell us how we can get back."

Jonah looked at Paul a moment before speaking. His eyes were full of kindness and sympathy. In a soft voice, he answered, "Paul, I think you already know where you are. Search your heart."

Paul stood there, frozen, unable to speak or breathe. The moment of silence was broken with violent sobs bursting out of Maria as she sank to the ground. "No!" she whispered. "This can't be true! We have to get Michael!" As understanding of her situation sank in, she began to panic, her chest heaving. Turning to her husband, she grabbed his leg and started to scream, "Paul! Paul! We have to get Michael! Don't you understand? We can't leave him all alone! Who will take care of him? How will he grow up without us? He is only twelve years old! He has no one!"

Paul sat down beside Maria and grabbed her, holding her. He closed his eyes, silent tears streaming down his face, and felt her body convulsing with her uncontrollable sobs. He felt helpless as all he could give her at that moment was his body to lean on.

Jonah, in anticipation of this moment, had already taken Lexy over by a tree and was showing her how the tree fruit could turn into gemstones one moment and back into fruit the next. "Lexy, do you understand where you are?" Jonah asked her.

"We are in heaven, aren't we?" she answered. Jonah remarked to himself how children often are able to grasp situations before adults can. They have less noise in their minds to distract them.

"Yes, Lexy, you are. But normally the Garden Region isn't the place where new arrivals come. I am going to contact a navigator to assist you and your family." He walked over to the back of the tree and pulled down one of the branches. Out popped a small white box. Jonah pressed a small button, and a loud voice answered, "Destination?"

"Local navigation, please," Jonah responded.

"Connecting," the voice answered back.

"Local navigation, Remus speaking."

"Remus? This is Jonah in the Garden Region. I have an interesting case for you. A family has unexpectedly shown up here. And, oddly enough, they are new arrivals."

"Jonah, this is a great relief. Central dispatch informed us earlier that there was an interruption in the flow cycle. We knew that they had crossed over, but we were unable to locate their entry point. I am sending a navigator now to assist them in their transition."

"Thanks, Remus. We await the navigator." Jonah replaced the white box into the tree branch. He took Lexy's hand and smiled as he spoke, "Lexy, someone will be here very soon who can help you and your family."

Lexy looked up at Jonah with tears welling in her eyes. "Will I ever see my brother, Michael, again?"

Jonah squeezed her hand. "Yes, Lexy. You will. I'm just not sure when that will be. The navigator can help us figure that out. Right now we need to help your mom and dad."

Chapter 2

Michael Ramon Garcia was sitting at his large polished cherrywood desk, staring at his computer in frustration. He should have left an hour ago, but he needed to close this deal with his new customer on their portfolio. This was a VIP client who would bring in millions for his firm. He was very adept at determining and resolving last-minute customer concerns, finding their areas of weakness, and then luring them into the "yes" decision. This customer had been particularly nervous to pull out of their existing pension investment fund and reinvest in a new fund with a completely different broker. After all, these were teachers who were counting on their pensions to fund their retirement. The customer wanted steady growth with little risk. They also didn't want any unsafe investments, like the whole mortgage-backed securities fiasco from a few years ago. Michael smiled to himself as he remembered how well he had smoothed the customer's nervous feathers. He just pretended he was speaking to his grandmother when he soothed and cajoled Mrs. Watson, the representative from the Teacher's Union. "I know what it is like to live with no security, as my parents passed away when I was twelve," he told her. "Adding to the misery, my parents left no life insurance or savings for me to live on. After growing up like that, I have made it my life's work to make sure that other people will not have to suffer that way." With that personal testimony to play to Mrs. Watson's need of assurance and empathy, Michael manipulated his new client to sign on the dotted line.

Michael's words, albeit constructed to be syrupy-sweet for the client's benefit, were nevertheless true. He did have a difficult childhood—brutal, in fact. But he turned his hardship into a personal vendetta to work hard and succeed in a big way. After finishing high school with straight A's, he left his foster home and supported himself while attending Northwestern. Upon graduation, he went to work for a large investment firm to "learn the ropes." Within two years, he was managing the most profitable portfolios in the company. Four years later, he struck out on his own when he had convinced enough of his clients to make the move with him. He was the original mastermind behind his firm's slick investment software, and he grew his company from the ground up. Now his firm manages investments for some of the biggest customers in his hometown of Chicago and all over the Midwest.

With rapid youthful success like his comes fame and fortune. Whenever he walked into a room, he turned heads. Every man wanted to do business with him, and every woman wanted to date him. To his surprise, his fame had grown to the point where he had to acknowledge that he was a celebrity and often found himself the topic of the local tabloids and gossip columns. Reporters surrounded him wherever he went, speculating on who his latest supermodel girlfriend was. It never ceased to amaze him—the fact that he attracted so much attention.

Oh, crap, look at the time! He nagged himself that he needed to call his latest girlfriend to let her know that he was going to be late. He still found women fascinating in that *they* were allowed to make *him* wait (for hours, sometimes), while he was not granted the same courtesy. He reached for his cellphone while cursing the large number of system updates that Microsoft had planned for this week. Normally he would just walk away and let the updates run, but he needed his laptop later that night. And, of course, he couldn't just close it and take it with him because his battery was low. While further cursing Microsoft, this time for their rotten timing on the updates, he dialed the number of his assistant, Cynthia, first. "Cyn, I need you to bring my computer to my home when you leave tonight."

"Sure thing," Cynthia responded. "You haven't changed the security code again on your front door, have you?"

"No, it is still the same as last month. Just leave it on the kitchen counter. Thanks a million! You are outstanding, Cindy!"

"Yeah, that's what all of the guys say, but then they never call me again!" Cynthia joked. Cynthia Longstein, his assistant, was much older than the average assistant, but there were none better in his estimation. He made sure that he paid her so well that she didn't even consider retirement. "So who is the lucky lady this evening?" she asked. "Are you still with Natália, or have you moved away from Brazil to models in a different country? I must remark that this is a quite record with you—three weeks, at least, with the same woman."

"Very funny, Cyn. Just remember that I determine your annual increase each year," he threatened with a smile.

"Michael, my dear, I don't need any more money," she laughed. "All threats of this manner are completely wasted on me. You need to invest more time in deep contemplation and reflection before attempting to intimidate me. I want to see improvement on your next opportunity." She was using her former schoolteacher's voice on him, and it almost sounded convincing. Working with her was like working with his grandmother, except that all of his family was dead. She was the dearest person to him.

"I will devote the rest of the weekend to meditating on the very topic. I will tell you all about it on Monday," he responded laughingly.

"Hmm, I don't think I want to know how you are going to be spending your weekend, so I will just picture you sitting quietly, fully clothed," she stated. "Have a great time at the banquet tonight. But don't drive too fast like you always do! And don't drink too much! And don't—"

"Thanks so much, Cyn," he stated, interrupting her litany of things that he shouldn't do but was planning to do anyway. He hung up the call and then dialed Natália's number. He waited in anticipation of her anger while listening to the ringing. It was at that moment that he noticed another of Cynthia's messages left on his desk. On the small slip of paper, he read:

> A wife of noble character who can find? She is worth far more than rubies. Proverbs 31:10 (NIV)

So Cynthia was trying again to influence him away from the usual women he dated. He smiled, picked up the slip of paper, and placed it on the stack of other similar messages from Cynthia in his desk drawer. The last message she left was an attempt to get him to stop pursuing material wealth:

> Do not lay up for yourselves treasures on earth, where moth and rust destroy and where thieves break in and steal, but lay up for yourselves treasures in heaven, where neither moth nor rust destroys and where thieves do not break in and steal. For where your treasure is, there your heart will be also. Matthew 6:19–21 (NIV)

It didn't bother him that she left these messages. In fact, it comforted him to know that someone cared about him—someone who didn't have an agenda or wanted something from him. Cynthia was a Christian, and so she took opportunities to try to share her faith with him. She was, in fact, sincere in her beliefs and concern for him, so he did not mind. He did promise to go to church with her one Sunday, just so that she would stop asking him.

"*Olá?*" Natália answered. "So nice of you to call me! You already keep me waiting for one hour!" She was not happy.

"Darling, I was kept late closing the deal I told you about this morning. I am sorry. I am leaving right now and will get there as soon as I can." He paused, calculating his next response, then added, "I have been anxiously waiting all day to see you in your new dress."

"Well," she exclaimed, her voice rising in equal pitch with her anger. "You will just have to be happy waiting more longer to see it because I put it back on the hanger while waiting for you! I don't want it to get with so many wrinkles while I am sitting here, waiting for you!"

He knew better than to comment on this logic. They were now in the nagging stage of their month-long relationship, which meant that it was time to end it soon. During the first week (the honeymoon stage), her pouting and little flares of temper were attractive to him. Now they were tiresome. But things were looking up. There was a new woman (yes, another supermodel, but from Italy) who had captured his attention in the hotel lobby during the conference he attended last week in Atlanta. She had slipped him her number, so now he would give her a call after this evening was over.

Walking out of his office, he took a quick look back in while shutting the door. Through the windows that spanned three of the walls of his office, he could see the most brilliant sunset in the distance, beyond the skyline of downtown Chicago. The shades of pink, purple, and orange were simultaneously separate, yet intermingled. Amazing that, after all of these years, he still couldn't enjoy sunsets. Too many bad memories were associated with them. It was while he was captivated by the beauty of a sunset that the police officers broke the news to him of the car crash and the deaths of all his family members. While looking at the glorious beauty of nature, his world had been cruelly ripped apart and changed forever. No, he wouldn't be fooled by any of that sentimental stuff again. Life is what you create it to be. And create it he would.

Michael slipped into his black Porsche 911 GT3 and started the engine. While the car purred its way to life, Michael selected a playlist on his iPhone. After pulling out into traffic, he wound his way onto Lake Shore Drive, heading to Natália's chic apartment in Edgewood. As usual, Michael was pushing the envelope on speed, going about seventy-five miles per hour, even though the speed limit was forty-five. Why have a Porsche if you never get out of first gear? Upon arrival at Natália's, he would change into the tux he had the foresight to load into his car that morning. Then he would take care to select his words to soothe Natália's anger. Thinking about how he was going to compliment her on her dress, he was reminded of an important task that was still left unfinished. *Damn, I forgot her corsage!* Well, that would eat more time and further fuel Natália's anger. While looking out the passenger window to scope out his options for changing lanes, he spied a clear acrylic box wrapped with a thick peacock-green velvet ribbon on the passenger seat. Reaching over, he picked it up and saw the white orchids peeking through the clear box top. Relief washed over him. Reading the note on the box, he saw that Cynthia had anticipated this situation and had picked up the flowers for him. *Wow*, he thought. *What would I ever do without her?* Smiling, he looked up just fast enough to notice that all traffic had come to a complete stop in front of him. He slammed on the brakes, but it was too late. After all, in the collision competition between a sleek Porsche 911 and a rock-solid Ford F-150, the truck wins every time.

Chapter 3

Paul, Maria, and Lexy were led into a massive hall with the tallest ceilings that they had ever seen, except that the ceilings were completely clear and proudly displayed the beautiful sky above. The most striking feature in the New Arrivals Hall was how brilliantly lit the room was: bright but not blinding. It felt like walking into direct sunlight, except without having to squint or shield their eyes to see. And, the room was comfortable, not hot like bright rooms can be. On the walls were enormous flat-screen-like monitors rising almost to the ceilings. The monitors were presenting a deluge of information—welcome messages for new arrivals, the latest news, and advertisements for various forms of recreation and entertainment. The hall was buzzing with the cacophony of sounds coming from the different monitors and the hundreds of people bustling about in the hall.

Every few minutes, announcements were made over some kind of sound system. The announcements were always preceded by three musical tones. Many times, however, Paul could not even make out the language in the announcement. He also found it odd that, although there were so many people in the hall, he didn't feel crushed by the crowd. There were all types of people in the hall; he heard dozens of different languages being spoken all around him. Studying the room around him, it became clear who the new arrivals were, as they were the people (like himself) who were gawking at everything and looking lost.

Paul grabbed Maria's hand in an attempt to comfort her. By the amount that her hand was trembling, he could tell that she was struggling to cope with their situation. Maria glanced up at him and tried to smile. Twice already, he had seen a tear slide down her cheek. Lexy, however, was enjoying herself by making silly poses and viewing her reflection in the immaculately polished marble floors. Their navigator, Lou, had just finished speaking with the attendant at the "New Cases" desk and was walking back to where he left them. He told them to hold all of their questions regarding their son, Michael, for their case manager. Lou had accompanied the family on their roughly twenty-minute journey from the Garden District to their present location in the New Arrivals Hall. They were still trying to understand how the transportation system worked (a high-speed "hover train"), as there were no visible tracks anywhere, yet the train smoothly sped them to their destination.

In Paul's mind, Lou's appearance was different from how Paul imagined people would look in heaven. Lou was young (twenty-something), had short spiked black hair and was wearing a bright-yellow muscle shirt, indigo-blue surf shorts, and dark-brown water sandals. Wrapping all the way down his right arm was a striking red-and-black dragon tattoo that seemed almost alive, like he was ready to leap from Lou's arm at any moment. As Lexy stared at the dragon, she let out a squeal when it appeared to blink and move on its own. Lou was very friendly, very smart, and also very relaxed about everything. Paul remembered how Lou had laughed when Lexy questioned him about the need take a *train* in Heaven to the New Arrivals Hall.

"Really? A boring old train? Surely everyone flies around in heaven, right, Lou?" Lexy asked hopefully. "When do we get our wings?"

"Well, Lexy," Lou explained, "some people do fly here. However, flying is a skill that has to be learned and earned. You are a new arrival, so you don't have that skill yet."

At that news, Lexy pouted and responded, "It figures. Even in heaven I'm too young for the good stuff!"

"No," Lou laughed. "It is not about your age. If you really want to learn to fly, then you can take the classes to learn how to do it. There is also a camp that teaches flying too."

Lexy brightened. "Wow! A camp? I always wanted to go to a camp! Mommy and Daddy, can I go?"

Paul, only half listening to the conversation, was relieved to turn Lexy's mind away from their problems, so he pasted on a smile and responded, "Sure, sweetie. We will look into it. Mommy and I might want to learn how to fly too."

Lou led them down the hall, past all of the large monitors, and into a waiting room. "We just need a few minutes until we are called in to meet with the case inspector assigned to your case. It shouldn't be long," Lou explained. "Do you want something to drink while we wait?"

Paul thought about that offer for a minute before responding. For the first time since the accident, he thought about his new physical form and realized that he didn't feel any different except that he had no discomfort anywhere. "This is amazing. For the first time in my life, I don't feel hungry or thirsty. I don't even need to go to the bathroom!"

"Neither do I," answered Maria. "This is so strange!" They were touching themselves and each other and noticed nothing different.

"Yeah, me too!" answered Lexy. "But I'll take something anyway! Do you have lemonade?"

Lou laughed. "Come with me, Lexy. We will go to the beverage waiter and get some drinks for you and your family." He then addressed Paul and Maria, who were still busy examining each other's forms. "By the way, what you are feeling is normal. Here we no longer *need* a continuous supply of food, drink, or anything like that, but we like to have it anyway."

Lou and Lexy walked up to the beverage waiter, a large circular silver machine with a video screen monitor about halfway to the top. Lou directed her, "Just say what you would like, but be sure to tell it if you don't want ice. The waiter loves to give too much ice sometimes!"

"Lemonade, please," Lexy requested. The waiter made a quiet humming sound and then a pink glass appeared, full of lemonade (and ice), complete with a little pink umbrella sticking out of the top. Lexy's eyes widened with excitement. "This is so awesome!" she squealed. She took the glass and took a sip from the silver straw. "Mmm! This is so good! Mommy and Daddy," she yelled across the room, "you have got to try this!"

Lou answered her, "Let me get them something. I think I know what they like."

After the drinks were collected, Lou and Lexy returned back to Paul and Maria. "Here you go, Maria." Lou handed her a cappuccino in an exquisitely crafted coffee cup.

Maria pasted on her best faux smile and took the cup from Lou. "Thank you." She took a sip, and her tear-swollen eyes widened with surprise. "This is outstanding! Perfect froth and not too bitter!"

An announcement over the sound system interrupted the conversation. "Arrival registration ready for John Orwell. Please report with your navigator to office 1899A." Two men stood up from their chairs and proceeded down a hallway.

"Paul," Lou said, "I think you will like this." Lou handed Paul a steaming cup. "Pure Colombian coffee." In a quieter voice, he continued, "None of that 'girly' coffee stuff, right?" Lou said and winked at Paul.

Before Lou had even handed him the cup, the aroma had already reached Paul, sending him into coffee bliss. Paul took a sip and briefly smiled. "This is really good," he said. "I like coffee, but this is way better than my normal cup I get every day."

Lou smiled. "Here all of your senses are enhanced. Colors are brighter, food tastes better, and you hear sounds more acutely. You also won't feel any pain or sickness."

"That is GREAT!" exclaimed Lexy. "Now I can eat as much candy as I want and never get a sick tummy!"

Lou laughed. "Here, Lexy, we enjoy many things, including food. But I need to clarify: we eat food, we enjoy food, but it is not really something that we spend large amounts of time doing. In fact, you could go for long periods of time without eating. Yes, food provides energy and nutrients, but here our forms are more efficient about using and storing those items. Although I haven't tested it myself, the theory is that you could comfortably go for about a month without eating."

"A whole month? But wouldn't you, uhm—"

"Die, Lexy??" Lou answered with a wink. "No, you won't die. You will simply feel tired and confused until you eat again." Lou was about to speak to Maria and Paul when another announcement was made, but this time in a foreign language.

"*Dàodá bàomíng zhǔnbèi jiàn ráo. Qǐng yǔ nín de dǎoháng yí bàngōng 321J bàogào.*" Paul watched as a man and a woman got up from their seats and proceeded down the hallway.

Lou looked at Paul and said, "Our appointment should be ready in just a few minutes."

"Lou," Paul asked, "why do we look the same *here* as we did on earth? I thought I would look different somehow. For example, I always imagined that people who died when they were old would somehow return to their young adult form in heaven. I also imagined people wearing long robes, having perfect features, you know what I mean?"

Lou thought for a moment before responding. "Actually, Paul, here your appearance is really meaningless. You can take on any form you choose—old, young, green hair, purple eyes—but others will always recognize you by your inner light."

Confused, Paul questioned, "Inner light? I don't understand."

Lou responded, "You won't because you cannot see it yet. That is one of the tasks to take care of during your arrival registration."

Another announcement came over the sound system. "*Registrazione Arrivo pronto per Giuseppe Piccolini. Si prega di segnalare con il tuo navigatore per ufficio 499Q-A.*" A plump, tall man wearing a long black coat and a wool fedora gathered his belongings and then followed his navigator down the hallway.

Lou continued, "Everyone has an inner light. It is the true essence of who you are, your soul, to use a different word. It is unique to each person and recognizable by everyone. Your inner light encapsulates all of the knowledge, experience, talents, and love you possess in your being."

"Are they really pretty, like a big Christmas tree?? Can mine be pink?" asked Lexy.

Lou laughed out loud at this. "Well, Lexy, your inner light color is one of the things that you cannot change here. But, yes, they are pretty." To all of them, Lou continued, "They are beautiful, really. The lights are one of the most wonderful parts of heaven. And when

HELP AMONG US

two or more inner lights are communing together with love, then each light shines even brighter than it does alone. This happens when family members and good friends are working together on projects or just spending time together. On earth, you felt it too. You just couldn't see it. It is that wonderful, happy feeling that comes bubbling out of you when you see your family or good friends. Or when you are praying to God and you feel His love."

"So it is something that we will be able to see soon?" Maria asked.

"Yes, in just a bit, if all goes well." Lou smiled.

Paul was still confused. "Experience, knowledge, talents… How about someone who didn't have the opportunity to acquire too many of those?" Paul asked. "Perhaps someone afflicted young with a disabling disease or impairment, like cerebral palsy? What do their inner lights look like?"

"Well," answered Lou, "soon you can tell me. I had Down syndrome on earth."

Both Maria and Paul stood for a moment in stunned silence at this. Then Paul started, "What? How are you so different now—" He was interrupted by yet another announcement.

"Arrival registration ready for the Garcia family. Please report with your navigator to office 211-Z."

"Hey, that's us!" exclaimed Lou. "Lexy, are you ready to see the brilliant glow of all of the inner lights around you?"

"You bet I am! I'm crossing my fingers that mine is pink!" squealed Lexy.

"Then follow me to office 211-Z!" Lou started down the hallway, and the family followed.

The case manager in office 211-Z was shuffling through files on her desk. She was of average height, wore glasses and a pretty teal-colored suit. She was young, attractive, and her blond hair was twisted into a perfect bun on the back of her head. She waved everyone in her office to have a seat in the comfy chairs in front of her desk. "Hi, everyone! I'm Janis, your case manager. And you must be Lexy! Would you like a piece of candy? I made it myself!" Janis opened up a beautiful box and placed it on her desk. Lexy smiled shyly and then took a piece.

"Lexy," Maria whispered, "say 'thank you.'"

"Th-ank goo," Lexy said through her mouthful of chocolate. "Dis is so goo!"

"I'm so glad you like it!" answered Janis with a smile. Then her smile disappeared when she turned to Lou. "Lou, I'm a little concerned. I've looked through their files, and I don't have their entry passes or initial assignments."

"Yes, the flow cycle and the transport systems were both down when they arrived," Lou explained. "All main systems had to be shut down temporarily when they brought up the new gateway this morning. It only took a few minutes, but, due to the timing, this family strangely ended up in the Garden District."

"The Garden District?" she laughed. "That's a new one!" Janis was reading the content of the family's file on the massive flat screen on the wall. "Well, we will have to complete their registration here first and then do their initiation and assignments. Their coordinator is Gus, and he just called and is on his way here."

"Cool, Janis." Lou smiled with his approval. "Gus is a great match for this family."

"I agree, Lou."

Paul couldn't help himself from speaking his thoughts. "Seriously? Even here you have systems issues? I really thought that there would be no problems or issues ever in heaven."

Both Lou and Janis laughed at this. Lou answered, "There are issues everywhere, Paul. Even here."

"But isn't everything 'finished' and 'perfect' in heaven?? I thought that was what heaven was all about," Paul responded.

Lou smiled. "Creation is eternal, Paul, even here. We continue to build His kingdom, making improvements as we go. And perfection is all about perspective."

"Sorry, but I thought that was what heaven was supposed to be—perfect. A place with no pain, no sickness, no evil, no worries, and everything in finished, working order. Every day is a day of joy."

"Well, much of what you described is here," Lou explained. "Every day here *is* a day of joy. But did you really believe that all we do up here is lounge around on clouds, listening to cherubs playing harp music? In the end, wouldn't that be a boring existence for everyone?"

Paul never thought of that. "Huh. Yeah, I guess that would get old after a while. But I must confess that I am a little nervous about system malfunctions *up here*. I really didn't expect that."

"You didn't expect any kind of imperfection up here, did you?" Lou answered. "That is what we all thought too. Remember, God is a 'Creator,' and He made us in His image to also create. The reality is that we have created a pretty amazing place here, as you will soon see. But it took the work of a lot of great individuals to make it happen. And there is still a lot more to be done."

Janis interrupted, "I'm sorry, but we have a lot of appointments today, so we must press on." Janis proceeded to register the family, which included some rapid data entry into the system. But, instead of typing, the system was voice activated, so Janis did not have move too much in her comfortable chair. In just minutes, a nonstop blur of data, pictures, and videos from their lives displayed on the large monitor. It seemed that every aspect of their lives was now documented.

Paul began to become uncomfortable with all of this vast data collection about him and his family. It must have shown on his face because Janis stopped what she was doing and looked at him and Maria.

"Don't be scared," Janis joked with them. "I can tell by your faces that you are wondering what we are going to do with all of this personal information about you." More seriously, she continued, "Remember, this is heaven, and God is in charge. This isn't an evil, totalitarian government with plans to use this data against you. Up here, everyone can access this information and see what is in all of the systems, including you. There aren't many secrets up here!" Lou nodded in agreement.

Next came the initiation process. At this point, Janis stood up from her desk and walked to the back of her office. "Please come forward and kneel here." She pointed to some cushions placed on the floor.

Paul, Maria, and Lexy knelt down, not sure of what to expect. Paul and Maria each took one of Lexy's hands and looked at each other.

"This doesn't hurt," Janis laughed. "Actually, what is about to happen is wonderful." She stood in front of the three of them. She closed her eyes, paused a moment and then spoke. "I will provide a quick summary of your earthly times. Each of you lived a human life of love and goodness on earth. You showed kindness toward each other, to friends, and even to strangers. You shared what you had with other people, even when you did not have enough for yourselves. You gave thanks to God for His blessings, asked for forgiveness for your sins, and you tried to show His love toward others."

Paul couldn't stay silent anymore. "Wait, stop, please. Maria and Lexy, yes, they are all of these things. But I know in my heart that I was not as good and kind as I could have been. There was so much more that I could have done. I—"

"Paul," Janis interrupted gently, "your life is the sum total of all that you have done and tried to do. Don't judge yourself by a few bad moments. While there will be a final judgment of us all one day, please remember that it is impossible to 'earn' your way into heaven. No one is capable of that," she said warmly. "The wonderful news is that Jesus already paid the price of your sins on the cross. The minute you accepted Him as your Savior, you were already saved." Then she walked behind them, placed her hands above their heads, and said, "Praise to God Almighty, the creator of all life and love. Praise to Jesus Christ, the Son of God and Savior of the world. Praise to the Holy Spirit, our powerful helping force of God on earth. Bless this family and guide them in their new life with us. From this moment on, each of them is now marked with Your sign as an initiate. Go forth, initiates, and use your talents according to His will."

With those words, Paul, Maria, and Lexy each felt a rush, like a wild wind, go through them. However, the wind didn't feel disturbing or cold, like normal winds (especially coming from Chicago). Instead, the wind was warm, comforting, as if an invisible force was holding them in a loving embrace. A brilliant light appeared and then it dimmed, showing a young, Middle Eastern–looking man in biblical robes. Without having to be told, they knew it was Jesus.

A foreign feeling overcame Paul. It took a moment for him to understand what this feeling was. The best word to describe it was happiness, the kind and measure he had never felt before. As his brain was grappling with adjectives that might possibly describe what he was feeling, Jesus looked directly at him. And time stood still. Those eyes appeared normal, but, looking deeper, they contained an infinite wisdom and a gentle understanding of everything that has been and will come. Without saying a word to Paul, Jesus was communicating His love. Then He smiled. Paul thought that his heart would burst from happiness.

Paul dropped to his knees, bowed his head, and tried to speak. "My...my Lord!"

Jesus smiled and gently said "Hello, Paul. Please stand, relax, and don't be afraid to look at me. I am so pleased to see you." Jesus opened his arms and welcomed Paul into his embrace. Paul could not control the waves of emotion overpowering him, as he was lost in the embrace of his Savior. After a moment, he pulled back and looked into Jesus's smiling eyes. Paul was still trying to grasp that he was having a conversation with the Savior of the world, so words were escaping him. Then he remembered all of the times of regret when he had a mediocre conversation with someone, only to remember some key facts *after* the meeting. *Don't let this be one of those occasions!* "Is momentary confusion a normal reaction, sir?" he managed to blurt out.

Jesus laughed. (Paul couldn't believe it—he was watching Jesus laugh!) "You can call me Jesus, Paul. And I don't think that there is a normal response for someone who suddenly finds himself in heaven. If it helps to calm you, I want you to know that I am so glad to see you. You were challenged by your faith, but you never stopped believing. You always clung to me when times got the toughest. I especially remember all of the moments when you felt alone, doubting yourself and me for brief moments. Believe me when I tell you, Paul, I didn't leave your side for a moment." Paul was speechless at this, unable to speak. Jesus continued, "Most importantly, I also remember how you shared your faith and your possessions with others."

"I am not this good," exclaimed Paul. "I did a lot of things that I am not proud of."

Those knowing eyes held compassion so deep that it almost made Paul cry. "Of course," He said. "But you learned from those mistakes, asked for forgiveness from me and the injured party, and moved on. Let me ask you a question, Paul. What do you think is the true measure of a person's life?"

Paul thought for a moment. "Well, using your life as the model, I would say it is the number of people we impact in a positive way, even after death."

Jesus nodded. "It is the amount of love given and received during the lifetime, both God's love and love from other humans. Your measurement is something to be proud of, Paul."

Paul felt simultaneously embarrassed and proud. A warm feeling grew in his heart. "Thank you, Jesus. I couldn't"—then he paused—"rather, I can do nothing without you." Then he added, "I don't think that it is quite adequate to say, but thank you for giving your life for mine."

Jesus turned very serious as he looked at Paul. "Even if you were the only human who had ever existed on earth, I would have died for you, Paul." The brilliant light came back, and Jesus's form began to fade. "There are a lot of people here who are anxious to see you, Paul. We will talk again."

Then, almost as soon as it began, the wind stopped.

After a moment, they opened their eyes and looked at each other. "I just spoke to Jesus!" Paul exclaimed.

"So did I!" Maria exclaimed. "I could not believe that I was standing before Him, and He was so gentle, so beautiful!"

"How is that possible?" Paul answered. "I didn't see anyone else there."

"Remember that all things are possible with God," Lou responded.

When they stopped focusing on the memories of speaking with Jesus, they turned their attention back to each other. They couldn't believe what they were seeing and feeling: each of them had a brilliant beam of light streaming out of them. The lights appeared to start in the center of their chests and extend far beyond them in all directions, like large halos fully encircling each of them. They were beautiful. More importantly, however, was what they were *feeling*. Never before had they felt so much love. It was God's overwhelming love for them radiating through the air and all around them. They could feel Jesus and sense that he was nearby. Paul, Maria, and Lexy were amazed at how much love they were suddenly able to feel.

While the family stared at each other, mesmerized by the changes, Lou provided an explanation. "Jesus is the light of the world. Our inner lights are a reflection of the love we feel for Him and for each other. All of this powerful love is pretty amazing, isn't it? It was there all along, but your human forms could not process it all. Now in your true form, you are able to love God and fully feel His love in return. And," pointing at them, he continued, "these are much more than just some pretty lights. As you will soon discover, each person's inner light contains vast amounts of information specific to that individual. This is why no two inner lights look the same. But don't just 'look' at the lights, concentrate on them," Lou instructed. "Soon you will be able to learn quite a bit about someone just from viewing their light. This is what we call 'reading' each other's lights."

Paul and Maria followed Lou's instructions. They stopped merely looking at each other's light and began concentrating on it, feeling it, absorbing it. They felt a rush of images come at them like a tidal wave of information. Within seconds, they each received an enormous amount of data about each other. "This is amazing!" Paul exclaimed.

"With a little practice," Lou continued, "you will be able to control your reading ability so that it won't feel like an explosion of information coming at you. Also, by reading deeper and interpreting the different parts of the light, you can learn each other's likes and dislikes, abilities, experiences, and even read many of their emotions."

"This is unbelievable!" exclaimed Maria, staring back and forth at Paul's and Lexy's lights. "I can read so much about you in your lights! Lexy, I see your love of animals and sweets. Paul, I see your vast medical knowledge and your love of baseball."

She turned to Lou and began to read his light. Sudden comprehension about him filled her, almost taking her breath away. "Lou! Your inner light is so beautiful! And you can do so many things. You speak so many languages, you can fly. Wow—you are an author! And"—she paused, reading further—"you are filled with so much love. Why, you already love us! This is amazing!" She paused, very serious for a moment. "Lou, I'm sorry to ask this," she continued. "How did you get some of these abilities when you had such serious Down syndrome on earth?" Reading more of his light, she went on with astonishment, "Why, Lou, your condition was so serious that you couldn't even speak."

Lou smiled. "Remember that you continue to gain abilities here. But even during all of my silent years on earth, God was working in me. While no one could really see it, He was there with me, loving me. Even when I couldn't communicate with my human parents, my schoolteachers, really anybody, He was there. As were my guardians."

"Your *guardians*?" responded Maria. "Who were they?" As she was about to ask Lou another question, she stopped. She felt different somehow—calm. She rubbed her face with her hands—dry cheeks. Strange, she was still crying just moments before. Now she noticed that her tears, her worry, and her deep emotional pain about Michael—they were gone. She turned to Lou and Janis. "Where is it? My worry for my son, my Michael, it is gone. What has happened to me? Help me, please. I know that I should be panicking and worrying right now because my baby is down on earth, all alone, and I am calm right now."

"Initiation removes the remaining facets of your human existence. All of your self-doubts, worry, pain—all of that goes away. Now you are able to calmly concentrate on what is important but without being burdened with the additional 'baggage' of human constraints such as worry and pain.

"Man," said Paul in amazement. "This really would've been handy during some of my harsher rounds of golf."

HELP AMONG US

"Be serious, Paul!" Maria said as she gently elbowed him in the side. Then, to Janis and Lou, Maria continued, "Well, can I find out anything about what is happening to him? Michael is completely alone down there. We have no family members who can take care of him. Both sets of grandparents are dead, and he has no aunts or uncles."

"He is not alone, Maria," answered Lou gently.

"What do you mean?" asked Maria.

"Some of us are down there with him, with everyone there, really."

"Some of whom? I don't understand."

"Maria, I think I will let Gus answer that." Lou turned to address a man who just walked in. "Gus, you are just in time. Please meet the Garcia family."

Gus was a thin, short man with long white hair and a white beard. His white robe was tied with a thin piece of rope and came down to his calves. His sandals looked as if they were constructed of rough leather and were strapped on with thin ropes winding around his feet and ankles. In contrast to everyone else that they had encountered so far, Gus looked every bit the picture of how someone should look up in heaven. He smiled as he walked forward to meet the family. "Hello, everyone, I am Gus, your coordinator. I have been assigned to your family for as long as you need me. My job, in short, is to show you around, explain as much as I can, and then give you your initial assignments." He turned to Lexy and smiled with a massive grin. "You must be Lexy," he said, shaking Lexy's hand and reading her inner light. "Yes, I see that the file on your family is correct. You do indeed have a huge love of animals, and you know quite a bit about certain breeds of dogs, cats, and horses. Your desire is to be a veterinarian. I think you will be a splendid one."

Lexy smiled in appreciation of his compliment.

"We have a need for animal expertise up here. We have animals here, and we need help training them, caring for them, and finding them homes."

"There are animals here? This place is GREAT!" squealed Lexy in excitement. She started jumping up and down as she spoke to her parents, "Mama, Papa, can we get a dog?" She turned back to Gus. "I ride horses too. Are there stables up here? Maybe I can work at one and ride every day and then have about four or five dogs and maybe a couple of cats, some rabbits, and fish… Oh, can I have some paper and a pen to make a list, please?"

While Lexy continued with her list of the animals that she and her family would soon acquire, Gus turned to Paul and Maria. "Well, I think Lexy is starting to adjust to being here." He spoke to Maria and shook her hand, "You must be the chef, Maria. I am extremely glad to meet you. Believe me when I tell you, we need all of the good cooks we can get up here."

"Glad to meet you, Gus," Maria replied. "But why do you say that?" she asked, very confused. "With all of the wonderful chefs who have already *died*—" She stopped and put her hand over her mouth. "Oops, is that the wrong word to say up here? I just would have thought that all of the cooking here would be nothing short of perfection."

Gus laughed. "Yes, you can say the word 'died.' We aren't 'politically correct' up here. We believe in stating the absolute truth at all times. But back to our food conundrum. The essence of the problem is not a shortage of great cooks. Rather, it is the opposite. *Everyone*, it seems, wants to try his or her hand at cooking. Even worse, the people who rush to be the first in line to do the cooking appear to be the worst at it. I think that I have eaten all of the fish and seaweed stroganoff that I can take. The fashion right now is crazy seafood dishes."

"Fish and seaweed stroganoff? That sounds pretty bad! I'm happy to make you something else some time. Do you like Italian, Mexican, French, Greek, what?"

Gus looked very happy. "Ahh… We will have to continue this conversation later." Becoming more serious, he changed subjects. "I believe we were talking about guardians when I walked in. But first I want to meet Paul, the heart surgeon." Gus smiled and shook Paul's hand.

"Hi, Gus," Paul said.

Gus took a moment to read Paul's inner light. "Wow, Paul. I am really impressed. Not only were you a successful doctor to your paying patients, you donated so much of your talent to the world. Thanks to you, many lives were saved."

Paul shifted, not comfortable talking about himself in any sort of bragging sense. "Well, especially when I was still paying off my medical school bills and starting my practice, I couldn't always afford to donate money to charity. So I donated my work instead."

"That is true," answered Gus. "But when you went to donate your skills in Mali, Chad, and other impoverished countries, you were doing well financially."

"Help is needed all around the world. I wanted to do my part," Paul answered softly.

"My husband is very humble, Gus. You will never hear him boast about himself," Maria answered, taking her husband's hand and smiling warmly at him. "Now please tell us about these 'guardians.' I really want to know who can help Michael since we are not there."

Gus walked back to the front of the office and sat on the edge of Janis's desk. "Please," he said, pointing to the chairs, "have a seat." After everyone sat down, he continued.

"Guardians are representatives from heaven down on earth. Their job is to spiritually assist those who are still in their human form. I'm sure you are familiar with the term 'guardian angel,' am I right?" They all nodded. "The guardians I am speaking of are not angels. Angels are a completely different group of God's messengers. Guardians are individuals from heaven who decide to return to earth to help guide those who have not yet died. Working with the Holy Spirit, each guardian is assigned to a human with the purpose of helping to steer the human onto the right track, toward goodness and to the Lord. However, remember that the 'other side' also has their set of guardians, also known as demons. So, in the end, there is a battle for the soul of each human. But, as each human is granted free will, the ultimate decision of which track to take completely resides with him."

"Can there be more than one guardian per human? And can the human see the guardian?" Maria asked.

"Yes and yes. While the human can sometimes see, even interact with the guardian(s), the human has no idea of their real purpose. Often, humans view the guardian as a just a kind person who is trying to help. Or, in some cases, the guardian is viewed as an annoying person who acts as their conscience. The objective is to place reminders of God's love out there for the human to see. Working with the Holy Spirit, the goal is to lead the human to salvation in Jesus." Gus winked as he continued, "As you may remember, humans are stubborn creatures and need a lot of reminding."

"So did we have guardians?" asked Paul.

"Absolutely," responded Gus. He read Paul's light. "Do you remember Dr. Hershall, your mentor during your first internship? He was the person who introduced you to the concept of donating your skills."

"Oh my gosh!" exclaimed Paul. "I honestly had no idea! He was a brilliant doctor and also very religious. He always talked about how we could use our Christian faith in our practice."

"When he was a human," Gus continued, "he was also a great doctor and a good man. He ran a clinic in Milwaukee that helped many poor people from the community. He is working with other interns now, although he has to alter his appearance and move around a bit to avoid any suspicion—"

"Gus," Maria broke into the conversation, "is there some way for us to see our son up here? I would feel much better if I knew who his guardians are and that he is safe."

"I thought that you would want information about Michael, so I looked it up before I left my office." Gus pulled out a small handheld device, similar to an iPhone, from his pocket. He pressed some keys, and a display of what looked like a hologram appeared above it. Inside the display appeared to be a live image of Michael sitting at a desk at school. "Michael is living in a foster home right now." Gus pressed a few more keys, and some data appeared beside the video of Michael. "As you can see, he is attending school and is getting excellent grades, according to his last report card." Gus pressed a few more keys. The image in the hologram changed to what looked like a computer screen. "Michael has been assigned two guardians right now. Both are at his school: his chemistry teacher, a Mr. Sanchez, and a Mrs. DiGiovanni, who works in the cafeteria. Both are reporting that, while Michael is adjusting to his new life, making excellent grades, he is struggling with the social and spiritual aspects. He appears to be immersing himself completely into his schoolwork, but nothing else."

"Wait, we have only been up here a few hours," Maria exclaimed. "How long has it been on earth?"

Gus responded gently, "I'm sure it doesn't surprise you to know that heaven and earth are not in the same 'time zone.' A few hours up here can translate to several years on earth."

"A few years already..." Maria just shook her head. "Sorry, but I just wish I knew why we had to be taken so soon, before Michael was ready to be on his own."

Gus thought for a moment and then answered, "People are taken for many reasons. One is that they are needed elsewhere, like up here. Hard to believe, isn't it, that your talents may be needed up here. Another reason is that it is simply your time to leave earth, and God alone knows when that is. Remember, everyone dies. The real mission is to accept Jesus as your Savior and then live the best life you can while you are alive, serving God by serving others."

"What happens if you don't live a good life? Does hell really exist?"

"Oh yes!" Gus exclaimed. "Hell exists just as heaven exists. The final judgment will come at the end of time on earth."

"Gus, I am concerned for Michael," Paul interrupted. "Without us there, he may not get the love and spiritual direction he needs to get onto the right track. Just thinking logically here, Michael may blame God for all of his problems."

"That is often the case. People tend to praise themselves when things are going well but then blame God when hardships arise."

"Very true. How can this be avoided when such a tragedy happened to him so young?" Maria asked.

"Maria, we were concerned about you and Paul too at points in your lives. Even Lexy too. But both of you got Lexy on the right track."

"Yes," said Paul. "But she is just a kid. That wasn't too difficult."

"Being good, Paul, is always hard, no matter the age. You should know that. You should also know that all humans have struggles in their life, which is part of the whole experience. Both of you went through some difficult challenges in your lives. Paul, you lost your parents when you were in college, and you had to find a way to pay for your education yourself. Maria, you were raised in a bad neighborhood where you were tempted every day to get into drugs, promiscuity, and crime. But both of you came out of these difficulties and became people who served others."

"Well," answered Paul, "we knew that we had to rely on ourselves to move forward. Waiting around for someone else to 'rescue us' was unrealistic. There was this really great church that we started attending and really turned around our thinking. We found our hope in Jesus and each other."

"Exactly," responded Gus. "Each of you made your own decision to turn your life into something good. It is up to Michael now to do the same thing. But remember, he won't be alone. Like both of you, he will have some help from guardians and other good humans."

CHAPTER 4

Michael woke up to the music of beeps going off at regular intervals, the pungent odor of antiseptic, and a serious level of pain in his body that he had never before experienced. Something kept tickling and stabbing at his face, so he tried to brush it away. That was when he learned that his right arm was completely immobilized. Not only could he not move it, he could barely move his fingers. He attempted to shift his upper body to turn his head, but the effort caused his ribs to scream out in agony. Realizing that his eyes were still closed, he blinked them open with much effort and slowly looked around the room. The monitors, IV unit, and breathing devices quickly alerted him that he was in the hospital. As he could not move his head without intense pain, he did his best to scan himself and his environment. He appeared to be in some kind of body cast, but a sheet had been draped over the lower half of his body. Pain was flooding into his brain from all over his body, especially his entire right leg and his left thigh. He appeared to be alone in the room, and, with dismay, the Call button was out of reach. It wouldn't matter anyway—he wouldn't be able to press it in his condition.

He was trying to figure out how he got here when a nurse arrived.

"Oh, Mr. Garcia, you are awake!" the nurse exclaimed. "Now don't try to move or anything. We have restricted all of your movement with various casts and braces all over your body. In case you haven't already figured it out, you are in the hospital. We have contacted your assistant, Ms. Longstein, and she is arranging to have your clothes and other essentials brought here. As soon as your breathing stabilizes, we will remove the ventilator mask from your face. For the moment, however, I need you to lie still and rest. In another hour,

I will give you another round of meds to help you rest easier." She took his temperature, his pulse, and his blood pressure while giving that speech. After recording his vitals on his chart, she gave him an encouraging smile and left the room. Even though he was confused and trying not to panic at his situation, he was amazed at how tired he was. Eventually, he drifted off to sleep again.

When he next awoke, he felt much less groggy and confused. That also meant that the meds were wearing off because he could feel much more pain than he felt earlier. It seemed to be radiating in his head, jaw, back, left thigh, and ribs. He was amazed at how helpless and scared he felt for the first time in a very long time. He needed to find out what happened to him, but he could not speak, flag anyone down, or even press the stupid Call button. As he groaned aloud in frustration, he heard a familiar voice.

"Well, hello, Sleeping Beauty!" It was Cynthia. Thank goodness! Just the sound of her voice comforted him. Smiling, she put down the book she was reading and stood up beside his hospital bed. "I must confess, Michael," she continued while folding her reading glasses, "that I am feeling a guilty pleasure in this situation. I can say anything I want to you right now, and you are forced to listen with no ability to respond with a clever retort." Cynthia appeared to be enjoying the moment. "Amazing. What pearls of wisdom shall I impart upon you right now, I wonder?" Even while trapped in a hospital bed with a ventilator mask strapped to his face, a neck brace, and bandages wrapped around his head, the look he gave with his eyes told her all he wanted to say.

She continued to smile for another moment, but then her eyes grew more serious. She gently put her hand on his arm cast, composed herself, and continued. "Don't try to talk just yet. Your jaw has been wired shut." She paused and took a steadying breath. "I'm going to give it to you straight: we weren't sure at first that you were going to make it. The accident was really bad." Her eyes were beginning to fill with tears as she continued, "You were sandwiched between an oversized van in front and a large pickup truck in back. You have been in an induced coma for a few days. The good news is that, while your concussion was pretty severe, there are no long-term injuries on your brain as far as they can tell. It looks like you have finally stabilized, so now you can start to recover."

She stopped speaking and just studied him for a minute. "Michael, blink twice if you understand me." Her face looked completely relieved when he slowly blinked twice. He was amazed again at how much effort that little movement took. Never before had he tried to convey so much to someone by only using his eyes.

She looked away for a moment and then went on, "There is something else you must know, and I don't quite know how to tell you." She paused for a moment, looking quite unsure how to continue. She closed her eyes, took another fortifying breath, and spoke. "Michael, I'm just going to say it. Your left leg was badly smashed. They worked for hours in the OR to try to save it." Her voice cracked with emotion during the last part of that statement. She stopped and couldn't look at him. The tears were pouring down her face, onto his sheets, and she turned her head. He had never seen her in so much pain before. Finally, she looked back at him. She knew what he was trying to ask her with his eyes. "No, Michael," she whispered. "Not the whole leg. Just below the knee."

Well, that certainly explained why he could only feel pain in his left thigh and not further down. He closed his eyes and shuddered with this news. "I know, honey," Cynthia responded soothingly. "It's going to be okay." She stepped back as a nurse came in to check his vitals and administer more meds in his IV unit. She stayed with him for a while until he drifted back to sleep.

The vitals check became a constant ritual, night and day. It seemed like only a few minutes had passed when yet another nurse would come in and repeat the steps: blood pressure, temperature, pulse. He began marking off the hours based upon the arrivals of the nurses. He also mentally ticked off the minutes by the rhythmic beeps of the different monitors in his room. Since he could neither move nor speak, he was prevented from reaching for or operating the remote control for the TV. It appeared to him that this was a deliberate objective to keep him bored; therefore, he would go to sleep.

But being in the ICU had its interesting moments. There would be some "excitement" in a room nearby and then he would hear the doctors and nurses yelling and scurrying about to address whatever emergency was going on. He was also a witness to the joy and the sorrows of the friends and families of other patients. His bed faced the doorway, so he had visibility to the hallway and could watch the ICU visitors walk past his room. It was fascinating how much he learned about the patients in the neighboring rooms by eavesdropping on the hallway conversations with the hospital staff and the visitors.

To his shame though, he was jealous of the love displayed by the family members of the other patients. He saw how much a particular wife loved her husband, as she seemed to never leave the floor. She was living for days on a diet of inedible hospital cafeteria food and endless cups of bad (but complimentary) coffee. He later watched as their family was finally reunited and saw the kids running toward their father's room, screaming, "I love you, Daddy!" at the top of their lungs.

The day that the now-recovered husband finally left the hospital, he found himself almost crying with happiness too. But, at the same time, he also felt so empty inside. There was such a dark void within him. He asked himself: Besides Cynthia, who else loved him that much? Had anyone ever loved him that much? No one except Cynthia came to visit him. Cynthia tried her best, on one of her visits, to gently explain that his relationship with Natália was over. Despite Cynthia's best attempt at a creative explanation, Michael could read between the lines and understood that the vain Natália could not be satisfied with a one-legged man, no matter how rich he was. Even worse, Natália could not be bothered to come to the hospital to deliver the message herself. Perhaps it was just as well. The relationship had been going nowhere anyway.

Finally, after three weeks, he was deemed well enough to have his jaw unwired. That gave him some new freedom because now he could finally (slowly) speak and start to ingest food normally again. Cynthia liked to show up and sneak him milkshakes, which were considered contraband within the hospital perimeter. Today she brought him a large chocolate Frosty from Wendy's. "Remember to go slowly with that," she told him.

"Hmm," Michael murmured as he watched her ferociously dig into her own large milkshake. "I'm trying to determine if you are only bringing me these milkshakes so that you can have one too."

"Of course, silly!" Cynthia responded between ridiculously large slurps. "Ugh!" she suddenly exclaimed, grimacing and grabbing her forehead with one hand. "Gotta slow down. Brain freeze…"

Michael laughed despite the pain in his ribs. He was sure that no one else had ever witnessed a dignified, well-dressed seventy-plus-year-old woman who still drank a milkshake like a kid. While he was still laughing, he heard a voice call out from the hallway.

"Hey! There he is!" the man's voice bellowed. "The man with all of the brains, most of the charm, and the one who can boast to being friends with some of the best-looking guys in town!"

"Hey, Trent!" answered Michael. "So good to see you! Where have you been hiding all of this time?"

Trent Wentworth was Michael's partner in the firm. Michael recruited Trent twelve years ago when he found that there simply were not enough hours (day or night) to do everything himself. Trent had recently completed graduate school and was Michael's coworker for two years before Michael broke away and started his own firm. Later, when his business started to take off, Michael persuaded Trent to join him in the venture. In the beginning, Michael focused on finishing up the state-of-the-art investment software that he created, while Trent concentrated on their existing clients. Once the software was finished, Michael passed the IT management to Trent while Michael concentrated his efforts on sales and building up their client base. Together they built the business from the ground up and turned it into a world-class operation.

"Dude, I've been busy running things since you decided to take a luxury vacation here," Trent responded, walking toward the bed. He carefully navigated his way through all of the various chords that were draping over the bed from the IV unit and monitors. He briefly put his hand on Michael's right arm cast and then quickly put it back into his pants pocket. "Seriously, Michael, we were really worried about you. I am really glad that you are going to be okay."

"Well, Trent, you don't look like you've lost too much sleep in my absence! Your hair is perfectly in place, as always, and your clothes barely look like you even drove here with them on. Not a wrinkle in sight." It was true. Trent always looked like he just stepped off of the cover of a men's fashion magazine. Even in a blizzard, Trent always managed to look pristine, all the way down to his perfectly manicured toenails. It was obvious that he was trying to appear casual today because he wasn't wearing his suit jacket. "So give me a sports update," Michael requested. "All I see on the TV here are the soap operas that all of the nursing staff wants to watch when they do their rounds." Michael then lowered his voice almost to a whisper. "Come closer so you can hear me, Trent." He took a quick glance at Cynthia, who was still sitting in the chair, working hard on her milkshake, and then continued in a desperate rant. "Trent, are there any issues that need my attention at the moment? I have been going absolutely crazy without any electronics in here! You try going weeks without a computer, iPad, or your phone!"

"Hang on a minute, Michael!" Cynthia blasted in, putting her cherished milkshake aside for the moment. "You are not supposed to do any kind of mentally strenuous work for another week. We have to make sure that your brain fully heals before you dive back into the sewer!" By the resuming slurping sounds, they could tell that Cynthia had returned to her milkshake.

Trent looked back at Michael with an incredulous look on his face. He leaned even more toward Michael, dropped his voice to an almost inaudible level, and said, "How did she hear us? It's like she is superhuman or something!"

"No, I'm just a regular girl," Cynthia said in a loud voice, suddenly standing right behind Trent.

Trent shrieked in fright, jumped back a bit, and nearly tripped over one of the monitor chords.

"Careful there, or you will wind up with your *own* room in these fine accommodations!" Cynthia responded, helping Trent with a steadying arm. "Well, I am sure that you two have a few things to discuss, so I will leave you alone for a bit. But just remember: Michael has to take it easy for a few more days." With that stern warning, Cynthia left the room.

"Wow, I feel like a guilty schoolboy who just had a run-in with the principal!" Trent stated, while Michael laughed.

"Cynthia is definitely overprotective, but that is one of the things I love about her."

"Well, personally, I never really cared for overprotective people—not even in my own mother."

"Ha! You just wish you had a mother who was like Cynthia!" Michael joked. Trent laughed, but Michael could see that the truth hurt. One of the things Michael and Trent had in common was a lack of parental involvement in their childhood. Michael's family died when he was twelve. Trent's parents, while very much alive, basically never involved themselves in his childhood. Trent's father was a successful businessman who devoted all of his time to his career. Trent's mother cared more about shopping, furnishing her luxurious home, and having lunch with her sophisticated friends than she did her only son. Trent learned early on that he had to rely on himself and that he really could *not* count on other people. To this day, Trent still had only a tiny circle of close friends. While Michael was essentially cynical when it came to trusting other people (and life in general), Trent took it to another level. Trent believed that most people were worthless and that you had to look hard for the "good ones." This strange bond formed their friendship and enabled them to work well together since they understood one another.

After Trent relayed the key issues going on at their firm, Michael gave him some instructions and then he left Michael's room. All alone again. Back to solitude and lots of time to think. These were the darkest days for Michael because everyone (including him) had to smile and pretend that everything was great. In reality, nothing could be further from the truth. Inside, hidden from everyone, his depression was growing exponentially each day. Sometimes he felt as if he was literally drowning in his despair.

As he was finishing the last bit of his milkshake, he noticed a small slip of paper that had been taped onto the cup. He managed to pull it off and then read:

> For I know the plans I have for you," declares the Lord, "plans to prosper you and not to harm you, plans to give you hope and a future.
> Jeremiah 29:11 (NIV)

Looks like Cynthia was still trying to encourage him. So, according to this verse, God was going to give him a future. Yeah, right. If his past was any predictor, he certainly didn't want his future. In any event, what good does some fluffy scripture passage written thousands of years ago do for him today? Who even was this Jeremiah prophet? Wasn't he speaking to the Israelites in this passage, if his memory from days in Sunday school served him well? So how could this be relevant to him today? Then he noticed that there was more on the slip of paper:

> Michael, in case you don't think that this applies to you, read the verse below:
> For the word of God is alive and active. Hebrews 4:12 (NIV)
> This means that God is still speaking to us today through His Word in the scriptures. Believe it, Michael!

There were times when he believed that Cynthia had certain extrasensory perception powers. This was just another example as she had accurately predicted his thoughts. He paused for a moment, reflecting on her message. This was all very nice but not very helpful at this moment. All he had to do was to look at the wreck that was once his body for all of the desperation and anxiety to return.

Today, though, he was moving beyond being sad; now he was angry. *Really* angry. He had stopped asking *Why me?* years ago. He already knew that life was unfair, and, for some unknown reason, his portion of misery seemed to be larger than for others. Obviously, life wasn't through beating him up. Why not? He had just put his life back together, so now it was time for it to be destroyed again. But this time he was going to have to overcome physical disabilities too, in addition to emotional pain. *Disabilities…I'm disabled. Dear God.* Even after all of these weeks, he hadn't fully internalized the fact that he was now disabled.

The dark forces were growling their pleasure at the sight of Michael's despair. "We are getting closer," they exclaimed to each other, their glee almost too much for them to contain without being audible for their human subject. "Soon," they said to each other. "Very soon he will belong to us!"

Chapter 5

"I want to be Michael's guardian," Maria announced to Gus, Lou, and Janis. Paul was busy looking at Lexy's massive list of potential family pets when he heard her request. He almost spilled his coffee when he spun around in his chair to look at her.

"Honey, are you sure?" he asked.

"Yes, Paul. I am absolutely sure," Maria confirmed.

"Well, then I am going with you."

"Me too!" Lexy exclaimed. "And we will bring some of our pets with us back to earth. I think a dog would work and maybe a smaller horse…"

Gus and Lou looked at each other. "Gus, I'll let you take this one," Lou said, putting his hands up.

"Maria, guardians' assignments are a complicated process." Gus explained. "First, guardians don't choose their human. Guardians are assigned by the Department of Guardianship. Second, guardians have to go through a three-week training course. At the end of the course, provided a passing grade is achieved, the guardian receives his or her human assignment. Then there is a one-day briefing to familiarize the guardian about the human and to create the assimilation disguise. Third, guardians are rarely, if ever, assigned to someone they knew when they were a human."

"Well, why not?" asked Maria. "Wouldn't that make the best kind of guardian, since you already know the person?"

"While that is a good point, you are forgetting something. Knowing the human will make it more difficult for you to maintain your disguise and objectivity. You will unwittingly make a gesture, relay an old joke, or portray some habit from your past that your human will recognize. Guardians must not be discovered."

HELP AMONG US

"What happens if a guardian is discovered?" Maria asked.

"Well, nothing disastrous like the destruction of the earth," Gus joked. "But if humans knew that we were there, it could compromise the whole basis of faith. Remember that faith is believing even without seeing the proof for one's self. Humans have a long history of focusing on and believing in the wrong things. For example, many humans still worship the earth (the creation) and not the Creator. They have this backward. We guardians are merely servants of God. We are neither holy nor all-powerful ourselves. Our main objective is to help humans find and strengthen their faith in God. We absolutely don't want humans to mistakenly worship us. Remember that the solution to the life experience is having faith to trust God in all things, especially when it seems hopeless."

"Which is why it is so hard to do," murmured Paul.

"Exactly," replied Gus. "When you have faith, you stop living just for yourself and for what the world offers. Faith in God drives all of the other essential elements such as service to our fellow men, and forgiving your enemies. Faith in God has built nations, freed slaves, and helped the poor. With faith, people believe that anything is possible. Therefore, they accomplish the impossible. Without it, you only have fear and hopelessness."

"Believe me, I understand what you are saying," Maria interrupted. "What if Michael didn't recognize us? We will alter our appearance, right?"

Gus sighed and tried again to explain. "Maria, you have no idea how difficult it will be for you to hide your identity. Even with the best of disguises. Adding to the challenge will be the fact that you cannot be completely impartial to the outcome when it is your own son. Going to heaven or hell is entirely up to him. You are only there to help guide your human onto the right path. In the end, you have to let him choose his own destiny."

"Gus, I don't mean to be difficult when I say this." Maria paused, stumbling to find the right words. "Somehow, Gus, I *feel* like I am meant to do this. I can't explain it. I just do."

"Maria, I can certainly understand feeling this way. It took me a long time to disconnect from the people I left behind when I first arrived here too. Regardless, I can tell you that I have never heard of guardians being assigned to humans that they knew."

"No, Gus, this is different," Maria answered, putting her hands to her face. "I don't know quite how to say this. I sincerely and completely believe that I was meant to do this. Like, this is why I died today."

Paul looked with amazement at Maria. "What? Maria, are you, I mean, are you *really* sure?"

Maria looked back at Paul. "Paul, I have never been more sure of anything before."

"Maria," Gus continued, exasperated, "I'm sure that this—"

"Gus! Hold on a moment!" Janis yelled out. "This is incredible," she exclaimed. "I have never seen this before. I'm looking in the DOG assignment system right now. Gus, it is true! Maria, Paul, and Lexy are already assigned as Michael's guardians!"

Chapter 6

Michael was sitting in bed, watching another episode of *As the World Turns* when he heard the nurse's voice outside of his room.

"He is right in there. As of this morning, he has only left his bed a few times for bathing and an occasional trip to the bathroom."

A deep, baritone voice answered, "Okay. Thank you. I will take it from here." A large African American man walked in. He seemed young, in his midthirties, and very confident. He was wearing a red Under Armour T-shirt that clung to his large chest. From the size of his biceps, it was clear that he worked out. His black sweatpants almost reached the floor above his trainers. For jewelry, he wore a small diamond earring and a cross necklace. From the way he navigated around all of the equipment, it was clear that he knew his way around a hospital room. He set down his large duffel bag and then walked to the end of the bed, reading Michael's hospital chart. After returning the chart, he walked to the sink in Michael's room and washed his hands. Then he approached Michael. Smiling, he spoke, "Hi, Michael. I am Dominic LeBrant, your physical therapist." They shook hands, with Michael's fingers sticking through the arm cast.

"Hi, Dominic," Michael answered. "Sorry I can't get up to greet you properly, nor can I offer you something to drink here."

Dominic laughed. "Believe me, the only thing I was expecting today was to find you awake and alert. Ms. Longstein, your assistant, contacted our office to get you started on some therapy. We will do what we can while you are still in the hospital and then we will move you back home for the remaining therapy there and at our facility downtown."

"Therapy so soon? I would have thought that I needed to heal more before we could do anything."

"Actually, Michael, the process is quite the opposite. We normally get started right away after surgery in order to reduce the amount of scar tissue buildup that would prevent your mobility. If it were up to me, I would have been here two weeks ago. But we had to wait for you to stabilize before we could do anything. Also, we needed to make sure that you didn't suffer any traumatic brain injuries in that crash." Dominic pulled out a penlight and began to do some basic eye tracking tests. "When did they take the wires out of your jaw?"

"Last week."

"Have you been given any exercises to do to work the jaw muscles?"

"Yes, just some basic stretches," Michael answered.

"How often are you doing them?" Dominic asked while examining Michael's un-casted arm.

"Twice a day."

"Show me what you do." Dominic assisted Michael in removing a couple of the temporary rubber bands holding his jaw together. Michael demonstrated how he was supposed to put a knuckle between his teeth in an attempt to stretch the jaw open a bit wider.

"Try it this way." Dominic demonstrated with his own fingers, and Michael mimicked it. "That's good," Dominic stated. "While you aren't ready to bite into an apple quite yet, you are able to open your mouth a bit wider than I would have thought at this point. I will instruct the nursing staff to make sure that someone can come and assist you with this after each meal." Dominic replaced the rubber bands and then washed his hands again. He then turned his gaze to Michael's neck and chest. Dominic gently touched the sides of Michael's neck just below his jawbone and above the neck brace. "Does your neck hurt very much these days?"

"Not so much. I can't turn my head very much in this brace, but it no longer hurts like it used to." Dominic turned his attention to look at the shoulder area above his broken arm. "Don't freak out, but I need to take a look at various parts of your body. How is the collarbone doing?"

"I haven't really tried to move more than just my arm, so I don't completely know. The couple of times that I have gotten out of bed—with lots of help, of course—it hurt."

"No surprise. You are pretty banged up. A couple of broken ribs and lots of bruising on your legs."

"One leg, you mean," replied Michael.

"No, two legs," answered Dominic, looking intently for a moment at Michael. Dominic continued, "Soon we are going to start some exercises for your legs, in bed at first. We will also start to work on getting your core muscles back in shape so that you can get up by yourself." Dominic pulled out his smartphone and pulled up his calendar. I have already scheduled you for a prosthetic measuring next week. That will give us a couple of weeks to get your core, quads, hams, and glutes ready for your new limb." Michael didn't look too impressed.

"Okay. Now that the chat session is over, it is time to get to work." Dominic walked back over to his duffel bag and pulled out some resistance bands, a rubber ball, and some light ankle weights. "Let's start with your grip on your good hand first. Then we will start gentle squeezing exercises on your hurt hand."

Over the course of the next three weeks, Michael worked with Dominic just about every day. The exercises were painful, and progress was very slow at first. Then Michael started to notice improvements in his strength and endurance. Michael was now sitting in a wheelchair, working with resistance bands to rebuild some strength in his good leg. "Very good, Michael. Tomorrow, we will add another ten reps to the regimen. Your prosthetic arrives in a couple of days, so I want you to start getting out of bed a few times a day. We need to get you used to sitting upright on your own again."

"Yes, and then you can really start causing trouble!" Cynthia walked in the room, observing the scene. "Hey, Dominic, you really are super, you know that? Michael looks better every time I see him!" Dominic smiled the biggest grin that Michael had ever seen on him. Around Cynthia, Dominic appeared to loosen up and have fun.

"He is working hard, and that is what counts." With a joking, pontificating tone, Dominic continued, "Remember you only get back—"

"What you put in," Michael said, finishing Dominic's sentence for him.

"Ahh, good! I see that my words are reaching you," Dominic laughed.

"Be careful," cautioned Cynthia. "Remember pearls before swine!"

"Hmm, there are three of us in this room. Not sure who are the pigs in this analogy," Michael responded with a smile.

"You need only look in a mirror, my dear!" Cynthia joked.

"Hey! You two need a referee!" Dominic laughed, stepping a little between them. "Just remember, Cynthia, it is going to be a few more weeks before the champ is ready to go ten rounds in the ring! But we do need to mark a major milestone. His temporary prosthetic leg arrives tomorrow. We still need to wait a few more weeks for the real one." At that announcement, the smile on Michael's face visibly dropped. He wheeled his wheelchair away from them and moved toward the window.

"Hey, Michael, are you okay?" Cynthia started to move toward him. Dominic gently pulled on her arm, stopping her, and silently shook his head no. He motioned to the door with his head, implying that they should have a private conversation outside.

"Michael is fine," Dominic answered loudly, really for Michael's benefit. "He just needs a rest from today's activity." Cynthia understood and motioned to Dominic to wait outside for her. "Michael, I will tell the nurse to help you back into bed."

Outside the room, Dominic shared some insight with Cynthia. "Behind that smile of his, Michael is struggling to accept this long aftermath of the accident, especially the loss of his leg. This is normal, by the way. However, he is going to need his friends more than ever now."

"What can I do to help?" Cynthia asked.

"Listen to him. Let him talk about how he feels. Help him to get his life back to a normal state. But mostly it is critical that you treat him as you always did before. Cynthia, I am not trying to pry into his business, but I need to know some things about him personally. Can I ask you some questions about him?" Dominic inquired.

"Certainly. What do you need to know?"

"What was he like before the accident? To aid him in his recovery, it helps to know what the person was like before the tragic event.

From the little time that I have spent with him, I'm guessing that he was pretty driven and independent."

"Actually, that is understating it. Michael is extremely ambitious. His work is his life." She paused for a moment. "I'm going to level with you. Underneath it all, Michael is fragile. His external image of strength and confidence is a facade, because he really defines himself by his latest accomplishment."

"That explains a lot. What about friendships?"

"He has very few friends and relies on no one except me."

"What about relationships? Is there anyone close to him? He hasn't mentioned anyone in particular to me."

Cynthia sighed. "Michael changes girlfriends like he does his underwear. Truthfully, he chooses women who offer him nothing more than their beauty."

"What about his spiritual life? Does Michael believe in God?" Dominic asked.

Cynthia shook her head no. "Unfortunately, God is not one of Michael's favorite beings right now. I think he has added the accident to the long list of things he is blaming God for."

Dominic paused for a moment, staring hard at Cynthia. "Cynthia, I am going to speak from experience here. Michael is going to need faith and friends right now. Depression is very common with people who have lost limbs. Many people experience feelings of helplessness and even perceive themselves as unattractive, even a freak. Part of the recovery challenge is helping him gain back his independence, hope, and feeling of self-worth. Oddly, there will even be times when we have to help him by *not* helping him. Especially because of his ambition and independence, he needs to be able to do things for himself."

"I understand. Thank you so much, Dominic. I am really glad that you are here to help us."

"Not a problem. Next week, we move him home and begin rehab both in-home and at our downtown facility. Be sure to call the clinic to schedule his initial appointment with Marti—I mean Dr. Robinson."

"I will. I am looking forward to meeting Dr. Robinson. We are so fortunate to have one of the best rehabilitation doctors in the country right here in Chicago. I wasted no time contacting the office right after the accident."

"You are now a part of this recovery team, Cynthia. Believe me, the people around the patient are just as important as the therapists and doctors. Have you arranged for his assistance at home, round-the-clock for a few months?"

"Yes. I have already hired a doctor and nursing staff to come by the condo several times a day for examinations and for help with bathing, dressing, and wound care. Strangely, his cook didn't want to stay on after the accident. We were even paying her despite the fact that Michael hasn't been there for eight weeks. However, I managed to get a great chef who is willing to live in the condo full-time, provided her eight-year-old daughter lives there too. She seems really wonderful and is willing to do some housework and will call the nursing staff should Michael need help. Oh, and the contractors are almost done installing all of the medical equipment and safety handrails." She paused, looking a bit guilty, and laughed. "Oh, all right! I will tell you! I just couldn't help myself! I took a bath in the new walk-in tub. It was the best twenty minutes of my life! It has the power-jet bubble generator which will massage all of your worries away!"

Dominic roared in laughter. "Well, it certainly sounds like you have everything under control. I will give you a call later on today to do a quick walk-through of the condo, just to make sure that we haven't forgotten anything."

Michael stared out the window at the sunset. Yet another depressing sunset to remind him of everything bad that keeps happening in his life. Sunsets lead to darkness, which is when the horrible loneliness really sets in. Then he would be all alone with his thoughts.

For reasons he couldn't explain, he thought of his family. He imagined his mother—What would she look like now if she were still alive? Would her hair be gray, or would she dye it? What about his dad? Would he still want to shoot hoops with him now? What about Lexy? She would be an adult now, possibly married and maybe a kid on the way. As the tears rolled down his face, he closed his eyes and imagined them all just as they were before their accident. They were even wearing the same clothes that they had on that terrible day. It is amazing what the mind remembers when a final memory has to last a lifetime. They were all gathered around him, hugging him. He heard his mother's voice telling him, *"Te amo, mi hermoso, Miguelito."* ("*I love you, my beautiful Michael!*") He heard his father's voice, telling him (like he always did), *"You can be anything you want to be, son. Just believe in God and yourself."* It was strange that he was finding comfort by imagining his family around him. Dominic's laughter from the hallway broke through the haze of his sorrow, and, despite his mood, he couldn't help smiling a little bit himself. Dominic was a bit like himself—intense—so every laugh had to be cherished.

Michael watched the last rays of sunlight creep below the horizon, marking the beginning of the night. He then prepared himself for the profound loneliness that would accompany him until dawn.

Chapter 7

Gus stood back and examined his craftsmanship. Not bad, really—the transformations were pretty good. The slender Maria had been turned into a plump middle-aged woman with big cheeks and dark hair with gray strands interwoven throughout. Paul, who stood at six feet, was now a short balding man with a little tummy. Lexy, who normally had straight dark hair, was playing with the long, springy curls of her shiny red hair. All three members of the family stood in front of the wall of mirrors, completely mesmerized by their transformed appearances.

The three weeks of guardian "school" had gone pretty smoothly, and the entire family was almost ready to begin their assignments. Now they needed to go over the particulars, including appearance transformation, personality traits, their specific roles/relationships, expectations, how to contact the subject (Michael, in this case), emergency contacts, etc. Gus, after fruitlessly trying to steer them on the next topic, smiled and paused to allow them time to adjust to their new physical appearances. *Rookie guardians... It happens every time*, Gus thought to himself.

"Awesome!" Lexy exclaimed as she pulled down on a long spiral curl, watching with glee as it sprang right back into shape. Her large eyes were changed from brown to blue, and her two front teeth, now with a gap in between them, were peeking out from her new set of braces. "Wow, braces! I look so cool!" Then she thought for a moment and spoke, "Wait a minute! These braces don't hurt at all! Why is everyone always complaining about them?"

"Remember, Lexy, that you no longer feel physical pain," answered Gus. "But, just to give you a taste of what you are missing, hold on a moment." Lexy stood in confusion as Gus quickly programmed something into the small transformer device and pointed it at her. Out from the device came a brilliant ray of red light that went directly to her mouth. Suddenly Lexy screamed and grabbed her face.

"Аннн!" she yelled. "Oh man! My teeth hurt like crazy! Make it stop, please!"

Laughing, Gus pressed another button, and the device projected a white light at Lexy's mouth. Instantly Lexy stopped wailing and looked at everyone in amazement. She was still breathing hard as she stared at her reflection in the mirror. "Wow. Now I know what all my friends were feeling!" She then turned back to Gus with a big smile and said, "That was so cool! Can we do this again? Or maybe I can choose something else, like my stomach. Can you program it to make me throw up or something?"

Gus couldn't help himself; he laughed out loud. Then, to Paul and Maria, he stated, "There is never a dull moment with her around."

"No," Paul and Maria laughed and answered together in almost-perfect unison.

"The transformer," Gus explained, "can be programmed for many things. Just now, we used it to change your physical appearances. Another use for it is to recreate the emotional and physical reactions of the human form, such as pain. This is useful because it helps a guardian prepare for his or her role. If your guardian role needs to have a particular ailment or emotional disorder, we can temporarily provide this to you so you learn how to behave. Remember, on earth, you are now free of any human ailments so that you can focus on your role in assisting your subject.

"Wow, I feel so different! Well, no more yoga pants for me!" Maria laughed, while examining her new fuller figure in the mirror. She looked over at Paul, who seemed unsatisfied with his new physique. "Don't worry, honey. You still look hot to me!"

Paul, who was a six-time marathon runner, was having trouble accepting his wider girth. "Gus, is it possible for me to just have some love handles? Do I have to have the pot belly?"

"I think it is cute!" Maria said, reaching over and patting his new tummy. Paul smiled, but it was clear that he was not amused.

Gus was laughing again. This was actually entertaining for him. "Sorry, Paul, but it is critical that you look nothing like your real self. And remember: your new name is Dr. Sheldon Sherman."

"*Sheldon*? Your new name is Sheldon?" Lexy snorted. "That is funny, Daddy!"

"That will be 'Dr. Sherman' to you, honey!" Paul answered with a wink. He turned back in horror to his reflection in the mirror. "Wow, I never realized how vain I really am."

Gus, the consummate professional, was trying to control his laughter and get the group back on topic. "Well, Dr. Sherman, this change may actually be good for you. Think of it as a growth opportunity."

Paul responded, "Growth? I never imagined this one. There is growth in the afterlife. When will I stop being surprised?"

Gus smiled. "You will catch on to everything in time, Paul. Everyone thinks that their personality was 'finalized' back on earth, in their human form. The truth is really the opposite. Free of all of your human limitations, you will change and grow substantially more here. I think you will be shocked by all that you can learn to do as well as how much deeper you will be able to feel and contemplate on everything.

"More importantly," Gus continued, "your relationships with the Father and Jesus will reach heights never achievable on earth. Our communion with Them and each other is constant and grows every day. In fact, our spirituality—our love—increases with every new person that arrives here. Love, you see, is a powerful force that grows exponentially with each additional person. Like a dessert or a good joke, it is best when shared with others." He then added, "I'm sure that you have experienced that feeling—the moment your heart 'grows,' and you discover that you are capable of feeling more love than you ever knew you had within you."

"When I saw each of my children for the first time, I felt that. Gus, I should need surgery from all of the times my jaw has dropped in shock and amazement," Paul answered. "Speaking of earth, how will we recognize each other when we are back there, especially since we look so different?"

"Your inner lights will be visible to you all, even down on earth. That is also how you will recognize other guardians there too."

"Right, other guardians. Are there a lot down there right now?"

"Absolutely. We have both a numeric target as well as a needs-based target that we maintain at all times. During periods of spiritual 'famine,' as I like to call it, we send down more guardians. Wartime, natural disasters, political and civil unrest—these are some of the times when the need is greatest. Remember, as you learned in your training, we are only there to help them in their journey to accept Jesus as their Savior. The choice, however, is completely theirs."

Paul nodded his understanding. "Right. Remember when you said that hell sends their own guardians, or rather demons, to earth? How does that work? How will we recognize them?"

Gus paused for a moment, then spoke. "You will know when you see them, as they are surrounded by the darkness and evil that fills their existence. Some of these demons appear in humanlike form and get to know their human target, while others remain invisible and provide a dark influence behind the scenes. But know this too: just as you can see them, they can also see you. They see God's goodness and love beaming out from your inner lights. Our lights remind them about their own destruction in the end-times. Confrontations with them can actually be a little frightening at times, but remember that you have help with you—from other guardians, angels, and from the Holy Spirit. Just call out to the Lord, and he will send help."

"Angels?" exclaimed Lexy. "Can they really help when they are so small?"

Gus laughed and answered Lexy, "It is clear that you have never seen a real angel. They are not only the Lord's messengers but also the fierce members of his legions of armies. They are true soldiers and an awesome force to be reckoned with. They serve as protectors and defenders to help advance God's will on earth."

Gus paused for another moment and then continued, "This is going to sound like something from books or movies, but it is nonetheless true. You are about to witness firsthand the ancient struggle for the soul. Minus all of the distractions of 'everyday life' on earth, it all boils down to one thing: the battle of good versus evil. The worst fate for anyone is to spend eternity separated from God.

"On earth," Gus continued, "humans are given everything that they need to live and be happy. Additionally, humans are also given free will, which allows them to choose their own path of good or evil. Unfortunately, humans persist in the same pursuits throughout their long history. The quest for material possessions and ultimate control over others dominates every civilization. It is most dangerous when people, and nations in particular, band together with these goals. That is why we focus on the *individual.* While it is very difficult to reach all the hearts of a large group of people, each guardian is assigned to help one person at a time. In your case, you three will all be assigned to your son, Michael."

"So," asked Paul, "is life on earth just some massive battle over which side—good or evil—gains the most souls?"

"Yes and no," answered Gus. "It is a battle for souls. However, we are not in the business of collecting souls like a child collecting baseball cards. To us, every soul—each person—is precious. To lose even one is a tragic loss, as that person is separated from God and us forever. You see, God knew each of us before we went down on earth. He created each of us individually. He loves us and wishes for us to return his love. In fact, that is all He wants—our love. The way to show our love to God is to help and love each other—on earth and up here in heaven."

"I don't mean to sound rude to you or to God, but I still don't understand," answered Paul. "Is life just some big test for each soul to prove their love to God? This sounds too harsh."

"Only God understands the true purpose of life on earth. If it is a test, then it is not entirely what you are thinking. Each person needs to grow and mature spiritually, which is only made possible by holding on to their faith in God while overcoming challenges, helping others along the way, and choosing good over evil."

"Yes, I can see that. But I still wonder if it had to be so hard sometimes. The suffering, cruelty, oppression—some people really endured a lot."

"Yes, and it is often at the hands of other people or even themselves," Gus explained. "People *choose* to mistreat others in their quest for power, material possessions, and revenge. It is easy to blame God when things go wrong. But, if God made all the decisions for everyone, why then would people need the free will that He gave them?

"Take something like the occurrence of a natural disaster," Gus continued. "This is an opportunity for people to choose to help one another. But again, some people choose to do nothing, or they choose to save themselves. This is where we, the guardians, come in and try to steer them toward the path of Jesus by showing them His love. But I don't want to focus just on the negative. Often the most amazing acts of kindness are performed during the most difficult of situations. The end result is that many people come to Christ when they experience Jesus's love through the selfless acts of churches, missionaries, and Christians reaching out to help during these crises."

Paul nodded. "Yes, that is true. A disaster brings out both the best and the worst in people."

Looking more serious, Gus put on his glasses and went back to the packet he had been holding in his hand. "Believe me, Paul, there will be plenty of time to answer all of these questions and more. But for now, we really need to get moving on the task list. First, you already know that the passage of time up here is very different than down on earth." Michael is now thirty-two years old. To their astonished faces, Gus clarified, "Yes, twenty years have just passed. However, he is in a lot of trouble, which is where you three come in. Please open your briefing packets, and we will discuss your roles and responsibilities."

Chapter 8

Michael looked around the waiting room of the downtown clinic, waiting for his appointment to begin. The room was tastefully furnished, with light maple furniture and dark green carpeting. A video explaining healthy cooking techniques was playing on a large flat-screen TV. Across the room was a large aquarium that took up almost the entire wall. A bevy of tropical fish were swimming in a constant pattern around the tank. It was almost hypnotic just watching the smooth floating motions of the fish as they explored their surroundings. Cynthia had just returned back to him from speaking with one of the receptionists at the big desk at the front of the room. She sat down in the chair next to Michael's wheelchair. "They are running a couple of minutes behind schedule, but they will get to us soon."

"Of course," answered Michael sarcastically. "We have to be punctual, but they can take as much as they need."

"Michael, lower your voice!" replied Cynthia in a whisper loud enough to wake the dead. This was confirmed by some of the other patrons in the room who were now looking at them with interest. "We are lucky to even get an appointment today. They are fully booked through the end of the month."

"Hmm," Michael answered. "My guess is that they figured out who I am and decided that they *could make the time* since I could afford to pay in cash, rather than receiving the less-than-full price with an insurance company."

"That is a horrible attitude," Cynthia scolded. "This is an extremely reputable clinic led by one of the best doctors in the country. Not only is she a renowned physical therapist, she is also a medical doctor with specialized training in brain trauma."

"Money is the key that opens all locks."

"I think Dominic pulled a few strings for us, if you want my opinion."

"Dominic, yes, and also the potential to have me listed as one of their clients. That will certainly give them some free publicity."

"You are really unbelievable today," Cynthia retorted. "I think I will play a game while you sit there and sulk."

Cynthia pulled out her iPad and began a fierce round of *Bubble Witch*. Michael found himself actually obeying her order, sulking, as he looked at his pathetic reflection in the aquarium glass. While he was contemplating how everything had come to this moment—his missing leg, him confined to a wheelchair, his independence gone—he heard a voice near him. An old lady, also in a wheelchair, had rolled on up to him. She had to be close to ninety years old.

"Son, I think I know what your problem is," she told him in a raspy voice. She was shaking an arthritic, bent finger at him but was also smiling. "I get that way myself sometimes."

Michael looked at her in complete confusion. Either she really did understand what he was feeling or she was a complete lunatic. Truth be told, he was not angry about being at the clinic. He really liked Dominic, so, by extension, Dr. Robinson should be great too. He was just angry at life, angry at not being in control of his life. "Well, I—"

She continued, interrupting him, even louder this time, finger still pointing at him, "I just tell myself to STOP IT. I am making myself and everyone else around me miserable, and it is wrong."

"Hmph!" agreed Cynthia, still engrossed in her game.

"Honestly, I don't mean to—" Michael attempted to interject but was again interrupted.

"You have to think of other people, not just yourself."

"Well, I—"

"Don't you agree, Ben?" She motioned to another patient, an elderly man across the room.

"I sure do, Rosetta!" Ben hollered back at full volume. "In fact, I was about to give him the same advice myself!" Other patients began to voice their agreement, nodding their heads and shouting things like: "Definitely!" and "You tell him, Rosetta!"

Michael could almost hear the triumphant trumpet fanfare from the smile on Rosetta's face. He was growing more and more uneasy as the entire room was now engaged in this scene. While his earlier behavior was less than perfect, he didn't need a room full of people diagnosing him. He looked over at Cynthia for some help, but she was still absorbed in her game. This was a strange experience for him.

Before the accident, Michael would have had no problem telling off everyone in the room. But he would have done it so smoothly, probably resulting in him selling investment plans to many of them. Feeling like an alcoholic at his first AA meeting, Michael answered, "Yes, I admit that I can be challenging sometimes, but I am still trying to learn how to live with what has happened to me."

Rosetta didn't seem to be listening. She took off her crocheted shawl and, with some effort, draped it across Michael's shoulders. For a man with very few friends, he was not used to complete strangers inserting themselves in his life and putting their hands on him.

"I am Rosetta. I have been coming here the longest of everyone you see in here. We are a family in this clinic." She gestured to the whole room. "You are our newest member. Your name is Michael, is it not?"

"Well, yes," Michael responded, his nose now full of the strong, strange rose-scented perfume from the shawl. He was so used to being famous (everyone knew who Michael Garcia was) that he was trying to adjust to being unknown here. While he was attempting to stifle a sneeze, she continued, grabbing his hands, unaware of his discomfort.

"Everyone takes care of everyone else here. That's the rule. Even though you came to this clinic alone today, you will never be alone again. We all work together. We make progress *together*." She lifted his hands into the air, almost screaming at this point, when she asked him, "ARE YOU READY TO COMMIT TO GETTING BETTER? ARE YOU READY TO CHANGE YOUR LIFE?"

Michael, eyes wide and trying hard to regain control of his hands without injuring her, exclaimed, "I—I'm not sure about all this...I need to—"

"Hold on, Michael. I have something for you," said Rosetta. She let go of his hands, calm again, and reached for her rather large handbag. She started digging around inside the bag, pulling out various items, and began to place them into his lap. First came a comb, then a hair dryer, next a large pair of women's underwear.

Michael's face paled with horror at this display. Cynthia, he noticed, was silently laughing so hard that there were tears streaming down her face. "Thanks, Cyn. Some help you are right now," Michael spewed at her.

"Here it is!" Rosetta shouted with victory. She proudly held out a bottle of Philips Milk of Magnesia and a spoon. "This is the answer to most of your problems. You are obviously suffering from some issues with your bowels." The other patients in the room nodded their approval.

"What?" exclaimed Michael, who had clearly had enough. "I don't have ANY issues with my bowels, thank you very much!"

"Well, I am certainly glad to hear that, Mr. Garcia," said a female voice. "Ahh. I see that you have met Rosetta. I am Dr. Martha Robinson, or Marti, as I prefer to be called."

Michael stared blankly at her extended hand that was waiting for him to shake. He then decided that if he were going to die, now might be an acceptable time to do so.

"Hi, Marti," said Cynthia, who stood up and diverted the attention away from Michael. "I am Michael's assistant, Cynthia Longstein. I am so glad to finally meet you!" She and Marti shook hands. "And, yes, this is Michael Garcia."

Michael looked up at Marti and extended his hand for the handshake. "Hi, Dr., uh, I mean Marti. Despite this less-than-desirable introduction, I am also glad to meet you." At that moment, to Michael's relief, Dominic arrived.

"Hey, Michael! Cynthia! Glad to finally see you both here!" Dominic hugged Cynthia and did a fist-bump-shake with Michael. "Hey, Rosetta, are you getting Michael into trouble already?"

"No trouble that a little bit of this can't fix!" Rosetta exclaimed, holding up the bottle.

"Oh, I see," said Dominic, trying not to laugh. "Looks like you are doing a great job, as usual, taking care of the patients here." He turned to Michael and continued, "Michael, Rosetta is one of our volunteers here in the clinic. She does a great job of keeping everyone fired up about working hard and making progress."

"Oh, you are a volunteer?" Michael responded.

"Been working here for fifteen years!" Rosetta replied. "I saw Dominic through some of his worst days."

"Yes, she did. And I am forever grateful to you for that," Dominic said in complete earnest. He leaned down and gave Rosetta a kiss on her cheek. Rosetta beamed with happiness.

"You were a patient here, Dominic?" Michael asked in complete surprise.

"Yes. You didn't know?" At that, Dominic lifted up his left pant leg, revealing a prosthetic limb. "I came here after leaving a part of myself in Iraq during the war. IED."

At that news, Michael was stumped into momentary silence. "Wow, Dom. I'm sorry. I didn't know."

"You didn't ask" was all Dominic said as he began wheeling Michael down the hall and into Marti's office.

The dark forces around Michael released a sharp hiss that was imperceptible to the humans around them. They did not like this place of positive feelings or these newcomers who were beginning to impact Michael's perspective, making him reassess his behavior. They will have to tighten their grip around Michael's soul and plan for sabotaging any effort for leading him toward the light.

Chapter 9

"Okay, Michael. You have been doing in-home therapy for three weeks now, and your progress is steady," Marti explained in her office. "The good news is that you have made it out of phase one, which mostly comprises exercises designed for scar tissue prevention while still letting you heal. From this phase, you have accomplished quite a bit. You are able to stand for a few minutes at a time, with assistance, in your temporary prosthetic limb. From the exercises you have been doing, the muscles in your left shoulder, collarbone, and ribs are healing and getting stronger. Soon we want you to be doing all of your transitions to and from the wheelchair on your own. From the latest measurements, your jaw is able to open pretty wide now. You have made amazing progress on that. Dominic will continue to tweak the exercises to get you back to full capacity."

Marti got up from her chair and walked around her large mahogany desk. She sat on the edge, facing Michael and Cynthia, who were sitting in the chairs in front. "We need to talk about roles and responsibilities." She looked first at Cynthia and then continued, "You, Cynthia, now need to change roles from caregiver to assistant. Michael needs to do all of his own feeding, wheelchair maneuvering, toothbrushing, etc." To Michael, she continued, "You should only need assistance now with transitions and anything that you cannot lift. You still have a home aide to help you in and out of the tub and to the bathroom, right?"

"Yes. For how much longer will that be necessary?"

"Hopefully only another few weeks. Once your ribs and collarbone are completely healed, you will be able to do this yourself. Now that you are able to start coming here to the center for therapy, we will create a new schedule for you."

While Marti continued on about the new schedule, Michael looked around the office. It looked like the normal doctor's office with a computer on her desk, bookshelves filled with medical books, journals, and mini statues representing various parts of the skeletal and muscular systems. On the wall was only one piece of artwork, a framed picture with the word "Believe" in the middle and then, directly below it, words from Scripture: "With God all things are possible—Matthew 19:26." He then studied Marti as she was discussing some dietary issues with Cynthia. She was younger than he expected, probably around thirty-five or thirty-six. Her red-rimmed glasses helped her to look a bit older, but not much. From her appearance, he could tell that she focused much more on her work than on her looks. Her strawberry-blond hair was pulled back into a ponytail, and she wore little to no makeup. The only jewelry she wore was a cross necklace that peeked over the collar on her white lab coat. He tuned back into the conversation when she pulled some papers off of her desk. "I will send off the results from today's digital scan of your stump to the prosthetics manufacturer. They will use the scan to customize the fit of the device to your body. This will minimize pressure points and will make wearing the limb more comfortable. We should receive your new permanent limb in a couple of weeks. Any questions?"

"None from me," said Cynthia. "We really appreciate your help."

"My pleasure, Cynthia. As funny as this sounds, my goal is to get you all to the point where you won't need to come back here," Marti laughed. She turned to Michael. "Any questions from you?"

"Yes. Who will be running the therapy sessions—you or Dominic?" Michael asked.

"It will vary, depending upon what we are doing. Sometimes it will be me, other times Dominic. And, on occasion, even both of us."

"Good. I am used to Dominic's style, and I was hoping that I would still work with him." Cynthia nodded her head in agreement.

"Definitely. Dominic is essentially my right hand in this clinic," Marti answered, gesturing to her hand. "He practically runs the place."

"I, uh, didn't know about his leg," Michael stated. "I feel pretty badly about never noticing, even after all of the time we spent together."

"Actually, I'm not surprised," Marti responded. "Dominic has worked hard to appear as though he does not wear a prosthetic device. His rehabilitation is so complete that in his mind I genuinely don't believe that he feels impaired at all. Years ago, after he completed his treatment here, he went back to school to become a therapist himself. He is an amazing person, one of the best people I've ever known and frankly one of the best therapists I've ever worked with. Even now, he is studying for an advanced degree in working with patients with traumatic brain injuries."

Michael was stunned again. He knew that he and Dominic were similar—intense, driven—but now he knew that they had even more in common; both had lost a leg. Looks like Dominic figured out how to live with the loss. For the first time in weeks, Michael actually had hope that he could too.

The dark forces around Michael swirled in anger at the new hope finding its way into Michael's heart. "We need to work harder!" the leader screamed at the others. "We can't lose him now after we have come so far!"

"Don't worry," one of them sneered in response. "I already have someone working on the final part that will seal the deal."

Chapter 10

Maria (guardian name: Joanna Flaherty) was cleaning the kitchen floor in Michael's penthouse apartment when Lexy (guardian name: Jackie Flaherty) came through the door. "Hi, Mama!" Lexy said as she stepped carefully to not walk on the freshly mopped parts of the floor.

"Hi, sweetie. How was your walk?"

"Good. I made some new friends today."

"Any with only two legs?" Maria asked.

"Well, do wings count as legs? If so, then no."

Maria sighed and laughed to herself. Since being back on earth for the last three weeks, they discovered that Lexy had a new talent: she could talk to animals. "Okay, let's hear it."

"Well," answered Lexy, "I learned that the best blueberry pie in the city is made in that corner deli on the street. Grim and Graw both like it there the best."

"Grim and Graw?"

"Yes. They are brothers, they told me, and their mother thought she was being funny when she named them."

"What kind of birds are they?" Maria asked, resuming her mopping.

"They are crows. Actually, you know them."

"I do?" Maria asked, curious now.

"Yeah, they are the two birds that always carry on so loudly in the mornings right outside Michael's window. Usually they are fighting over scraps from the dumpster behind our building. But they also just like to make noise and wake everyone up."

"Sounds charming," Maria said, shaking her head as Lexy grabbed a freshly baked cookie from the plate and scampered off to watch TV on the couch. The really good news, thought Maria, about *not* being human when on earth is that she was no longer worried about Lexy's safety. Her only concerns now were to not reveal their true identities and to help Michael.

Michael—that was another topic. Again, she was very glad that she could no longer feel any painful human emotions, because the Michael that she encountered now was unrecognizable to her. Yes, twenty years had gone by since the last time she saw him, but that would only age his appearance and make him more mature. Yes, he had been in a serious accident, so his body was damaged. However, it was his spirit, his personality, that she found so different from the loving, always laughing, and outgoing boy that she knew before. The "old" Michael that she knew would have given anyone the shirt off of his back. The "new" Michael, while polite, was reserved and only seemed concerned about his ambition.

Even more alarming was what she read in his inner light. Instead of a brilliant glowing flame, Michael's inner light was only a tiny glow surrounded by a thick band of darkness. What she read was pain and bitterness, with barely any love for anyone, himself included. She also read that Michael blamed God for all of his troubles, thereby cutting off the primary source from which all love comes. She could see the fierce, dark bands encircling, almost suffocating his light, like thick clouds of black smoke. The darker the clouds, the stronger the forces.

After their first few meetings with Michael, she, Paul, and Lexy had overcome their initial shock of seeing actual demons firsthand; and Michael had several standing guard around him at all times. Demons are very clever, she knew; their main weapon used on humans is the poisoning of minds against any positive thoughts about themselves and especially God. Unfortunately, guardians cannot permanently chase away demons; only the human can do this by accepting Jesus and calling on the power of the Holy Spirit. In his inner light, Maria read Michael's accomplishments, of which there were many. But she had to look hard to find any works of selflessness or charity, except for those that could be used as tax write-offs. While he was not completely bad, Michael was in trouble.

She finished mopping and walked to the laundry room to rinse out the mop. On the way, she couldn't help but admire the apartment. It must have cost a fortune, especially with the tall ceilings and the long walls of windows in the living and dining rooms opening to the city below. Chic dark leather furniture furnished most of the rooms, complimenting the light hardwood floors. Interesting amenities could be found throughout the place, such as a Jacuzzi in the media room, a conservatory hosting exotic plants and flowers (complete with a breakfast table), and a full-circle fireplace in the middle of the dining room. Much like the man who lived in the apartment, it spoke of accomplishment yet felt empty. Maria noticed that, despite the enormous care that had gone into the interior design, including expensive paintings and statues, there was nothing personal anywhere. No photographs of friends or family (them!) to be found. The apartment was beautiful but sterile, more like a museum than a home.

Since her responsibilities as Michael's cook resided in the kitchen, Maria gave herself permission to place a Bible on the counter. Sometimes that Bible would find its way to the kitchen table on the occasions that Michael would take his meal or coffee there. Maria would then smile to herself when she would peek over and notice Michael reading the page that she had turned to—for his benefit, of course. This spiritual war for Michael would have to be won by daily chiseling away at his resistance through the Word of God and by examples of love. This was the hard part as a guardian—she could only help steer Michael in the right direction; everything else was left up to him.

"I still can't believe how many TV channels there are now, Mama!" Lexy (Jackie) yelled from the living room.

Maria moved quickly into the living room and gave Lexy a stern look. She lowered her voice when she spoke, "Jackie, dear, remember not to give us away."

Lexy gasped and then covered her mouth with her hands and nodded. She then mouthed the words "I'm sorry!"

"It's okay, pumpkin. Just remember to think before you speak," Maria responded in a soft voice. She started to return to the laundry

HELP AMONG US

room when she heard the intercom buzzer go off. She walked over to the console in the kitchen and pressed the Talk button. "Yes, Mr. Garcia?"

"Mrs. Flaherty," Michael's voice sounded through the speaker, "would you please bring some coffee and a light snack to my office? Enough for me and my guest, please."

"Certainly, sir. I will be there as soon as the coffee finishes brewing."

"Thank you," Michael answered.

Maria went to work to prepare the food. Now that Michael had recovered enough, he started working at home, just a few hours a day. When everything was ready, she made her way to his office and knocked on the door.

"Come in," Michael's voice called through the thick wooden door. Maria opened the door and wheeled in the cart carrying the tray through the doorway. Michael and his guest, Trent Wentworth, were busy at work at Michael's desk. "Please put the food down on the table over there." Michael gestured to the table next to his desk.

Maria set everything up, including pouring the coffee, and then left the room. As she walked down the hall, she adjusted her hearing, as she learned in her guardian training, so that she could hear through the walls. This was not a complicated thing to do. It just took a little bit of concentration so that she could pinpoint the very direction in which she wanted to focus her hearing. It was almost like turning the dial on a radio until she found the clearest signal on the desired station. Soon she could hear them.

"Trent, I still don't understand all of these expenses." Michael's voice sounded agitated. "I know that I've been gone for over three months, but I don't understand what could create this amount of charges."

"The majority is for the new construction at the Garcia Lodge—materials, labor, permits—you know how that goes. The rest is for utilities, insurance premiums, taxes, and penalties because we got behind in our quarterly payments. Remember, Michael, that I have been doing both of our jobs right now. I need you to sign these checks, and I will make sure that we get caught up on everything." There was a momentary pause and then Michael spoke again.

"All right. I guess the new construction charges plus three months' worth of expenses and penalties can add up to a large amount." Maria could hear the sounds of shuffling and the pen writing on the papers.

"Oh, Michael, there is one more check and form to sign."

"What? I thought we just took care of the outstanding expenses."

"No, Michael, this is good news," Trent answered. "This is the agreement and the projected setup up costs for the Chicago Business Summit next month at the lodge. This is going to be a huge event, Michael. Melissa worked her tail off to secure our lodge for their conference. We should make a lot on this."

"Wow, Trent, that is great news! I was hoping we could start hosting that annual event! This draws people from across the country and all over the world. This should open the door to booking some national events, especially with the elections coming up. Make sure that we give them the best of everything." Michael's voice sounded mildly happy for the first time in all the weeks that Maria had been there. From the guardian briefing, she remembered that Garcia Enterprises also owned a large resort (called the Garcia Lodge) that hosted many conferences and events.

"I will personally pass that message to Melissa," Trent answered.

"I'm sure you will since she is your girlfriend!" Michael answered with a laugh. "Hey, pass me my coffee and sandwich, please. And tell Rensalant Construction that I want to set up a meeting with him by the end of the week. I want a full briefing on the status of that new construction at the Lodge. Now that I can sit up for longer periods of time, I want to start really working again, initially from here and then hopefully back in the office soon."

"Yeah, Michael. It will be really great to have you back," Trent's voice answered back.

Chapter 11

"How does that feel now, Michael?" Marti asked. She showed him another way how to wrap his stump to minimize swelling and to prevent blisters. Then they put on his new permanent prosthetic limb. With Dominic behind him, Michael was standing between the parallel bars in the workout room inside the clinic. He took a couple of baby steps, and, unlike his temporary prosthetic, this new one didn't hurt.

"This feels like it is almost attached to me," Michael answered as he continued to make his way down the length of the bars.

"That is how it is supposed to feel," Marti answered back.

"It still feels like I am walking on air though."

"You will get used to that," Dominic answered, assisting him from behind. "Soon you will be able to adjust how you move so that you don't notice it as much."

"At first, Michael, you will lead with your good leg. Once you get used to shifting your weight onto your prosthetic, this will change, and you will lead with your prosthetic. Now let's spend a few minutes standing in place and just shifting your weight. Start on your good leg."

Michael leaned on his good leg and then shifted his full weight onto his prosthetic. While it felt better than his temporary prosthetic, it still didn't feel like his old leg. He quickly realized that learning to fully walk again was going to take some time.

"Don't get discouraged, Michael," Marti said, reading his face. "This takes time, roughly three to nine months to just get comfortable walking around. Then, if you really want to be able to move around like you did before, we have advanced training with a true obstacle course."

"Sounds like boot camp," Michael said, shifting his weight back to his good leg. He was amazed how tiring this was, despite the fact that he was doing nothing more than shifting his weight. He stopped for a break and took a look around him. If he did not know that he was in the Robinson Rehabilitation Center, he would have thought that he was in a world-class gymnasium. Rows of treadmills, elliptical trainers, and cycling machines lined one wall, while free weights and a circuit training area filled in two more. In the corner was a stretching area with balancing balls, disks, foam rollers, and resistance bands. Windows were everywhere, including on the ceiling, giving the room a positive atmosphere. "Wow," Michael exclaimed. "You could really get a great workout here."

"That is the goal for both our clients and our employees," Marti answered. "In fact, most of our employees use this facility on a regular basis—no need for a gym membership when we have this right here in our work space."

A young African American boy, probably around twelve years old, walked up to Marti. He wore the Richardson Clinic T-shirt, just like everyone else who worked in the building. "Excuse me, Marti, but there are a bunch of TV cameras and reporters in the hallway over there." He was pointing at the glass doors. "They are trying to get in here to take some pictures of you and Mr. Garcia, I think. I just locked the doors."

"Thanks, Ethan. Dominic, can you call security? Looks like they forced their way into the building again."

"Again?" Michael asked.

"Yes. Looks like the paparazzi have found you here. We will need to beef up security during your appointments."

From the corner of his eye, Michael began seeing rapid flashes of light. He was still trying to figure out where it was coming from when Marti pointed to the glass doors. Soon they could hear the sounds of banging on the doors and muffled voices calling for Michael.

"Well, I've certainly given them some new material," Michael spewed. "They used to fight to photograph me standing on the Red Carpet. Now they are clambering over each other to film me in my struggle to stand on a prosthetic leg or sitting in my wheelchair."

HELP AMONG US

Dominic and Marti shared a knowing glance. "Dominic, can you get rid of the ones right behind the doors?" Marti asked.

"Sure thing, Marti. I will also clear them all out of the hallway," Dominic yelled as he sprinted off.

"Don't hurt anyone, Dominic. We aren't insured for that!" Marti said, laughing.

"I'll be gentle!" Dominic yelled as he went out the glass doors into the hallway. After a few seconds, they heard Dominic's voice, calm but firm, directing them all to move out of the hallway, as they were in violation of the fire code.

"Seriously, Marti. Will Dominic be okay? I've seen some of these paparazzi guys in action, and they can really be tough. Maybe we should help," Michael suggested.

"No, we would only get in the way," Marti answered. "Dominic actually works better alone."

Without warning, they heard a loud THUD against the glass doors. Next, a man's body was pressed up against the glass and was slowly sliding down the door. They could hear Dominic's voice outside shouting "Whoa, sir! Looks like you fell down!" Then, with dripping sarcasm, "Oh no! Your camera looks broken to me too. What a shame."

Marti tried hard to hide her laughter. Ethan was watching this with keen interest. "Marti, did Dominic just break that man's camera?"

"No, Ethan. Dominic is smarter than that. However, I would bet that he 'orchestrated' in helping that man trip over himself, fall face-first onto the glass door, and land on his camera. And all without laying a finger on him."

"That is so cool!" Ethan said, unable to take his eyes off the scene just behind the door.

"While this is very entertaining, Ethan, my guess is that you still have homework to finish."

Ethan's momentary enjoyment came to an abrupt end. "No way! Can I do it later?"

"No. Finish it now because you have soccer later," Marti told him. "Oh, go out through the locker room so you don't have to go through the hallway. And I want to see your homework on my desk in one hour."

Ethan grumbled and walked toward the locker room. Michael noticed that he walked with a limp.

"You help him with his schoolwork? That is nice," Michael said.

"Schoolwork. And everything else. I am his foster parent right now."

"Foster parent? That is incredible."

"Not really," Marti responded. "Both of his parents are dead. He had been living on the streets for years. I found him by chance four years ago when I was visiting the hospital for another patient. Ethan had just arrived the day before and almost died from the beating he received from the street gang he was working for." Michael's eyes widened.

Marti continued, "Ethan had an interesting job. The street gang would pay him, and other young kids, to break into cars and apartments and steal items such as car stereos, cell phones, jewelry, wallets, anything not nailed down. At first it seemed like easy money to Ethan. But the gang kept raising the stakes. One day, Ethan apparently didn't steal enough to satisfy them. Being a homeless orphan, they knew that they could do whatever they wanted to Ethan."

Michael was rendered speechless for what Marti was telling him about Ethan, so he listened in silence. He couldn't help but make the comparison to his own childhood and, for the first time, felt a twinge of guilt for being so bitter. While it was very cliché to admit, his brutal childhood could have been much worse.

Marti paused for a moment, in deep thought. "I am not sure why, but I saw something in his face, even though he was asleep. I was drawn to his bedside, and I just looked at him, trying to find him through the maze of the various machines hooked up to him. He seemed so helpless, so alone. Yet there was something so angelic about him. Each time I returned to the hospital, I would stop by. Eventually, I learned the severities of his injuries and knew that he would need rehab in order to walk again. So I offered my services to him—for free, of course. One thing led to another, and now I am his foster mom."

Stabs of humility, awe, and guilt coursed in Michael's gut. He had never considered the foster parent relationship from the parent's point of view. What an enormous sacrifice that these people make, *choose* to make, to help someone in need: someone like him, often a complete stranger. He thought about his former foster parents and wondered how they were doing now. Another surge of guilt swept through him as he realized that he had never taken the time to find out. "That is such a great story, Marti," he managed to blurt out. "Is it hard being a parent?"

Marti gestured that they needed to continue the session. "I will only answer your questions if you keep working." After a few moments of the weight-shifting exercises, Marti moved him back to taking baby steps, using the parallel bars for support. She then continued the conversation, "It is always challenging to be a parent, even more so when the child is partially grown and not your own. But in many ways, I feel that I am the lucky one. Let me just state that no one should ever underestimate Ethan. He is highly intelligent and has actually become a big help in the clinic. For example, he figured out how to work the appointments and billing computer systems all on his own."

"A computer genius. That will serve him well," Michael said between steps.

"It will. He wants to be an astrophysicist."

"Really?" Michael exclaimed.

"He is going to do it too. He can already tell you more than you ever want to know about black holes, supernovas, antigravity, and neighboring galaxies."

"Wow, Marti. I'm really impressed. That is a long way from stealing radios for a street gang."

"Life is a journey, Michael. You need to always think about which path you are going to take." Just at that moment, Marti's cross necklace caught the light and seemed to sparkle.

"Yeah, maybe. But for some people, that path leads to a dark alley," Michael responded, looking at her necklace.

"It doesn't have to," Marti answered.

"For some of us," Michael continued, "we have no control over where our path leads us. Despite our best efforts, no matter how much we have already endured, disaster always finds us."

"Sometimes, Michael, the dark alley leads to a new street, one that you would never have found on your own. Finding new streets can be scary at first. Be patient with yourself." She stopped for a moment, thinking. "Michael, are you a spiritual person? We are a holistic clinic. We treat the entire person—body, mind, and soul."

"No, Marti, I am not spiritual," Michael answered with a trace of anger in his voice. "God has not exactly endeared himself to me. I don't know how much you know about my past, but if you know any of it, then you will understand why I am not religious."

"Well, there really isn't anyone in Chicago, possibly even in America, who doesn't know something about you," Marti answered. "But I did do a little research on you to learn more about your past. I'm sorry about your family."

"Thanks," Michael answered, shifting back and forth between the parallel bars. "Honestly, I'm not looking for sympathy here. In fact, talking about my past is not something I like doing." He struggled back to his wheelchair, and Marti helped him into it. "I will just sum this up quickly and then we won't discuss it again. The truth is, every time I finally get my life back on track, something terrible happens. Sometimes I think that I should just stop trying."

Anger and frustration fueled the speed with which he wheeled himself toward the men's locker room and away from Marti. Once inside, he felt something dripping onto his arm, so he looked up and around to find a ceiling leak without success. When he saw another drip, his hand went to his face, and he felt the hot track of tears that were sliding down his cheeks. Wheeling around to his locker, he wiped his face with his towel and closed his eyes, leaning his head against the locker door. No, he wasn't angry with Marti. Rather, these were tears of shame for his behavior—past and present.

Marti stood by the parallel bars and watched him wheel away. She gently grabbed her cross necklace. "Please, Jesus," she whispered a silent prayer. "The enemy has him in his grip and is deliberately hurting him to make sure that he stays angry and blames You. Help him find You through the midst of his anger. I don't know what Your plan for him is, but help me to guide him onto the path to You."

CHAPTER 12

"Jackie," Maria called to Lexy, "you can't bring them in here! This is not our apartment."

"But, Mama, they followed me here!" Lexy answered.

"Then you will just need to take them back down the elevator and outside."

"But they could starve, Mama! Who will feed them?" Lexy cried out.

Michael wheeled himself out of his office and down the hall. "What is going on, Jackie? Are you okay?"

"Michael—" Jackie (Lexy) started.

"Mr. Garcia—" Mrs. Flaherty (Maria) interrupted.

"Michael is fine," Michael answered.

"Yes, Michael." Lexy looked happily at her mother. "On my way home from school, I passed by some mean boys tormenting these two little kittens. I asked them to stop, but the boys wouldn't listen. One of them even pushed me down." She pointed to a scrape on her knee.

"Jackie! You could have been hurt!" Maria exclaimed.

"I'm all right, Mama, really." Then, with more excitement in her voice, she continued, "Just when I thought that there was nothing I could do, a really cool thing happened. A group of stray dogs came by and started to growl and circle the boys. It was really weird, but they seemed to be protecting the kittens. One of the boys tried to kick the dogs, but they bit his pants and pulled him to the ground. The other two boys ran away. I then walked over to the dogs and got them away from the boy. I don't know why, but the dogs weren't mean to me. They even let me pet them." She smiled softly, as if recalling the memory. "The last boy finally ran away. That is when I pulled out the remaining ham from my lunch box and gave it to the kittens. The rest of my lunch went to the dogs, of course, as a reward for their bravery," Lexy said proudly. "After that I walked home."

"So how did the two kittens end up here?" Maria asked.

"When I got on to the elevator, they got in before the doors closed. I didn't even know that they followed me." She paused to think hard for a moment. "Wow, I wonder how they crossed all of those streets?"

Michael was trying to imagine how all of this was possible, when the two kittens jumped up into his lap and starting purring, rubbing their heads against his hands. "Oh no, you don't!" Michael said. "While I admit you are both very cute, you can't worm your way into my house!"

"Wow, Michael! They like you!" Lexy exclaimed.

As if on cue, the littlest kitten with brown tiger stripes yawned and settled down in the crook of Michael's arm. It could not have looked cuter. The other kitten mewled loudly at Michael as if to say, "Let us stay with you!"

Maria looked at the scene in horror and then shot a knowing glance at Lexy. Lexy gave an innocent smile back at her mother, but it didn't work.

"Well," said Michael, "they can stay until tomorrow. We will decide what to do with them then."

"Hooray!" celebrated Lexy. "I already bought some food on the way home! I will go back to the corner store and pick up a litter box and some litter!"

"Hold on, young lady," Maria said. "Bring the kittens, and help me pen off an area in the mudroom for them."

Michael laughed. "I will be in my office, if anyone calls."

Maria waited until Michael was back in his office and on his phone. "Lexy, what happened here?" she asked her daughter. "You know that you cannot have all of these pets. We have only been here a month, and already we have acquired a fish and two hamsters. Thankfully, both of those live in your room. These kittens, however, are going to roam the whole house. They will wreck the furniture, the carpets, the drapes, literally everything. And they could eat the other pets!"

"No, they won't, Mama. I told them that they have to behave in order to live here."

"Lexy, do you really expect me to believe that they understand what this means?"

Lexy called to the two kittens that were lounging on the floor, cleaning themselves. They both stood up and walked over to her. She spoke to them in a strange sounding voice and used a language that even Maria couldn't comprehend. However, it was clear that the kittens understood. "Mama, I am going to prove to you that they understand." Maria waited and watched.

"I am going to say it first in English, Mama, and then in their language," Lexy explained. Maria nodded.

"Kittens," Lexy said to the kittens in English, "meow three times and then take two steps backward if you understand that you cannot destroy anything in this apartment." Lexy then spoke in their language. To Maria's amazement, the kittens both meowed three times and then took two steps backward.

Maria was satisfied, at least for the moment. "So I am guessing that those 'miraculous rescue dogs' were following your commands too, right?"

"Certainly, Mama. I talk to them every morning on the way to school, so I was able to call out to them after that mean boy knocked me down. I told them only to scare the boys, not to hurt them." She paused, looking down at the fake injury on her knee, and then continued, "You know, Mama, it is really wonderful that we cannot get hurt or feel pain anymore. I think that fall might really have hurt me otherwise!"

Maria hugged her daughter but was still trying to understand the new gift that she had obtained. Somehow Lexy could communicate with animals. She also wondered how many more pets they would have before this adventure ended.

CHAPTER 13

Dr. Sherman (Paul) finished examining Michael. "Good news, Mr. Garcia. Your collarbone is almost fully healed, and your ribs are back to normal. You should be able to start moving around completely by yourself now. Just take it slow and be careful, as your shoulder needs more time to completely heal. I will instruct the home health aide to merely assist you, as you should be doing all of the work now."

Michael smiled a little at this news. While it was only a little smile, it warmed Paul's heart. While he could no longer feel painful emotions as he could when he was human, it still bothered him to witness how his son had changed from a happy, loving boy to a reserved and deeply unhappy man.

"Thanks, Dr. Sherman. I must say that I am looking forward to some privacy again, especially in the bathroom. Nothing like having an audience around for some of your most personal moments."

Paul laughed. "I can well imagine how you feel. It is experiences like these that make us grateful for all the little things in life."

"Yes," muttered Michael as he began wheeling himself back to his desk. "Especially when those are all you have left."

Paul's heart broke when he heard Michael's comment. But speaking of little things, both kittens chose that moment to jump back into Michael's lap, snuggle next to his hands, and start purring. In the three weeks since they moved in, the kittens had bonded with Michael. In fact, he had become quite protective of them as they slept in his room and were always nearby. Maybe Lexy's new talent with animals had a great side effect by giving Michael something to care about.

"Well," laughed Paul, "you may not get any privacy with these two around!"

"True." Michael smiled, petting both of them. "However, these two won't tell anyone about what they see," Michael joked.

Paul smiled but had to choke off his laughter. The kittens kept Lexy informed of Michael's every move. That is how Paul learned the depth of Michael's unhappiness. Paul packed up his medical bag and took out his cell phone, scheduling an appointment. "I will be back at the end of the week to check up on you again. Does 2:00 p.m. on Friday work for you?"

Michael grabbed his cell phone and checked his calendar. "Yes, that is fine. By the way, I want to start working back in my office downtown next week. Is that okay?"

"So long as Cynthia is there to assist you, should you need help," Paul answered. "She has my phone number on speed dial in case of an emergency. But I don't foresee anything. See you on Friday." He waved, walking out of the room and closing the door to Michael's home office.

Paul walked down the hall and found Maria and Lexy in the kitchen. "Tune your ears so we can hear if he is coming near us," Paul said, voice lowered.

"I can hear him now," Maria answered. "He is on the phone right now, so he should be occupied for a few minutes, at least."

"Excellent," Paul answered. "The good news is that his body is healing well. His ribs are healed, and his collarbone is just about there. He will need more time with his shoulder, so he will still need the home health aide to assist him for some things. But he is ready to start doing most everything for himself. Obviously, he still has several months of therapy before he is ready to walk and move around completely without the wheelchair."

Maria exhaled in relief. "Any bit of positive news can attempt to penetrate the armor of the dark forces controlling him. I think that the longer he feels helpless, the worse his depression and bitterness becomes. This good news should give him back some independence." She got up and put on a pot of coffee to brew.

"I agree. We need to find a way to get past those demons surrounding Michael and feeding him with self-destructive thoughts."

"You are so right about that," answered Cynthia, who just arrived in the doorway. "Sorry I am late to the meeting. I got caught in some brutal traffic." She smelled the air and her face lit up. "Oh, wonderful! You make the best coffee, Maria."

"Thanks, Cynthia! I just made a blueberry pie. Would you like a slice?"

Cynthia's eyes doubled in size. "Are you kidding? Your pie is the best in town."

"Both Grim and Graw agree with that," Lexy said proudly. "They used to like the pie in the corner deli the best, but when I gave them a slice of Mom's, they changed their mind!" Lexy added with a smile.

"So that is where those missing slices of pie have been going!" Maria laughed. She served each of them a warm slice and then put another slice onto a tray for Michael. She then filled up cups of steaming coffee and set them on the table along with containers of creamer and sugar.

As if on cue, Grim and Graw flew onto the ledge in the kitchen window and began to caw gently, almost begging. Lexy walked over, slid open the window, and began cawing back to them in a language that no one (except the two crows) understood. Lexy turned around, smiling at her mom. "They smelled your pie as you were cutting into it. Is it okay if I give them a small slice to share?"

Everyone started laughing. "Well, all right!" Maria said. "But they have to eat it on the windowsill."

Lexy cut them a small slice, put it onto a piece of aluminum foil, and carefully set it on the windowsill. Both birds cawed their thanks and then dug into their slice. Lexy went back to the table, picked up her plate, and went back to join her feathered friends.

"Incredible," Paul exclaimed, watching his daughter engaged in a conversation with two crows.

"Her new talent with animals is becoming very helpful to us," Cynthia said. "Speaking of amazing, where is Gus? I thought he was supposed to be here too."

"Sorry I am late!" answered Gus in the kitchen doorway. "I am still not used to driving on the wrong side of the street. My last assignment was in Scotland, where they drive on the left and 'correct' side of the road!"

"No worries, Gus. You are just in time. Have some pie and coffee." Maria smiled and waved him in.

Gus walked in a sat down. He took a bite of pie and then closed his eyes, savoring the experience. "Wow, Maria," Gus exclaimed when he could speak again. "This truly is a little slice of heaven down here!"

"Why, thank you, Gus!" Maria said, bowing her head in acknowledgment of his praise.

"So, Maria and Paul, how have you been adjusting the past few weeks?" Gus asked.

"Fairly well so far," answered Paul. "It certainly was a bit of a shock at first to return to earth but not as a human. At first we couldn't get over how different everything appears once you can see all that is really there."

"Yeah, we can see everyone's inner lights now," exclaimed Lexy.

"That is right, honey," Paul said to Lexy. Then, back to Gus, he continued, "I still cannot get over how you can actually *see* good and evil. As a human, we could detect that someone or something was evil because we got a creepy kind of feeling. But now we can see the dark bands crowding out the inner lights and, even worse, dark shadows—demons—literally surrounding people, whispering into their ears all sorts of negative and self-defeating thoughts."

"Exactly, Paul. And know this: the darker the bands encircling the inner lights, the greater the control that evil has over that human. As a guardian, you can now detect both good and evil with all of your senses."

"All of them?" squealed Lexy. "So does that mean that we can *smell* evil too?"

"Pure evil has a distinct odor, Lexy," explained Gus. "Once you smell it, you will never mistake it again for anything else."

"What is also surprising, Gus," said Maria, "is that now, after a few weeks, we must be somehow accustomed to seeing all of this. At first when I looked at humans, all I noticed were their inner lights and any light or shadows around them. I had to really force myself to not stare and react to what I was seeing. Now, however, I find myself looking past all of it and acting 'normally' again."

Cynthia smiled. "Yes, it is the same with all of us. You'll get used to turning all of that stuff on and off."

"Well, it sounds like you all are adjusting well," remarked Gus between bites of pie.

"So, Gus, what is your disguise name going to be here in this assignment?" Paul asked.

"Gus," responded Gus. He pointed to the name tag he had on his home health care aide uniform that clearly read "Gus."

"Seriously?" Paul answered. He took a moment to observe Gus's appearance, noticing that, other than the clothes, Gus looked exactly as he did in heaven, including the long beard. His uniform consisted of a navy-blue hospital shirt and pants. Despite the guardian "disguise," Paul still found it very strange, however, to see Gus wearing sneakers. "So you aren't going to transform yourself for the role?" Paul asked.

"No need. My last assignment was over sixty years ago and in a different country. Other than Cynthia, no one here would recognize me," Gus answered. Then, with a wink, he leaned over to Paul. "You still can't get over your new big tummy, can you?"

Paul glared back at Gus.

"Bah if it'll be makin' yew feel better, ay'll be speakin' with me ol' Scottish brogue while ay'm here," Gus answered in a thick Scottish accent.

Both Maria and Cynthia laughed at that.

Suddenly, Maria stood up. "Uh-oh, Michael is off the phone. Let me bring in his snack so that he will be occupied for a little while longer."

"Better bring in a couple of slices and some extra coffee. Trent has an appointment here with him in a few minutes," Cynthia answered.

"Ah, good idea." Maria cut another slice of pie and then poured some coffee into a thermos. After placing everything onto the tray, she carried it out of the kitchen and down to Michael's home office. Upon entering the room, Michael directed her to place the food onto the little table near his desk. Maria set the table with napkins, forks, spoons, and coffee cups. Then she placed the full coffee thermos, creamer, and sugar into the center of the table. Lastly, she placed the two plates, each loaded with a steaming slice of pie, onto the table.

"Thank you, Mrs. Flaherty. This looks great," Michael said, eyeing the pie with some gusto. Maria inwardly smiled because her blueberry pie was one of Michael's favorite desserts when he was a boy.

"Let me know if you need anything else, Mr. Garcia." Maria picked up the empty tray and left the room. As she was walking down the hallway, back to the kitchen, she heard the doorbell ring. Maria then heard Cynthia's voice from the hallway, informing everyone that she would get the door. Maria had just set the empty tray down on the kitchen counter when she heard some loud yelling from the doorway.

"This is the SECOND time that this has happened!" screamed Trent Wentworth.

"The second time?" Cynthia's voice answered.

"YES! The last time I was here, Tuesday I think, it happened too!"

"Okay, okay, calm down. We will get you some towels. Please go into the bathroom over there, and wash up. I'll be right back."

"What in the world, Cynthia?" Maria inquired when Cynthia entered the kitchen. Maria was already handing her some towels as she listened to hear what the commotion was about.

Cynthia started to explain but then started laughing. "Give me a second, please," she answered. She composed herself and then continued in a low voice, "Apparently, the last two times that Trent has come here, he has gotten pooped on by one of the crows that hang out on the penthouse roof."

"Oh! So that is where they went!" Lexy exclaimed. She then began to talk to the two crows who had recently returned to their blueberry snack.

They all tried to control their laughter. "Good shot too," Cynthia chortled while trying to speak softly. "It landed right on his perfectly coiffed hair and dripped onto his suit coat." Cynthia started taking deep breaths to calm her laughter. "I better go back and see if he needs anything else."

"They don't like him," Lexy announced to everyone.

"Who doesn't like whom?" Cynthia asked, pausing before leaving the kitchen.

"Grim and Graw," Lexy answered, pointing at the crows. "They just told me that they don't like him. That is why they poop on him."

"Ah, Lexy, you are a *communicatoris*," exclaimed Gus, staring at Lexy. He walked over to her and studied her. "Yes," he said, pausing for a moment. "I knew that you had the potential to communicate with animals. However, looking at your inner light, I see that you now can speak to many different species already." To everyone, he continued, "It is rare that someone develops this skill so quickly and without any training." He looked back at Lexy and smiled. "This is a divine gift, Lexy. Make sure that you give Him your thanks and use it well."

"I will," Lexy said, smiling.

"Oops! Gotta go!" Cynthia said as she darted out of the room with the towels. After she helped Trent clean up, she led him down the hall and tried to brighten his mood. "Lucky you," she said as they walked toward Michael's home office. "Mrs. Flaherty just made a blueberry pie. There is a slice with your name on it waiting for you in Michael's office."

"Well, that does sounds great," Trent answered as he opened the door and walked in.

"Hi, Michael," Cynthia said as they entered the room. "I'm in the kitchen with Mrs. Flaherty and Dr. Sherman. We are speaking with your new home health aide, Gus Winters. Let me know if you need anything."

"Thanks, Cynthia," answered Michael.

Cynthia walked back to the kitchen, adjusting the tuning in her hearing so that she could monitor the meeting with Michael and Trent. She was really glad to have all of the new guardians here to help her with Michael. This was a tough case; not as bad as some of the others she had in the past, but still difficult. "Hey," she said as she entered the kitchen and sat down at the table. "Their meeting has started, so, unless they need something, we have a little time to discuss our next steps. Let's start with observations. What have you all noticed during the last week?"

"He is very polite to all of us, but other than that, he is still pretty reserved," Maria answered. "I'm trying to determine if this is somehow normal for him or if he is just not responsive to us because we are 'the help,'" Maria answered.

"No, that is Michael," Cynthia responded. "While he is polite and very kind at times, he has very few friends. It takes him a long time to open up to people. It took me over two years, working with him almost every day, to get him to trust me as a friend. From what I have seen, it usually takes some kind of crisis in order to push him to trust someone new."

"New… How ironic for us to be 'new' to him," Maria said.

"Oh, gosh, Maria. I didn't mean—"

"It is okay, Cynthia," Maria patted her hand. She thought for a moment and then continued, "He doesn't make it easy, as he offers little to no conversation in general. He still won't eat with us, even though we invite him to every day. The only person he has opened up to a little bit is Lexy. In a strange way, I think he likes all of the craziness with the animals. Without a doubt, those silly kittens have helped him to have something, besides himself, to care about. Otherwise, he sits in his office all day, either working or just staring out the window. From what the kittens have told us, his mood worsens after dark, and he becomes very depressed at night, even sleeping with a light on."

"Physically," Paul answered, "he is healing well. In fact, his jaw and ribs healed very quickly, so that is good news. However, I think that the only reason he is glad to get better is so that he can finally be left alone."

"Gus, I believe that you have already familiarized yourself with the two therapists we hired for Michael, Dr. Marti Robinson and Dominic LeBrant," Cynthia stated. "I had to look all over town to find Christian therapists who specialized in cases like Michael's. We really got lucky. They are not only great therapists, they are kind and caring humans. Both are strong in their faith in Jesus, and I believe that they could be a great help to Michael—physically and emotionally. However, both have told me that he is not challenging himself in his sessions or at home, and they are afraid that he will impair his own rehabilitation. I don't think that he cares about much of anything anymore other than work," Cynthia said with a sigh.

"I never see him trying to walk here at home, not even a little bit," Maria said. "We have handlebars installed in every room, in the hallway, and he has some parallel bars set up in his bedroom. He has no interest."

"That isn't good. Deep down, I think he feels like a one-legged freak. And to top it off, I think he is afraid of working hard to only get hurt again. I hear the evil forces whispering to him, convincing him about how hopeless everything is. He believes every word," Paul answered.

"Humans are so ready to believe the worst about themselves that it really doesn't take much work for the demons to plant powerful negative thoughts in their minds," Gus mused. "To put it simply, without God, humans have an identity crisis. They value themselves by the fickle world standards of money, status, achievements, etcetera. Without God, humans operate from a place of 'empty.' They are constantly trying to fill their tanks (or hearts) with the love and acceptance they so desperately need but can never be supplied by the world. Once Michael understands that he is *already* loved and valued by the most powerful being in existence, he will operate from a place of 'full' rather than 'empty' and will no longer need nor want the world's acceptance. This is the peace that only comes from God. With this, he will be equipped to combat any negative thoughts from demons or the world."

"This boils down to a change in perspective, Gus. It is basic psychology, like the techniques used with cognitive behavior therapy," Paul reflected.

Gus smiled. "That is the world's explanation, and it is limited to only what the world can provide. What has always fascinated me is the volume of books, courses, and research on the topic of the human mind when God already provided the original self-help book—the Bible. It is packed with wisdom and direction on how to live. But don't forget that, with God, you also get the power of the Holy Spirit living inside you on earth to help you through everything."

"Our plan is to direct him toward positive influences and experiences to drown out the negative thoughts and beliefs," said Cynthia. "We have a good start already by selecting Marti and Dominic to provide his therapy. As both of them are strong Christians, they can reinforce the messages that we are already giving him. Next, we need him to see what God can do in his life if he will only trust in Him."

"I wish that we could just read his thoughts," Lexy said, licking her plate and fork clean. "Then we wouldn't have to guess how he is feeling."

"Only God can read our thoughts, Lexy," Gus answered. "Just keep your ears and eyes open for more clues of how Michael is feeling. So often when it seems darkest, that is when God is working the hardest in the background for all of us. We just have to be smart enough to listen and learn from what He is trying to tell us. Let's pray again to the Holy Spirit for wisdom and guidance."

"Uh-oh! Speaking of keeping your ears open, Michael's meeting with Trent is not going well. They are having an argument," said Cynthia. "Tune in, everyone."

"What do you mean, Trent, that Rensalant Construction can't meet with me again?" Michael yelled. "I clearly asked you, two weeks ago, to get a meeting set up with him! He works for me, not the other way around!"

"Michael, I am doing the best I can," responded Trent, flustered. "Rensalant has several big construction projects all going on at the same time. He sent over these projections this morning and needs your signature now on their latest bill. It includes some additional, unforeseen expenses that have come up at the last minute."

A moment of silence passed before the eruption.

"Are you *kidding* me?" Michael screamed. "They are now two months BEHIND schedule and yet they are OVER budget by half a million? You tell him that they will not get another cent from me until I see a revised construction schedule, putting us back on track. I will not pay for their mistakes!"

"Michael, Rensalant told me that they will stop the construction if we don't pay the bill. I will press them to prioritize us, but—"

"No, Trent," Michael yelled. "Not another cent! They will prioritize our contract and eat these additional charges!"

"Michael, that is not how it works! If we don't pay them, they put us at the back of the line. They are the best contractors in town, and everyone wants to do business with them. They get to set the rules."

Silence followed. Michael spoke again, closing his eyes in an attempt to control his anger, "Trent, I will not sign anything until I meet with Rensalant personally. I will call him as soon as you leave. If I cannot get through to him, you will go to his office and give him my message."

"Michael, we can't just—"

"Trent, yes we can! This is completely unprofessional. Rensalant won't meet with me or even return my calls, yet he sends over more bills on work that is nowhere near completion. Do you have any idea how many conferences we have scheduled two months from now? Rensalant assured me, personally, that this work would be done by now! I cannot cancel on these events or the Garcia Lodge will be ruined!" A moment of silence passed. Michael continued, "You know, I've changed my mind. *You* will go now to Rensalant's office, AND I will call him when you leave. That way, he will get the message, one way or the other."

The group of guardians around the kitchen table looked at each other with raised eyebrows. "Wow," said Cynthia. "I've heard Michael angry before, but he has never yelled at Trent like that."

Rapid footsteps down the hallway followed the loud crash of the slamming door. "I guess I'd better see Trent out," said Cynthia as she stood up and walked out of the room.

"Trent," Cynthia called out. "Are you okay?"

"Uh, sure! Just have to run a quick errand, you know how that goes!" Trent responded without stopping or looking at Cynthia.

As a result of the earlier commotion with the bird poop, Cynthia did not get a good look at Trent until now. She noticed, for the first time ever, that Trent was not his usual pristine self. His shirt looked like he had slept in it, and his eyes had puffy bags under them. "Are you all right, Trent? You look like you haven't slept in a while." She caught up to him and handed him his dirty suit jacket, which she placed into a plastic bag.

"Oh, uhm, not really. Lots to do." Trent ran a nervous, shaky hand through his hair. "I really can't stay and talk, so I'll see you in the office tomorrow." Trent motioned to Michael's room. "Hopefully he will be in a better mood then."

"Okay, then. Call me if you need anything," Cynthia said. Trent nodded, turned, and left the penthouse. Cynthia walked back to the table and joined the others but was unable to focus on the conversation. She couldn't put her finger on it, but something didn't seem quite right with Trent. From his inner light, she could see his usual thick band of darkness surrounding the almost-faint glow of light. This signaled a low level of hope and love and a high wattage of evil influence. However, today, it seemed darker, almost shutting out his light entirely. *Poor Trent*, she thought. *He must be suffering*. She knew Trent had a history with a gambling addiction; perhaps he was in real trouble and needed help. She would ask Gus for his opinion on how best to help Trent. She was still deep in thought when Maria left the table and announced that she would go collect the dirty dishes from Michael's home office.

"Gus, what do you suggest we do to motivate Michael to engage more in his rehab exercises?" Paul asked.

Gus opened his mouth to respond, but then they heard Maria running back down the hall, screaming, "Paul! Paul! Michael is unconscious!"

Everyone ran to the room. They found Michael slumped over his desk. The phone was off the receiver and dangling toward the floor. Paul gently lifted Michael's listless head and examined his eyes, pulling back the lids. Paul noted that Michael's face had taken a gray hue, and his fingernails were starting to turn blue. "Cynthia, please call an ambulance. Everyone else, help me get him to his bed," Paul ordered, holding Michael's head steady while starting to push the wheelchair toward the office door. "Lexy, go to the kitchen and bring back my medical bag." When they arrived in Michael's bedroom, everyone grabbed a part of Michael and quickly moved him onto the bed. Lexy ran into the room and handed her father his medical bag.

Paul began rescue breathing on Michael, tilting back his head, pinching closed the nostrils, and breathing into his mouth. "Michael! Michael, can you hear me?" Paul shouted after a minute of the breathing. Michael appeared to wake up a bit but then fell immediately back into unconsciousness. "Guys, it looks like an overdose of some sort, I'm guessing his painkillers. I am going to hit him with Narcan to stop the progress of the overdose." Michael quickly dug into his bag and located the small box containing the Narcan nasal spray. After resuming the rescue breathing on Michael, Paul sprayed one dose into each nostril and turned him onto his side in recovery position.

"How long does this take to work?" Maria asked.

"It can take several minutes. We may need to administer more before the ambulance arrives. Oh, go get a bucket and some towels as Michael may not feel so well when this stuff kicks in."

"Ambulance is on the way," Cynthia announced.

Paul nodded his thanks. After three minutes which seemed like an eternity, Michael began to stir. He opened his eyes and looked around, completely confused. After another few seconds, he groaned and grabbed his stomach, not looking well. Paul grabbed Michael and leaned him against himself in a semi-sitting position. Maria positioned the bucket, and Michael vomited.

Just then, the doorbell rang. Cynthia let in the EMS crew, who immediately went to work, placing Michael on a stretcher and carrying him out to the waiting ambulance.

CHAPTER 14

"Looks like an overdose of OxyContin," the doctor in the emergency room announced. Paul, Maria, Gus, and Cynthia looked at each other. "It is a good thing that you had some Narcan with you," he continued. "Otherwise this could have been much worse." After a moment, the doctor asked Paul, "Do you have any idea what happened here?"

"No," answered Paul. "None of us knows how this happened. In fact, Michael stopped taking the painkillers several weeks ago."

"When he wakes up, we can ask him what happened. He is going to be all right, but he needs to remain here until morning," the doctor explained.

"I am his primary care physician, so I will go home with him tomorrow and monitor him for a couple of days," Paul answered.

"A psychiatric evaluation may be in order," the doctor added. "In case we suspect a possible suicide attempt."

"I understand," answered Paul. "I will observe him and decide if this is necessary."

As the doctor left the room, Michael's guardians looked at each other and then at Michael.

The dark forces had multiplied their strength and were swirling around Michael in triumph at the close call on his life. Like sharks circling their prey, they were eager to escort his soul to hell.

"You aren't going to win, you know," Gus emphatically whispered to the demonic forces surrounding Michael. With an authoritative voice, Gus continued, "In the name of Jesus Christ, I command you evil spirits to leave Michael and get out of this hospital!" In response to the name of Jesus, the forces violently shook Michael's bed as they left him. They emitted a shrill cry as they soared up to the ceiling, ripping the curtain above the window in the room.

As the demons left the room, they hissed, "We will be back! He belongs to us now!"

"Gus," asked Paul, "why don't we just chase the demons away all day, every day? Wouldn't that buy us some time to work with him without all of the negative influences?"

"No, that won't solve the problem. Demons will always come back to try to get their influence over their targeted human again. The key is to make the human self-sufficient by arming them with something much stronger: with love, protection, and authority over evil forces from Jesus and the Holy Spirit. This is only possible, however, when the human decides to follow Jesus."

CHAPTER 15

"Well, hello, Sleeping Beauty!" Cynthia's voice echoed in Michael's head the following morning. He opened his eyes and saw her seated next to him. It took less than one minute for him to realize that he was, again, in a hospital bed. In horror, he tried to sit up.

"No! Not again! Am I okay?"

Cynthia gently pushed him down. "You are fine. You are not injured at all."

Michael instantly felt relieved. "Then why am I here?"

Cynthia's facial expression clearly showed him that there was something wrong. "Michael, you overdosed on your painkillers—OxyContin."

"Overdosed?" Michael was clearly confused. He thought for a few minutes, remembering the meeting with Trent. He replayed the events in his head. He remembered yelling at Trent, being angry at Rensalant, and feeling woozy by the end of the meeting. However, he knew that he didn't take any painkillers. "Cyn," he exclaimed, "I didn't take any painkillers yesterday. I stopped taking them after my first week back home."

From Cynthia's face, he could tell that she didn't believe him. Dr. Sherman and Mrs. Flaherty walked in. "Michael was just telling me that he didn't take any painkillers yesterday," Cynthia told the group.

Dr. Sherman studied Michael and then spoke, "Are you sure, Michael? Is it possible that you confused that medicine with, perhaps, some aspirin or something?"

"What? Absolutely not! I wouldn't make that kind of mistake. But this much I do know: I didn't take any kind of medicine yesterday," Michael persisted.

"Well, we do know that you were pretty upset in your meeting with Trent yesterday." Cynthia added, "Perhaps you didn't realize what you were doing—"

"Didn't realize that I was taking a deadly quantity of highly addictive opioid prescription painkillers?" Michael interrupted, incredulous. "Do you seriously think that I am insane or something?"

"No, not insane," Cynthia said gently. "But possibly very depressed."

"Well, of course I'm depressed! Who wouldn't be, with everything that has happened! But not enough to try to take myself out!" Michael and Cynthia stared at each other for several minutes. Never before had Cynthia seen such a look of desperation on Michael's face. As she studied his eyes and his expression, she did not see any sign of lying there.

"Michael," Cynthia said slowly, "okay, I believe you, although I can't explain what happened to you. Painkillers don't just jump into someone's mouth."

"No kidding, they don't," Michael added. "So that means that someone *else* gave them to me." He looked around at all of them with a bit of accusation in his eyes. "Any ideas just who that might be?"

CHAPTER 16

Michael spent the next few days back at his home with orders from the collective group of doctors to get some rest. While he was still a bit on edge with everyone about the mysterious overdose, he decided to seclude himself in his room and concentrate on his work. Other than his therapy sessions at the clinic, he spent his time reviewing the expenses of the various operations under the Garcia Enterprises umbrella. Being out of commission for almost three months, a thorough analysis was required to understand how things were going during his absence. He still didn't understand the large expenses from the construction project on the lodge. Rensalant was still unreachable, and Trent wasn't able to get a revised projection from him. Michael made a mental note to call his attorney later that day. The threat of legal action should make Rensalant more responsive.

He spent the next two hours going over the investment analysis reports. Strangely, he found some discrepancies with the client investment account balances. He couldn't understand some of the transactions. It looked like money was being added to some of the client accounts, but without any explanation. Normally, those balances increased due to monthly contributions, dividends, or other investment gains. These transactions had no explanations for them. He started doing some digging, going back several months, and found many more of these strange transactions, some quite large.

Even more alarming, he found transactions that removed money, thankfully only small amounts, from the client accounts, but with no explanation again. He packaged up his reports and questions and fired them off in an urgent email to Trent. Hopefully, Trent already knew what was going on and was resolving the problem. Michael kept thinking about how this could happen; maybe it was a systems glitch. If so, he would personally make the corrections in the code. Otherwise, if an employee was doing this, he or she should be fired immediately. Touching client money without client authorization could result in criminal prosecution for him and his company. He started running some detailed reports, going back even farther in time, and was about to review the results when Gus knocked on the open door and walked in.

"Hi, Mr. Garcia. Are yew ready ta go to yewr therapy session? We'd better leave noow if we dinna want to get caught in traffic." Gus's Scottish accent was fairly thick at times.

Michael cringed at that announcement for a couple of reasons. For one, he didn't see much purpose to the therapy sessions. After all, he really wasn't making much progress beyond shifting his weight between his good leg and the prosthetic limb. Second, riding in a car with Gus at the wheel was enough to make him want to crawl the whole way there, prosthetic leg be damned. "Not today, Gus. I think that I will cancel the appointment. Can you call them and tell them that we will be there at next week's session?"

"I can, Mr. Garcia," Gus hesitated a bit. "And forgive me for speakin' me mind ta yew here, but unless yew are physically nah up to it, me professional recommendation is that yew should go."

Michael was a bit astonished that a home health aide would be so bold as to state his opinion so freely. However, Gus Winters stated his opinions quite regularly. In fact, to Michael, Gus was more like a grandfather, albeit a very strong grandfather, than a mere employee in Michael's home. In the short time that he had been around Gus, he couldn't help but like him. "Gus, I know that you mean well, but I really don't want to go today. If you don't make the call, I will."

Gus knew from the tone that Michael's decision was final. "Ay'll make the call, Mr. Garcia. But know that ay'll be makin' veerry sure that yew dinna miss next week." With that, Gus left the room.

Michael smiled a little as Gus left the room. Oddly, a bit of guilt set in as he thought about all of the people who were trying to help him, like Gus. He also thought about everything that Marti and Dominic were doing to try to motivate and push him toward success. While thinking, he began to pet both of the kittens, who chose that moment to jump onto the desk and walk on top of his reports. After a moment, he set them both down on the little bed that Lexy created for them next to his desk.

As he thought, he honestly wished, for all of the people who seemed to care about him, that he could be motivated, even energized to push himself in his therapy. But he simply saw no point in trying. For what grand purpose was he going to put himself through the torture of learning to walk again? For now, his life was about his work, and that he could do very well in a wheelchair. As for the future, who knew? First, why would anyone want to share her life with someone who would always require "extra" maintenance? Second, even if he learned to walk again, it was only a matter of time before life would unleash another tragic event on him. He was a "disaster magnet" after all; anyone who gets too close will themselves suffer collateral damage in the impending destruction.

He had just turned his attention back to his report when Cynthia arrived at his open door, along with uninvited guests Marti and Ethan.

"Hello, Michael," Cynthia said as she knocked on the door. "You have some company here to see you."

Michael looked up at everyone, feeling quite a bit guilty but swallowed it down. He switched to a defensive tactic. "Hello, everyone." Michael proceeded smoothly, "I am sorry that you all wasted your time coming here, but I really can't spend the afternoon on therapy today." He gestured to the stacks of paperwork on his desk and continued, "As you can see, I am literally surrounded by unfinished work."

Before anyone could say anything, Lexy came running through the door. "Ethan, Ethan!" she shouted. "Let me show you the kittens! They are so cute!" Lexy grabbed Ethan's hand, and she pulled him around Michael's desk. "See this?" Lexy pointed to the kittens' bed. "I made this bed for them, and they love it!" Ethan and Lexy sat down on the ground next to the bed (which was really just a basket filled with several soft blankets and a pillow). Lexy picked one of the kittens up and placed it into Ethan's lap. "They follow Michael—oops, I mean Mr. Garcia—around everywhere!"

Michael forced back the smile that was trying to form on his face. While he was annoyed that Jackie's arrival had actually brought the entire group further into his home office, he was mesmerized at the expression of joy on Ethan's face while holding one of the kittens.

"Hi, Michael," Marti said as she walked toward Ethan. "Sorry about this. You see, we don't have any pets at home, and Ethan loves animals." Marti paused for a moment, then continued speaking, "As you can guess, I deliberately came here, unannounced and uninvited. And I brought Ethan with me as a sort of 'peace offering' because I know you two get along."

She exhaled and then went on, "From our last few sessions and the events over the last few days, it is apparent to me that you are losing interest in your therapy, and possibly more. While I cannot make you *do* your therapy, it is my job to try to figure out what is going on with you in terms of mind, body, and spirit." To the kids, she spoke, "Jackie, I have heard that you are quite an expert with animals. Would you please show Ethan how you feed the kittens? Maybe even let him brush them?"

Cynthia took the hint and stepped forward at that point. "Yes, Jackie. Let's give them some milk in the kitchen, shall we?"

"Oh yes, Ethan. They LOVE milk!" Lexy exclaimed, getting up and grabbing the other kitten. "And sometimes it gives them gas afterwards! Wait until you see that part!"

"Cool!" Ethan shouted.

Cynthia rolled her eyes. "Gee, I can't wait."

Michael and Marti watched the small entourage leave the room, laughing at the scene. Then came the uncomfortable silence of dealing with the problem. Michael decided that the best defense was a good offense, so he initiated the conversation. "Marti, I really appreciate what you are trying to do here, but this is something that I have work out on my own. Plus, I am a bit surprised that you would leave the clinic just for me."

Marti smiled at that. "Actually, since we were scheduled for two hours today, I thought we would still use the time—just in a different capacity."

Michael sat for a moment, arms folded across his chest. Then he narrowed his eyes, took a quick glance at the clock, and spoke, "So, with the hour we have remaining from my original appointment, you expect me to break down, spill my guts, and tell you everything that is troubling me. Then you can impart your brilliant wisdom, essentially 'saving' me, after which our therapy sessions will resume with renewed vigor. As an added bonus, I will be added to your impressive portfolio of patient success stories."

Marti sighed but only smiled at his rudeness. "No, Michael, you guessed poorly." She opened her purse and pulled out a set of car keys. "During our last couple of sessions, you complained about Gus's driving. I think it is time for you to start driving on your own again." She examined him, noticing that he had a slipper on his foot and was wearing a T-shirt. "You will need to put on a sweatshirt and change your shoe to something you can drive in. And don't forget to put on your prosthetic limb." She turned and walked out of the room.

Michael was stunned. Of all the things that she could have said or done, he certainly didn't expect this one.

CHAPTER 17

"Great work, Lexy!" Cynthia whispered proudly as she and Lexy did a high five back in the kitchen. Ethan was busy feeding the two kittens some milk on the other side of the large kitchen, so Cynthia and Lexy could speak out of his hearing range.

"No problem, Cynthia!" Lexy smiled and whispered back. "I knew that having Marti bring Ethan over and then getting him involved with the kittens would do the trick! That way, Michael would *have* to talk to Marti!"

"You are almost as good at this stuff as I am!" Cynthia laughed.

Marti walked into the kitchen. "Cynthia, are you okay to watch Ethan for a couple of hours? I am taking Michael out of the apartment. I will call you when we are on our way back."

"Absolutely!" Cynthia responded. "We are having fun here, so don't worry about us!"

Ethan turned around, smiling, "Marti, are you sure you don't want to stay and play with these kittens? They are so awesome!"

"I'd love to, but duty calls, Ethan. But I definitely want to play with them when I get back!" She walked over and gave him a quick hug.

"Mrs. Flaherty," Marti asked, "where are Michael's crutches and prosthetic limb?"

"Oh, I put them in the closet next to the front door," Maria answered. "Cynthia, can you help her with them?"

"Sure thing." Cynthia led Marti out of the kitchen and down the hall to the closet. They pulled out the new and state-of-the-art prosthetic limb, a fresh stump sock, and the gel liner. Lastly, they grabbed the crutches and waited for Michael, who was wheeling himself down the hall.

Meeting them by the front closet, Michael surrendered himself to spending a couple of hours with Marti. "Okay, Michael," Marti said, holding out the prosthetic limb, sock, nylon liner, and gel liner. "Put these on, and we will go."

Michael glared at the prosthetic limb but took it and began to push up his empty sweatpant leg. He exposed his stump, which was wrapped tightly to prevent swelling. He first pulled on the cotton stump sock followed by the nylon stump liner, taking extra care to ensure no wrinkles. Any bunching would produce sores when the stump rubs against the prosthetic socket. He then inserted the gel liner into the socket of the prosthetic to provide extra cushioning. Finally, he pushed his stump into the prosthetic socket and tightened the straps. After a couple of minutes of shifting his weight inside the socket to adjust the position, he felt comfortable.

After observing this success, Marti pushed the crutches toward Michael. "Stand up, take these, and we are on our way. We will bring the wheelchair as a backup, but I want us to walk today."

Michael looked very unsure. After all, they hadn't spent much time actually walking any real distances before.

"I can tell by your expression, Michael, that you don't think that you are ready for this," Marti said. "Believe me, you are."

Michael resigned himself to her judgment. He slowly stood up and took the crutches. Marti opened the front door and then walked behind him, ready to push the wheelchair. "After you," she said.

Michael looked at the doorway and began taking deep breaths to slow down his racing heart. Unbelievable to him, he was scared. This would be his first literal step out of the penthouse since the accident three months ago. All other times, he had been riding in the wheelchair.

"Remember, Michael," Marti said, "the only person holding you back right now is *you*." She let that thought marinate for a few seconds and then continued, "Walk with these crutches. Don't lean on them like you would if you sprained your ankle. Lead with your good leg to start with. Then, when you feel a bit more confident, start leading with your prosthetic. We will be doing exactly what you have been doing in the clinic, only we won't be using the parallel bars today."

Marti whispered to Cynthia as she was leaving the apartment. "Wish us luck, Cynthia. We need all the help we can get." Then, as an afterthought, she added, "Any prayers you can say on our behalf would be greatly appreciated!"

"Oh, I'll be praying for you both, all right!" Cynthia said with a smile and complete seriousness.

"Thanks!" Marti returned her smile and left the penthouse.

Michael held himself up with the crutches, took a deep breath, and then stepped out the doorway with his good leg. Once he had his balance, he then stepped with his prosthetic leg, slowly sliding it past his good leg. Taking his time, he repeated the process, moving down the hallway toward the elevator. By the time they reached the elevator, he was feeling a bit better and confident enough to lean over and press the Down button. He turned to Marti, who had been following him with the wheelchair.

The elevator doors opened, and he let her go inside first. He then stepped inside while she held the Open button. After pressing the button for the garage level, he looked over at her. She was forcing down a smile and was trying to maintain a businesslike demeanor, he could tell. Strange, he thought, but this was *easier* than he had imagined taking his first steps outside the clinic to be.

As they approached her car, she unlocked it and told him to get into the passenger side while she folded up and stored the wheelchair in the hatchback. Again, Michael was shocked at receiving no assistance from her with this. Clearly she was forcing him out of his comfort zone and thereby getting him to learn that he could do this *himself.*

She drove them out of the garage and took the highway toward the university where she taught classes once a week. Upon entering the campus, she drove for a while until she found a fairly empty parking lot with lots of space next to a beautiful park. She stopped, put the car in neutral, and unbuckled her seatbelt. "Well, Michael, it is showtime." She looked over at him and gestured to his seatbelt. "Unbuckle, get up, and we will switch seats. It is now time for your driving lesson."

"Driving lesson? I thought you were kidding before," Michael asked.

"Yes, a driving lesson. And, no, I was not kidding." She looked him directly in the eyes. "It is time for you to stop feeling sorry for yourself."

"Feeling sorry—" Michael started to protest but stopped himself. He realized that she was right. He was wallowing in self-pity and had been so for the last three months. Marti got out of the car and walked around to his side, waiting for him to get out.

He unbuckled his seatbelt, opened the car door, and braced the crutches on the ground to support him. He stood up and made his way to the other side of the car. It was getting easier all of the time. Balancing mostly on his good leg, he opened the back door and slid the crutches across the floor. Opening the front door, he then sat down by holding onto the handle above the door and bracing himself on the seat. Buckling himself in, he turned and looked at her.

"Well done," Marti said. "I was waiting for you to ask me to assist you with the crutches. But you figured out what to do on your own. Your confidence is building."

"You're right, it is," Michael said, his hands on the steering wheel. It felt great to be sitting in the driver's seat of a car again. For the next moment, he almost forgot that he had the accident. He went into autopilot, adjusting the seat and mirrors, and figuring out where the various controls were.

"Well, I think we are ready." Michael began to drive the car around the parking lot. Since the car had automatic transmission, he didn't really have any problems driving again, as his right leg was still there. He just had to take it easy with his shoulder and turning his head, as these were still healing from the accident.

"Lucky for you, you lost your left leg," Marti said as they drove around the parking lot. "This means that you don't have to learn how to control the pedals with your other leg."

"Yeah, but it also means that I can no longer drive a stick shift car, like my Porsche," Michael answered bitterly."

"Horse manure," Marti said. "There are all kinds of driving devices created for people with prosthetic limbs and other challenges."

"Really?" Michael asked as he drove. "Like what?"

"For example, there are clutch controls that can be installed on the steering wheel. Or, if you prefer, there are push-button clutch controls that are mounted on the stick shift itself. Either way, you are engaging the clutch while you shift."

"Do you need a special car for this?"

"No. These devices can be installed in any vehicle. Some cars even have paddle shifters already installed, so there is no special order involved."

"That is so great!" Michael answered, smiling for the first time since she met him. "I can drive a Porsche again!" Michael drove for a moment in silence and gratitude. "Thank you, Marti. I can't tell you what this means to me." Michael wasn't impressed easily, but she amazed him.

"Save it," she said, laughing. "Go over there." She pointed to the edge of the beautiful park with cars parked all along the street. "Prove to me that you can parallel park between those two parked cars over there."

Now it was his turn to impress her. Michael drove beyond the two cars she had selected. Instead, he chose a more challenging space between two large vehicles. With unbelievable ease, he whipped her little Mazda M3 into the tiny spot between the Suburban and the Hummer.

"Nice job!" Marti said, opening her passenger side door and confirming the appropriate distance with the curb. "I think you need to give me some lessons on how to do that!"

"It would be my pleasure," Michael said, feeling good for the first time in weeks. "I need to repay you somehow."

"Nonsense," Marti said. "I'm just doing my job."

"No, Marti. You changed my perspective today," Michael said with seriousness. "Not two hours ago, I was depressed, thinking that the only thing I had left in my life was my work. Now I am able to walk out of my home and drive myself anywhere I want to go. Soon I can go anywhere in my Porsche too. He paused for a moment. "I finally have some independence again."

Marti smiled. "I'm glad to help, Michael. How about we take a little walk by the water? There is a smooth trail that starts right over there." She pointed through a row of trees.

They got out of the car and made their way to the water on the trail. It was a beautiful spring day with the sun reflecting off of the water. The flowering trees were bursting in full bloom while a gentle breeze was blowing through the grass. Funny, being trapped indoors for three months, he didn't even realize that the seasons had changed from winter to spring. They found a bench right next to the trail and sat down for a little while. For just a moment, they sat in silence. Not an awkward silence but a moment of pure peace, feeling the warm breeze blow on their faces while listening to the birds singing their joy and watching the sunlight glistening on the water. Michael could not remember feeling so relaxed.

After a while, he looked over at Marti, who was playing with a flower that she had picked. He realized in that moment that he had never looked at her before. She was so different from other females in his acquaintance. The most obvious difference was her lack of concern about her appearance. She wore very little makeup, and she always wore her strawberry-blond hair in a ponytail. It wasn't that she was sloppy or dirty; rather, it was that she was preoccupied with other tasks, and her appearance fell low on the list. Marti looked up at that moment and smiled.

"What are you thinking about?" she asked.

"Well," he paused, buying some time to think of a topic, "how did you get into physical therapy?" Michael asked, lying a little, but he was curious to hear her reply.

"By accident," Marti answered, now playing with a stick she picked up off of the ground next to the bench. "I already had my medical degree and was doing my residency. While taking care of various patients admitted to the hospital, I began to take an interest in people who suffered a severe brain trauma, like a stroke or a serious head injury. In talking to some of the families of the patients, I discovered, to my horror, that in many cases, there was not always a clear plan identified for what to do, especially in cases requiring long-term rehabilitation."

"What do you mean?" Michael asked.

"When they were discharged from the hospital, the patients were given pretty general guidelines of what to do next. However, there was little to no instruction explaining which therapies to take, how aggressively to pursue them, how to fight when the insurance company or government programs like Medicare or Medicaid drops the patient if sufficient progress isn't made—"

"Wait," Michael interrupted. "What do you mean by 'dropping the patient'?"

"It is exactly what it sounds like, Michael, and it is cruel. Coverage for the therapy ends if the patient hasn't made 'sufficient progress,' as defined by some bureaucrats in an office somewhere."

"*Sufficient* progress? That sounds horrible, kind of like socialized medicine where a panel decides if your potential value to society is worth the expense of your treatment."

"Well, in many ways, it is," Marti answered. "And think about it… Most stroke patients are older, so they would be wiping out their retirement savings to pay for treatment. Most wounded veterans certainly don't have the money to pay for this, and neither do most people who were in a serious accident and can no longer work.

"So," she continued with a smile, "back to why I decided to go into this field. There are very few clinics that offer a holistic approach that assesses the complete needs of the particular patient and then design a comprehensive program of therapies to work together. A lot of therapy, in contrast, is done in a vacuum, with no consultation with other therapists that a patient may be seeing. Depending upon the patient, therapy comes in the following forms: speech and swallowing, physical therapy, occupational, vision, bladder—the list goes on and on. My goal was to create an 'all-in-one' clinic."

"But how can you offer a clinic like this, especially considering many people can't afford to pay for it?"

"Great question, Michael. After I got started, I created a charitable organization, the Richardson Angels of Hope, which raises funds to help many patients to continue their therapy. We hold fundraisers every year at some of the art galleries around town."

"Really? Why don't you hold an event at the Garcia Lodge? That would also generate more publicity, as so many events are held there," Michael asked.

Marti smiled and answered, "I've tried—many times, in fact. But the Lodge is too expensive. In the end, we would net very little holding it there."

Michael visibly winced at this. "Well, I happen to know some people in the organization who might be able to help you with that."

Marti smiled even bigger and winked at him. "That would be great. Tell him or her that we would really appreciate it."

"So, Michael, to make a *short* story very, very *long*," Marti said, laughing a little, "I went into therapy because I wanted to work with the patients that the other clinics and programs dropped. This may sound strange to you, but I believe that I was called by God to do this work."

"Called by God? How do you know?" Michael asked, honestly trying to keep the cynicism out of his voice.

Marti smiled. "Once you decide to follow Jesus, you will receive an incredible gift, Michael. You get the powerful presence of the third person of God, the Holy Spirit, living in you every day, 24-7."

"What is so special about the Holy Spirit?"

"Remember that there are three persons of God: God the Father, Jesus the Son, and the Holy Spirit. All three are God, and all three are desperately needed for the roles that each performs. The Holy Spirit gets shortchanged in many churches and seems to play a lessor role to the other two persons. This is especially sad since the Holy Spirit is literally *here* with us right now! He was sent to us after Jesus ascended to heaven to be our comforter, teacher, conscience, guide, protector, and healer here on earth. I am not even stating all that He does for us, but that is a quick list."

"That is quite a list of characteristics."

"More than just a list, Michael! He is the most powerful energy source in the universe, and through Him all creation was made. Throughout the Bible, He is referenced as 'the Spirit of God' who performed many roles to carry out Father God's plan, some of which included empowering humans with special wisdom and knowledge and imparting visions to the prophets. At the beginning of Jesus's ministry, the Holy Spirit descended onto Jesus to assist in the miracles of healing people, raising the dead, casting out demons, feeding the multitudes—you know the stories. But a key point to know is that the Holy Spirit supplied the energy to resurrect Jesus's body from the dead, and now that same Holy Spirit lives in you once you accept Jesus!"

Marti reached down and picked two more long-stemmed flowers to join the one she already held in her hand. Michael watched as she wove them together into a little braid as she spoke. "The miracles from the Bible," she continued, "they happen even today because of the power of the Holy Spirit working through those who believe in Jesus. He is your direct connection on earth to Jesus and is your constant companion, your conscience, and your best earthly friend, if you allow it. And, if you pay attention, the Holy Spirit will speak to you and guide you through the rest of your life. He is the powerful energy source of love that changes hearts and transforms the lives of people on earth once they let Him in." She paused for a moment, laughing. "Sorry, Michael, but once I get started talking about this stuff, it is hard to stop!"

Contrary to what he would have believed, Michael didn't mind hearing about this. He had never heard anyone speak about the Holy Spirit like this—like a friend who helps you figure out which paths to take. "Go on, Marti," he answered.

"For me, I felt an overwhelming impulse to continue visiting the stroke and brain trauma patients at the hospital and even after they had been discharged. I became almost obsessed with learning more about their situations and wondering how I could help. Every time I would pray to the Holy Spirit for direction, the same answer kept coming back—to change my career path to help these people."

"You really believe that this came from God?"

"Absolutely! I never would have thought of this on my own or even believed that I was capable of doing all of it! Trust me: God is working in my life, and you can see the evidence. So, with this decision, I went back to school to study physical therapy and advanced treatments for traumatic brain injuries. So now, at the Richardson Clinic, we help stroke patients, wounded veterans—"

"And amputees," Michael added.

"That's right."

Michael paused for a moment, really thinking. "That is quite a story, Marti. While I still have some doubts about this whole 'called by God' thing, I really respect all that you have done. Honestly, I didn't know how tough it could be for some families to have no options for care."

"Michael, most people have no idea what it is like to be a caregiver or a patient until it happens to them. Some of my patients are fighting every day to relearn how to do simple things like speaking, swallowing, sitting up, walking. Heck, some of them are fighting just to relearn how to button a shirt by themselves. And remember, this affects the whole family, not just the patient."

"Oh boy. I feel a guilt trip coming on," Michael said, but he wasn't joking.

"Well, I didn't say all of this to make you feel guilty. But, in truth, I hope it makes you feel grateful for all that you are physically *and* mentally able to do." She then looked him directly in the eye and continued, "In your case, Michael, you have the potential to make a full recovery. How fast and how far you go is completely up to you."

Michael just stared back at Marti, thinking about what she just said. It was true. Despite all that had happened in the accident, he was pretty well off. With her and Dominic's help, he would be able to learn how to even run again. For the first time in weeks, he felt like a great burden had been lifted.

"Are you okay, Michael?" Marti asked. Just at that moment, the sunlight chose to shine directly on the cross on her necklace, creating a brilliant glow.

"Yeah, Marti," Michael answered, looking at the cross. "I think I am better than I have been in a long time."

"That is good, because I think we locked the keys inside the car!" Marti stood up, checking her pockets.

"Are you sure? I handed them to you, just like you asked," Michael answered.

"I know, I know," Marti answered, checking all of her pockets. "This is my fault. I went back into the car to grab my cell phone, and I think I left them on the seat. I will be right back," Marti answered, and she took off in a sprint toward the car.

A couple of minutes later, she ran back to their bench, confirming the disaster. She pulled out her iPhone and dialed a number. "Hey, Cynthia? Marti here... Brilliant me! We are in the park at the university. I've locked my car keys in my car. Would you please put Ethan on? I need his help."

Michael was trying to figure out how Ethan could possibly help with this problem when Marti continued the conversation.

"Hi, Ethan. I need your assistance. Cynthia is going to take you back to the apartment. I've locked myself out of the Mazda again."

Michael listened to silence while Ethan was speaking to Marti.

"Hey, you!" Marti laughed. "Two can play that game! What about this morning when you spilled your juice all over your homework? Did I laugh at you? Can you grab your tools and meet us in the park at the university? We are on the bench in our usual spot by the water... Great! See you, then." Marti ended the call and put her phone back in her pocket.

"Aren't you going to call AAA or something?" Michael asked.

"Oh no, Michael. That will take too long," Marti answered matter-of-factly.

Oh, right. Silly me, thought Michael, very puzzled indeed.

After about twenty minutes, Cynthia's car pulled up. Ethan jumped out and ran down the trail to their bench. "Hi, Marti. Hi, Michael," Ethan said, smiling, and pulled out a tool from his bag. This particular item was really a long thin rod.

"Hi, Ethan. We are parked over here," Marti said, getting up and putting her arm around Ethan as they started walking toward her car. Michael got up too, and the group walked back down the trail to her Mazda.

Ethan immediately went to work. To Michael's amazement, Ethan had the skills of a master. He quickly slid his tool down into the thin crack between the window and the car door. Next, he pulled up on the tool and the group heard the telltale CLICK of the door being unlocked. Ethan then opened the door. The whole process took less than five seconds.

"Thanks, Ethan. You've earned an ice cream!" Marti said, hugging him.

"Actually, you owe me *two* ice creams now." Ethan smiled.

"Ah! You are right—I forgot about last weekend. We will get one of them now." Marti turned to Michael, who was still surprised by Ethan's skill. "Are you able to join us for ice cream right now?"

"Sure," he answered, shaking off his disbelief. "I think Cynthia will want to come along too. She has quite a fondness for sweets." To Ethan, Michael said, "Where did you learn how to open up a locked car door?"

"From Master T," Ethan answered. "He taught a bunch of us how to break into cars and steal stereos, cell phones, fuzz busters, GPS systems. Basically anything that they could sell on the streets, on the internet, or even pawn."

Marti filled in the gaps in the explanation, "Master T was one of the leaders of the brutal gang that used Ethan and other boys to steal 'merchandise' for them."

Ethan was momentarily sad at the memory, but then he brightened up, adding, "Master T used to beat us if we didn't bring back enough stuff for him. Still, I have to admit, he was an expert. He could break into any car or truck ever made. We even timed him once. He was so good that he could break in, disable the security system, and then completely strip a truck in less than three minutes. You should have seen it!"

Michael struggled to match Ethan's admiration for this ability but smiled anyway. "Yes, Ethan. That would be something to see."

Chapter 18

The next two days in Michael's penthouse were very different; for the first time in weeks, Michael felt like he had a real goal: to live again. While he still cared about his work, he spent most of his time practicing his walking in his prosthetic limb. His goal was to return to his office later that week—almost fully functional. To that end, he even engaged Jackie (Lexy) in silly games of clocking his progress in all sorts of activities such as walking down the long hallway as well as putting on and removing his prosthetic limb.

But the key difference was that Michael's mood had changed—toward himself and everyone around him. He no longer kept to himself in his room. Instead, he hung out in the kitchen and invited conversations with Jackie, Mrs. Flaherty, Dr. Sherman, and Gus. He found himself smiling, laughing, and enjoying the company of the people in his penthouse.

How different and wonderful the last two days have been! Maria thought to herself while cooking dinner and looking over at Lexy and Michael playing an intense game of checkers on the kitchen table. The dark forces surrounding Michael had taken a massive hit and no longer had complete control over his thoughts. Marti, through a little bit of tough love, showed Michael that he could be self-sufficient again. This had made a huge dent in the demonic armor and was allowing new thoughts of hope to enter Michael's mind. Maria's heart warmed as she saw her two children spending time together again. She wondered if Michael remembered playing checkers with his little sister. She laughed to herself at the memory of how the two of them spent an entire summer playing each other. Michael had generously taught Lexy all of his tricks, so the two of them were almost evenly matched.

"Hey!" laughed Michael as Lexy triple-jumped him. "That is one of my moves!" he accused in jest.

"Well," laughed Lexy, as she removed his "captured" checkers from the board, "I had a great teacher a long time ago who taught me that one."

Maria almost choked up at that point. She forced herself to focus hard on the enchiladas she was preparing.

Michael laughed at that one. "How dramatic that sounds, Jackie! You are only eight, right? It couldn't have been that long ago."

Lexy recovered well. "I guess it just seems like a long time ago. Are you ready for another game?"

"Absolutely! I have to redeem myself. I haven't lost this much since I was young and played against my little sister."

At that moment, Paul (Dr. Sherman) walked in. "Hi, Michael. Gus let me in."

"Hey, Dr. Sherman." Michael smiled. "Take a look! I am not in my wheelchair!" He gestured toward his prosthetic limb.

Paul looked at Michael and then glanced at Maria, who gave him a large smile and returned to making dinner.

Paul took in the scene, his two children laughing and playing checkers again, and schooled his face to show only a little emotion. "I noticed that, Michael. That is fantastic. Can you show me how you are getting up and around? Sorry, Jackie, but I just need to evaluate Michael's progress."

After a brief examination, Paul pronounced the good news to Michael. "It looks like you won't be needing my services much anymore. Your shoulder is just about healed, thanks to the rehab exercises that you have been doing. Your collarbone is also almost healed. Lastly, your jaw now opens at almost full capacity. In short, Michael, you are close to well again."

Michael smiled at the good news. "That is great news, Dr. Sherman. But, if you don't mind, I would like you to come around once a week for a while longer. This is just for my own peace of mind. I will let you know when I think I am done with the home visits." Funny, he thought. He really didn't need to have Dr. Sherman come around the penthouse anymore, but he really enjoyed the company. For some reason, he felt a connection with him.

"That is fine, Michael."

Michael noticed how Dr. Sherman was eyeing the dinner that Mrs. Flaherty was preparing. It certainly smelled delicious. "Dr. Sherman, would you like to stay for dinner? As you can see, Mrs. Flaherty is an excellent cook."

Paul smiled inside. He glanced at Maria, who smiled while continuing to mix the guacamole. "Please call me Sheldon. And, yes, I would love to stay for dinner." Paul noticed that there was another place set at the table. It looks like Michael was including Gus in the dinner tonight too. This was a great change, indeed. "Let me put my things away and wash up before dinner."

Paul walked down the hall and found Gus. "What a transformation in Michael!" Paul exclaimed with joy. "He is almost like his old self."

"Yes, Paul," Gus said. "God is working in his life through Marti. A critical change in him has now occurred. He no longer feels sorry for himself and is now inspired with a new goal to get better and to be with others. This is a very effective weapon against the enemy."

"Gus," said Paul, deflated, "you don't seem as happy about this as I would have thought. Am I missing something?"

"I am happy, Paul. However I need to set your expectations. In short, this change, while good, is not complete. I'm sure you noticed the difference in his inner light. The thick darkness that was practically suffocating all his happiness has dissipated. The tiny glow of light that was almost unnoticeable, is much brighter now, displaying the growing love he has for others and himself. While he still isn't trusting in God yet, there is hope now. However, now the hard work begins."

"Begins?" asked Paul. "I was hoping with this new inspiration that he was over the hard part."

"Inspiration, such as the kind that Michael feels at the moment, ebbs and flows like the tides, Paul. Right now, Michael is feeling good. But, at the first real test, he could crash back down with despair and become worse than before. That is what happens when the inspiration is not based on anything that is lasting. Real inspiration only comes from following Jesus. With Jesus, Michael will stop living only for himself and his own interests. Instead, he will find himself living to help others. In return, he will obtain the love, freedom, and happiness that he has been seeking his whole life. That is when he will permanently change. Helping Michael to accept Jesus as his Savior is our main task, Paul."

"I am ready to help however I can. What are the next steps?"

"Several things. To start, keep praying! Never doubt the power of prayer to bring wisdom and results! Next, keep trying to get Michael to church. I know that he has been resistant in the past, but he may be more open to the idea now. Also, lead by example. Let Michael see the wonder of a faith-filled life through all of us. Make opportunities to speak to Michael about Jesus and the true peace that only He can offer. Lastly, we need to keep Michael in the company of those who follow Jesus. We are so fortunate to have Marti and Dominic as the power of the Holy Spirit is strong in both of them. The demonic forces always cower a bit in fear whenever they are around. We need to encourage Michael to spend as much time in their company as possible."

CHAPTER 19

Cynthia had just opened a yummy bag of crisp cheese puffs and was about to dig in when she heard the *DING* of the elevator and then the distinctive rapid-paced *click-click-click* of high heels walking across the marble floor. Whoever it was, she was in a hurry. Melissa Butano turned the corner and quickly walked up to Cynthia's desk. Melissa was the events manager at the Garcia Lodge and also Trent's girlfriend. From the brief scan of her physique, Cynthia could detect a serious lack of sleep and mountainous levels of stress in Melissa. In truth, she looked bad despite her perfect hair, expensive suit, and the four-inch Jimmy Choo heels that she was wearing.

Cynthia put down the cheese puffs and focused her attention on Melissa, who seemed lost in her own thoughts at the moment. "Hi, Melissa. I'm gathering that you wish to see Michael."

"Yes. Absolutely." Melissa paused, remembering her manners. She smiled a little while continuing, "Sorry. Hi, Cynthia. Is he in?"

"Yes, Melissa, but he is not alone. Trent is with him. Shall I let them know you are here?" Cynthia asked, reaching for her phone to call Michael.

"No!" Melissa blurted out, slamming her hand on the edge of Cynthia's desk. Then, trying to compose herself, she took a deep breath, closed her eyes, and then said, "Ahh, sure. I'll see them both. It really doesn't matter anyway."

Cynthia, concerned, paused for a second with her finger right above the phone's Call button. "Are you sure about this? I can tell Michael that you need to see him alone."

Melissa swallowed and shook her head. "Trent will find out anyway. With Michael there, it might be better that way."

HELP AMONG US

Cynthia didn't move for a few seconds, trying to give Melissa time to change her mind. When Melissa did not respond, Cynthia mentally shrugged, pressed the Call button, and dialed Michael's number.

"Hello?" Michael answered via speakerphone.

"Hi, Michael," Cynthia responded. "Melissa is here and wishes to see you. Are you available right now?"

"Sure," Michael answered. "Actually, this is good timing because I want to go over the status of the new construction and the schedule for events at the Lodge, now that I am finally back in the office."

Over the speakerphone, Cynthia and Melissa could hear Trent's voice, clearly annoyed. "Do we need to discuss this, Michael? I told you that I was in contact with your attorney and he was putting together a case against Rensalant."

"Trent," Michael answered, "I decide what we discuss. Right now I want to hear Melissa's input on the construction work, or lack thereof, and how any project delays will impact the multitude of events scheduled for the next couple of months. We may need to shuffle events to other buildings at the Lodge or possibly rent a location elsewhere."

Cynthia interrupted the discussion before Trent could respond. "Uh, Michael, I will show Melissa in." Cynthia pressed the Call button to end the call. She got up from her desk and walked Melissa to Michael's large office door. She put her hand on Melissa's arm as she spoke, "Please let me know if you need anything, Melissa. I mean it."

Melissa stared at her for a second, her mouth open like she was about to speak, but then she looked down at the ground. Cynthia could sense that Melissa really wanted to share something with her but was not able to.

"Thanks, Cyn. I'll see you later." With that, Melissa opened the door and walked in. Cynthia walked back to her desk and tuned her hearing so she could follow the conversation. Cynthia was a bit uneasy now. Even more disturbing than Melissa's disheveled appearance was the new darkness that had crept into her inner light and some new powerful demonic forces swirling around her. Melissa was in more trouble than she realized.

Chapter 20

"Hi, Melissa," Michael smiled as he saw her enter, glad to see her. He directed her to join them at the large cherrywood table at the back of the office. As she passed the large windows, she could see the city streets fifty stories below her and wished that she could somehow escape into the hustle and bustle.

Melissa first addressed Michael with a genuine smile. "I am so glad to see you back in the office, Michael." Etiquette forced her to quickly glance at Trent, and she managed a weak "Hi, Trent" as she took the seat nearest to Michael.

"Hi," Trent barked back, refusing to look up at her as he continued to shuffle through the stack of paperwork in front of him.

Strange, Michael thought. Trent didn't look happy to see his girlfriend. "It is great to be back, Melissa. I was going nuts in the hospital and then at home." Michael pointed to his chair. "As you can see, I am no longer using my wheelchair. Soon I will be able to drive myself here too. Just need to check with the dealership about when I can pick up my new car."

"Porsche again?" Melissa asked.

"Is there any other car?" Michael answered.

"For you, I guess not," Melissa answered with a weak laugh. She looked down nervously at her lap for a few seconds. Then she regained her professionalism. "Where shall we start, Michael?"

Michael felt the brewing tension in the room between Melissa and Trent. Something was wrong between the two of them, but now was not the time to discuss this. Sometimes it was a bad decision to mix personal and business relationships. "Let's start with your general perspective of the construction progress."

"The lack of progress, you mean," Melissa answered, shifting a bit in her seat. "Virtually nothing has been done in the last three months."

Michael noticed the visual exchange between Trent and Melissa when she answered the question. "Is the work crew even showing up to work each day? I am going tomorrow to check it out."

"No, Michael," Trent answered in haste. Michael turned his head to stare at Trent. Trent composed himself and continued, "We can go together. I will pick you up after lunch. Just tell me what time works for you."

Michael continued to stare at Trent, trying to figure out what Trent wasn't sharing with him. "Sure. That will save me cab fare. I'll check my schedule and get back to you." Back to Melissa, Michael stated, "Please continue."

"Well"—Melissa hesitated, stealing glances at Trent—"workers show up, but they aren't seeming to make any progress. They keep insisting that they have to rework the foundation because of cracks and weather-related damage, but I never see any progress."

Michael was taking notes, mostly for his attorney. "So what do you think this does to our events schedule? Do we have capacity to just shuffle around the events within the Lodge, or do we need to rent out another facility?"

"For the rest of this month, I have rearranged the events to avoid this. However, I think we will need to move some of the smaller events to another location next month when we host the Chicago Business Summit."

"Melissa, I'm sure I don't have to tell you that the Summit gets top priority. Let me know if you are having trouble booking other locations. Lastly, I will need the projected costs of the entire disruption to present to our attorney as part of the case against Rensalant."

"Sure, Michael. I can get those to you by the end of the week."

Michael looked at Melissa and then at Trent. He decided to give Melissa a chance to speak to him alone. "You came here to see me, Melissa. If you give me a few minutes, I can finish up with Trent and then we can speak alone." Michael watched the exchange between

Trent and Melissa. She looked back down at her lap and then turned back to Michael.

"No, Michael, I'm fine. Actually, I was downtown anyway, so I thought I'd drop by and give you the update in person." Melissa stood up, grabbed her purse, and walked to the door. "I'll be sure to send you the projections and the list of upcoming events over the next three months." With that, she turned and walked out of the door.

Michael turned and looked at Trent, who was busy with something on his iPhone. "Problems with Melissa, Trent?" Michael asked.

Trent looked up from his phone. "Uh, the usual, Michael," Trent responded with a weak laugh. "She wants to get married, and I am not ready yet. In fact, we are probably breaking up right now. At least I am."

"Really?" Michael asked, still unsure if this was in fact the real issue. But he would take his friend's word for it. "Trent," he counseled, "while this is none of my business, she is a great girl. I'm not sure there are many better out there."

"Wow, that is rich, especially coming from you," Trent replied.

Ouch. "Sorry, Trent," Michael responded. "Not sure what you mean."

"Come off it, Michael. You don't stay with the same woman for longer than three weeks. Once you know the basic facts about her, you grow restless and move on to the next one. Believe me, you have broken a lot of hearts. You're just too busy to notice."

While true, Trent's comment still stung. "I guess you are right, Trent," Michael answered, thoroughly chastised. "I am hardly the expert on women or marriage."

"Truth is, Michael, Melissa was getting too clingy for me. I felt like I was being watched and nagged incessantly for the last six months. All we do is fight now."

Michael looked at his friend, feeling like a jerk that Trent had been miserable, and he was just too self-absorbed with his own problems to notice. "I had no idea, Trent. I am really sorry that I have not been there for you."

"That's okay, Michael," Trent said, with an honest smile now. "Now that you are better, we can get back to the way things used to be, going out on weekends, carousing the town."

Wow, thought Michael. He must have missed a lot during the lengthy hospital stay and the time he was chained to his apartment. The last time he saw Trent and Melissa together, they seemed really happy. True, Trent only came around to visit Michael a couple of times each month during his recovery. Once Michael was able to do some work, Trent came over more often, but they never discussed Melissa. "Okay, Trent. Well, I guess I have to get used to thinking of you as a single guy again. I'll call you later to tell you what time we can visit the Lodge construction area tomorrow."

Trent stood up and walked to the door. "Oh, Michael, don't forget that you need to attend the fundraiser ball on Friday. Black-tie affair. You need to find a date."

"Oh, right! I completely forgot," Michael answered. Ugh. In the past, women were lining up to date him. But now finding a date as an amputee would pose new challenges. And he had burned many bridges (as confirmed by Trent) with the women in his past. For the first time in his adult life, Michael was no longer confident in his appeal to women.

CHAPTER 21

"No, no, NO, Nick! You have to answer in the form of a question!" Rosetta hollered, shaking her finger at everyone in the room. "What is the Giza Plateau?" Rosetta proclaimed, loud enough for everyone to hear.

"What is the Giza Plateau," answered the male voice of contestant Joe on the flat-screen TV. A rerun of *Jeopardy!* had been turned on, and the whole waiting room of the clinic was engrossed in the game.

"A-ha!" shrieked Rosetta, clapping her hands in obvious delight at her correct answer.

"Alex, I'll take Ancient Cities for $200," contestant Joe stated.

"That Alex Trebek was so foxy!" Rosetta announced to the room.

"You said it, Rosetta!" answered Merle, who was somehow able to keep knitting while fully watching the game.

Michael had been in the clinic for about five minutes now. He was still remembering his entrance. Everyone clapped and cheered when he *walked*, not rode in a wheelchair, into the waiting room. He smiled to himself. It was true, he thought; the people in the clinic were becoming a family to him. Especially Rosetta—she was the biggest supporter of him in the room with her applause and cheering at his progress.

"This ancient city is located in a Central American rainforest, and its name is translated to mean 'the Water Hole,'" said the voice of Alex Trebek.

"Rainforest, rainforest...," said Rosetta, in deep contemplation.

"Where was that big city that used to be a huge trading post long ago?" asked Nick.

HELP AMONG US

"Trading post?" responded Merle.

"Yeah! Long ago, all of the traders from China and other places used to stop there. Before they used ships."

"Do you mean Timbuktu?" asked Rosetta.

"Yes! That's it!" shouted Nick.

"Great answer!" yelled Ben.

"Sure, except Timbuktu is in Africa and in the middle of the desert!" said Rosetta.

"What is the city of Tikal," said Michael.

"What is the city of Tikal," said contestant Joe, who was on a winning streak.

"Tikal is correct!" confirmed Alex Trebek.

"How did you know that, Michael?" asked Rosetta.

"Well, I'd love to say that I have a vast knowledge of ancient cities," Michael answered with a smile. "But the reality is that I have been there."

"That is CHEATING!" screamed Ben.

"No, it isn't!" yelled Rosetta. "If Michael has been there, then he has the RIGHT to know the answer!"

That was the end. Ben was angry now. "The point of the game is supposed to be about knowing all kinds of crazy stuff that you should know NOTHING about!" Ben was now jabbing his cane in the air at Rosetta like a sword, stabbing with each syllable. "If you have any *personal* knowledge of the subject, then you should excuse yourself from the round of play!"

"What kind of insane logic is that?" Rosetta screamed. "If they followed your rules, there would be no one who could play this round, as it would exclude all tourists, teachers, historians, flight attendants…"

Michael was trying hard to suppress his laughter. After coming here for the past few weeks, he was used to the frequent squabbles in the waiting area.

At that moment, Marti stepped into the waiting room, observing the scene. "Ah, looks like someone illegally turned on *Jeopardy!* again." She walked over to the cabinet below the TV screen, found the remote, and switched the channel back to a video describing the health benefits of various yoga positions.

A collective "BOO!" hissed through the room. Marti turned to everyone, controlling her laughter, and held up both her hands. "Now hold on, everyone! You know that *Jeopardy!* brings out the worst in all of you!"

Protests and promises of better behavior were being voiced in a general roar.

"We can try it again next week. But I think we need a cooling-off period for today. After all, we don't want to scare away our new patients, do we?"

Marti walked over to Michael in the midst of the grumbling. "Hi, Michael. Let's go."

Michael stood up, grabbed his crutches, and walked with Marti to the gym.

"You are getting better at standing up!" Marti exclaimed. "Each time I see you, you have made great progress. Keep it up, Michael, and soon you will graduate out of here!"

Michael smiled but then he felt a small rush of sadness at the thought of not returning. As crazy as it sounded to him, he would miss everyone. Dominic, Marti, Ethan, and even the nuttiness of the waiting room with Rosetta, Ben, Merle, Nick, and the others. "Well," Michael said, "maybe I will come back to visit at times."

Marti smiled at that. "We would love to have you here anytime." She pushed open the door to the gym, and they walked up to the indoor track. Dominic waved them over. He was wearing shorts, showing off his running blade while he was navigating the obstacle course he had set up on the track. Michael had never seen Dominic in shorts before, so he had no idea how muscular he was. Michael watched as Dominic jumped two hurdles and then ran around various cones set up on the lanes on the track. Again, Michael was impressed by Dominic's athleticism.

Dominic stopped and ran over to Michael and Marti. "Hey, Michael, the changing room is over there. Get on your running stuff, and we will fit you with your new running blade."

Michael was pretty excited. While he certainly didn't expect to be performing anything close to Dominic's level today, he knew that he was on his way to getting back into shape and, really, getting back his life.

Michael changed and then emerged from the locker room. "Sit over here," Marti called out. She pointed to a chair next to the track. On the ground, Michael could see his new running blade.

"Let's switch out the prosthetic leg for the blade," Marti explained. "You will do this transition yourself, with us talking you through it."

After Michael put on the running blade, he stood up and took a few steps. "This feels so weird! It is longer than my prosthetic, so I think it is going to drag on the ground."

"That is because the blade has to bend a lot to support you while you run," explained Dominic.

As Michael started to feel more comfortable, he started to run a little. Surprisingly, Michael found the running blade pretty easy to use. After a few minutes, he was able to jog a bit.

"Come over here, and let me check out the fit," Marti shouted out as Michael ran past her. He jogged over to her and took a seat in the chair next to her. She spent a few minutes examining the socket to gauge the fit and to determine how it was rubbing on his stub. After a few minutes, she smiled and looked up at Michael. "The fit is really good, Michael. We were fortunate to create such an excellent scan of your limb to send to the manufacturer. From how quickly you are able to run in it, it seems like it is working for you. How does it feel?"

Michael smiled back. "It feels really good! It is an adjustment, of course, because it feels like I am running on air. But I don't feel any major rubbing points, nor do I feel like I'm sinking down into the socket."

"Excellent, Michael. Getting the proper fit for a running blade can be a challenge. Let me know if we need to make adjustments." Marti stood up. "I think you are ready to be set loose! Take it away, Dominic!"

"Okay, champ! You've done enough resting! Let's hit the track!" Dominic led them out on the track. Together they started doing some basic running and stopping drills. Nothing too fancy or complicated, but Michael felt great. This was the first time that he had been doing more than slow walking in months. He felt like he could fly.

Too soon, though, Michael was ready to stop. It would take some time and effort to regain his cardio strength. Dominic moved them on to do some weight training and then exercises to strengthen his core. "Remember, Michael," Dominic said, "to get back in shape, you have to be fully committed to this. You need to do regular cardiovascular exercise, weight-bearing exercises, and core conditioning in order to be able to do what you want on your blade."

Marti walked over as Michael was doing crunches with a fifteen-pound weight on his chest. "Do you have any weights at home?" she asked. "And something like a treadmill or a stationary bike? You will need to do some form of exercise every day if you are serious about using your running blade to its full extent."

Michael stopped the crunches for a moment to answer. "Yes, I have a mini gym in my apartment. Actually, before the accident, I was in pretty good shape. I used to run half-marathons and other races."

"Wimp," Dominic responded with a smile.

"Wimp? What do you mean?" Michael asked, laughing.

"Half-marathons are for wimps. Try a *real* race, like sixty miles or so."

Marti rolled her eyes. "Oh man. The testosterone festival is beginning!"

"Seriously, Dominic," Michael puffed, between crunches, "I would like to shadow some time with you when you lift weights, run, and work your core. I just want to get an idea of your routine."

"Well, how about on Fridays after work, around 6:00 or 7:00 p.m.? You can meet me here, as this is my gym."

"Really? That would be great!" Michael was so amazed. He finished his last set and then sat down in the chair to take off his running blade.

"I'm always looking for a training buddy," Dominic answered.

"Great!" Then Michael remembered. "No, wait! Not this Friday. I have to go to a fundraiser."

"That's interesting," said Marti. "I'm going to a fundraiser too. It's the annual Children's Unit Ball for the hospital."

"Yeah," said Michael, smile fading. "That is the one." He was mentally picturing his arrival. In the past, he would step out of his

Porsche in his Brioni tuxedo, hand his keys to the valet, open the door for his gorgeous date, and then begin posing for all of the cameras on the Red Carpet. Events like these in the past churned great publicity for his company. What a scene it made: the handsome successful businessman with the latest high-fashion model on his arm—the paparazzi ate it up. This time, however, it would be very different. He would step out of his car alone and walk on his prosthetic leg. There was no time (in two days) to find anyone whom he could ask to accompany him. He had burned too many bridges with his past girlfriends.

Marti noticed his mood change. "You don't seem happy about going, Michael. From all of the pictures I've seen of you in the newspapers and magazines over the years, I thought you liked those events."

Michael looked up at her and gave her a smile that didn't reach his eyes. "You're not going to like my reply, Marti," he warned her. "The truth? I did not especially like the events. But they were really good for business."

"That is pretty callous," Marti said. "Did you ever go with the goal of actually *helping* the cause for which the event was held?"

"Back then? No. I was a pretty selfish jerk," Michael answered. And, not for the first time since he met her, he felt ashamed of his past behavior.

Marti took a second to parse his words, then stated, "You said the words 'back then.' What about now?"

"Now..." Michael exhaled, embarrassed, running his hand through his thick black hair. "Now I'm going because I made a commitment to the hospital that I would be there. You see, having Michael Garcia at your event generates enormous publicity and increases the contributions."

Marti smiled. "So you are going because you are honoring your commitment. This sounds like personal growth to me, Michael. Congratulations."

Michael smiled a little at that.

Marti then looked guilty and then laughed. "Sorry, Michael, but I have been requested to ask you a question. Otherwise, I will never hear the end of it from my friends who read all of the celebrity gossip magazines. So here it is: Which supermodel will you be taking this time?"

Michael answered firmly, "None."

"'None' as in not a supermodel? So is she an actress or pop star?"

"Marti, I am going alone. I will stay only as long as necessary to fulfill my commitment and then I will leave."

Marti's smile vanished. "Really? That will certainly generate some news."

"Yes, unfortunately, it will." He returned to taking off his running blade, imagining how cruel the paparazzi and celebrity gossip columnists will be when they see him arrive at the ball as an amputee and without a date. Things were certainly going to be different from now on, so he would just have to buck up and deal with it.

Dominic, who had remained silent during this conversation, finally spoke up. "Michael, did you know that Marti is also going alone?"

Marti looked at Dominic and smiled. "Very funny, Dominic. I hardly look the part of a supermodel or pop star." She turned to Michael, smiled, and continued, "Michael, I go to this event every year *alone*—by choice. So I'll see you there." With that, she started to walk off, back to her office.

Michael started to pull off his running blade and then had a thought. "So you always go to this event alone, Marti, by design, right? Even if you were asked, you would still say no, is that true?"

Dominic's interest in this conversation peaked, and he couldn't help but smile.

Marti stopped and turned back around. "Well, I would go with Dominic if he asked me, but his fiancée, Keisha, would have my head." She smiled and winked at Dominic.

"Keisha is a beautiful and jealous woman!" Dominic laughed.

Take Marti, Michael thought. This was actually a great idea as it would certainly solve his problem with the unforgiving paparazzi. Since she was a highly renowned doctor and therapist, the gossip columnists would not be so quick to judge her, like they would an unknown person. And, truth be told, he liked Marti. She was the first person he could talk to, and she happened to also be female.

Michael pulled from his significant experience with women to figure out the best way to persuade her to go with him. At her innermost core, Marti was someone who was driven by her desire to help others. He decided to appeal to this need in her. "Well, unless you have strong objections, I would consider it a great personal favor if you would accompany me. Facing the paparazzi with a missing limb will be easier if I have someone with me, especially the first time." *How could she say no to that?*

Marti looked at him for a moment. "Michael, are you being serious? Or are you just having fun by teasing me?"

Michael put his hand over his heart. "I'm completely serious, Marti. But if it would make you uncomfortable, then do not feel obligated."

"Hmmm..." Marti paused, thinking. "So does that mean we will be surrounded by crazed cameramen and journalists?"

Michael answered with all seriousness, "Without a doubt. Sorry." *Wow*, he thought. *She might actually turn me down.*

She surprised him with a smile. "If it will help you out, I will accompany you. But, in exchange, I get to wear my Groucho Marx glasses," Marti answered, laughing.

Michael did a double take. "What?"

"Marti, if you go through with that plan, we will hang a picture of the two of you in the waiting room!" roared Dominic.

"Trust me on this. If she wears them," laughed Michael, "you will have to move to a private island to escape from all of the pictures of us plastered on every magazine and newspaper cover as well as splashes of us on every news channel!"

Marti changed the subject. "Dominic, are you still okay to give us a ride from Michael's apartment to the Porsche dealership? Michael's car is ready for pickup."

"I really appreciate this from both of you," Michael said. "None of my friends are able to drive a stick-shift car, believe it or not!" Michael paused for a second. "Well, that is not entirely true. Gus can handle a stick shift, but he still thinks he is in Scotland, driving on the left side of the road!"

"I can believe it and not a problem, Michael," Dominic answered. "But you will just have to let each of us drive it sometime!"

"Uh, sure!" said Michael, forcing a smile on his face. *Hopefully they know how to drive a high-performance car.*

Dominic laughed when he read Michael's nervous expression. "Don't worry, Michael. I have driven in war zones while being shot at from all directions. I think I can handle your car on the open road!"

Chapter 22

Michael and Marti walked through the doors of the Porsche dealership. Dominic, while only obligated to drop them off, parked and joined them to get a look at Michael's new car.

"Hey, it's not every day you get to see machines like these!" Dominic explained when they saw him approaching. He was so excited, like a kid in a toy store, and it became obvious that he knew a lot about cars. He and Michael began discussing the different models, engine sizes, features, etc. At that point, Marti tuned them out and began to look around the room. While she understood, Marti did not share their love and fascination with cars; after all, she grew up in a garage with two brothers who souped up cars as a hobby. After a few minutes, the salesman walked up to Michael.

"Mr. Garcia, good to see you again." The two of them shook hands. Michael introduced his friends, and they all exchanged pleasantries. "Well," said the salesman, "are you ready to take home your new car?"

"Absolutely!" Michael and Dominic said in unison. The salesman, Mr. Davens, led the way out the doors and around the corner into the parking lot. Suddenly, there she was—Michael's new shiny black Porsche 911. The car literally glistened in the evening sun. Marti laughed to herself as she looked back and forth between Michael and Dominic, struggling to determine who was more excited. It was incredible; they were almost drooling.

Mr. Davens ceremoniously handed Michael the keys. Michael cradled them lovingly in his hand for just a moment. He then turned and handed them to Dominic. "I want you to be the first to try her out."

Her? Marti laughed to herself. *It is as if the car were a prized thoroughbred!*

Dominic's eyes grew wide with gratitude. "Thank you! It has been a little while since I was in one of these." Dominic unlocked the door and slowly sat down in the soft leather-covered driver's seat, closing his eyes in the sensory symphony of the feel of the new car. From his expression, one would think that Dominic had never sat in a seat before. The new-car smell wafted out of the vehicle and made its way over to Michael, who closed his eyes, breathing in the sweet perfume. Marti, observing all of this, laughed, rolled her eyes and looked heavenward for strength.

"It happens every time," Mr. Davens quietly told her with a huge smile.

Dominic adjusted the seat and the mirrors. He then inserted the key and turned on the ignition. The car initially roared and then purred like a large tiger as Dominic shifted the car into first gear. Both Michael and Dominic smiled knowingly at each other, clearly glorifying in the sound of the finely tuned engine. Michael closed the door to allow Dominic to absorb the experience for a few minutes. Very soon, they could hear music playing, intermixing with the soft purr of the engine as Dominic maneuvered the car around the lot.

"I am impressed, Michael," Marti said, smiling. "I can only imagine how difficult this was for you to wait."

"Well," answered Michael, "her first experience should be with someone who really appreciates her beauty and power," Michael said. "I promise that I will take better care of her than I did my previous one."

Mr. Davens piped in at that point. "Well, unless you had cut your *own* brake line, I don't know how you could have prevented your accident."

Michael whipped his head around toward Mr. Davens. "*What?*" Michael asked, stunned. It was as if a large bucket of cold water had been thrown on him; his reverie from the new car vanished. "Did you say that my brake line was *cut?*"

Marti was confused; she had not heard this before.

Mr. Davens looked at Michael in complete surprise. "Why, yes…" He hesitated. "Didn't your friend tell you?"

Michael was still having trouble. "Sorry, Mr. Davens. Did you mean 'cut' or just that it was severed, somehow, maybe from the crash?"

"No, Mr. Garcia. I meant that it was definitely cut before the crash. Despite all of the damage, our mechanics could tell that the line had been cleanly cut." He shuffled through the paperwork until he came to the page regarding the trade-in details for Michael's crushed Porsche. "Yes, here it is. I told a Mr. Wentworth about this issue a couple of months ago, after you placed the order for the new car. When the dealership did the complete inspection on your trade-in, they discovered the cut brake line. I thought it was interesting, and I wanted you to know in case you wanted to inform the police."

Michael grabbed the side of his now-throbbing head and had trouble balancing for a second. Marti reacted, grabbing his shoulders to steady him. "Whoa, Michael," she said. "Let's go back inside and sit down for a second."

"No, no," Michael said, pushing her away gently. "I am just having trouble processing this." He turned to Mr. Davens. "Are you saying that someone may have tried to kill me?"

Mr. Davens looked a bit nervous at that point. "Well, I'm no homicide detective, but this looks pretty suspicious to me."

Just at that moment, Dominic pulled up, rolled down the window, and smiled at everyone. "There are no words to describe my euphoria right now!" When no one responded, he narrowed his eyes and evaluated everyone's expressions. He got out of the car and went to them. "What is going on? Are you all right, Michael?"

"Dominic, we just learned that Michael's car accident might not have been an accident. Someone might have tried to kill Michael," Marti explained about the cut brake line.

Dominic's instincts started kicking in at that moment. "Michael, I think we need to finish up here and get you home. I am coming with both of you. It is time to start piecing together what has been going on."

Marti looked concerned. "So you think that there may be more to this?"

"Absolutely," answered Dominic. "Remember the mysterious 'overdose'? And if we don't get this figured out soon, Michael may not be around long enough to give us time."

CHAPTER 23

"Now do you all finally believe me? Just as I didn't cut my own brake line, I certainly didn't take a whole bottle of OxyContin," Michael declared at the kitchen table. Everyone was called in to discuss the issue—Cynthia, Dr. Sherman (Paul), Mrs. Flaherty (Maria), Jackie (Lexy), Dominic, Marti, Ethan, and Gus. Trent was on his way and would join shortly. Ethan and Lexy were playing with the kittens on the floor, but they were both listening.

The whole group exchanged glances with each other, and Michael knew that there had been some level of belief among them that he had attempted suicide.

"Well, I think I can speak for everyone here by saying that we all believe you now. I think we should call the authorities," Dominic said.

"I agree, Dominic," said Dr. Sherman. "If someone is trying to kill you, Michael, then that means that they may try again. It also means that whoever it is has access to you, your apartment, and your car."

Michael shuddered at that thought. "You are right about that."

Dominic got up and went to another room to call the authorities. Just at that moment, Michael's doorbell rang.

"I'll get it," said Cynthia, who got up from the table and walked to the door.

"Michael, we're needin' ta ask yew some questions. Do yew have any enemies that yew know of?"

Just as Michael was about to answer, the group turned to hear shouting from the doorway. "Argh! Those two damned crows tried to crap on me again!" It was Trent, and he was roaring angry. "But

I was ready for them. I brought my umbrella this time. Now I just need to wash it off."

"Trent, control your language! There are children here!" Cynthia scolded.

Lexy and Ethan both burst out in laughter. Maria gave Lexy a quick glare.

"What is this all about?" Marti asked.

"Well," said Maria, deliberately looking away from Lexy, "there are two crows that have nested, I think, in the roof of this building. We can't explain why, but every time Mr. Wentworth comes to the penthouse, the birds, uh, well, poop on him."

Marti started laughing. "Are you serious?" she asked and then, remembering her manners, she schooled her face into a serious look and continued, "How horrible!"

Cynthia rejoined the group at the table after helping Trent wash off his umbrella. Looking into her empty mug, she murmured to Gus, "I think I need something stronger than coffee after that scene!"

"I may be joinin' yew in that!" he answered. "Now, Michael, yew wehr aboot ta answer me question."

"Wow, Gus," Michael answered with a sigh, rubbing his hand down his face. "Truthfully, as a successful businessman, I'm sure that I've made some enemies," Michael started.

"Yes, and most of them are women!" Trent answered, laughing at his own joke. He walked into the kitchen and pulled a chair up to the table.

The group winced at that comment.

"Well, there may be some truth in that, Trent," Michael said, forcing a laugh. Michael couldn't help but look over at Marti. She smiled at him.

To break the tension in the room, Maria made a grandiose gesture of getting up, walking over to the kitchen island, and pouring a cup of coffee. To Trent, she asked, "Cream or sugar?"

"Both, please," he answered.

Maria placed the steaming coffee cup in front of him and sat back down. Paul, knowing well all of his wife's expressions, read her anger at Trent and protectiveness for her son. He thought to himself that Trent is lucky that she only put cream and sugar into his coffee.

Dominic walked back in at that moment. "A detective is on his way. I also called a buddy of mine in the FBI. I'm going to speak to him later tonight to see if he can find out anything more for us."

"Thanks, Dom," Michael said.

"Don't know if you are aware, Michael," Marti said, "but Dominic trained with the FBI before he decided to become a physical therapist."

"FBI? So you are an academy dropout?" joked Michael. He was impressed. *What didn't this guy do?*

Dominic laughed. "Yes, I am. My heart was into physical therapy, so I left before graduation. However, I made several great friends while I was there. A couple of them can help us out, if necessary."

"You are an invaluable source of so many things, Dominic," Michael said. "I think I would hate to have you as an enemy!"

"Dominic, what do you recommend for Michael's protection?" Paul asked.

"Well, Sheldon, I would recommend a pistol, but it would take some time to get a concealed carry permit within the Chicago city limits," explained Dominic. "I have a permit, so I can help protect him when he is with me. For now I will see about getting some police protection. But I'm thinking that we may need a bodyguard—I can look into that for you. I know of several good people who can help."

"Ugh," said Michael. "I was always hoping to avoid the whole bodyguard thing."

"Sorry, man, but it may become necessary."

At that moment, the doorbell rang. Cynthia answered it and let in the detective. She walked back into the kitchen and pulled up another chair to the table. "Everyone, this is Detective Jenkins." To the detective, she continued, "Detective, I think everyone should introduce himself or herself. However, the main person you are here to interview is here. This is Michael Garcia."

"Glad to meet you, Michael," said Detective Jenkins as the two shook hands. After all of the introductions were made, the group described the two events that precipitated the call, paying special attention to dates, times, locations, and all of the people involved. Dr. Sherman relayed the story of the overdose, noting the empty prescription bottle and the fact that no strangers had entered the apartment. Michael and Dominic shared the details of the cut brake line, even showing the detective the inspection paperwork from the Porsche mechanics that stated their assessment of the crashed vehicle. At that point, Trent chimed in.

"Oh yeah, I remember that. The car dealer, I'm forgetting his name now, called me several weeks ago and told me about the cut brake line in the crashed Porsche."

"Mr. Davens," Michael inserted.

"Right, Mr. Davens," Trent answered. "While I heard what he said about the brake line being cut instead of torn or smashed, I guess I didn't process it as being important. There was so much going on at that time with Michael being so seriously hurt and me trying to run Garcia Enterprises without him I guess I just forgot." Trent looked around the table. "I really apologize, everyone. I honestly didn't think about it at the time."

"No worries, Trent," answered Cynthia. "We were all going crazy at that time."

"Don't be silly, dude!" Michael answered.

"Trent, this is normal," Detective Jenkins replied. "Often the key to solving a case lies in a small detail that gets overlooked at the time. That is why we question people multiple times to see if we can jar their memory."

Trent appeared to feel better after that. Cynthia was glad because she could tell that Trent was overwhelmed with everything that was going on.

"So what about some police protection until we can get a bodyguard?" Dominic asked.

Detective Jenkins, who was recording the conversation on his iPhone and taking notes, put away his pen, phone, and notebook into his suit jacket pocket. He looked up at Dominic. "I will have someone assigned to watch this building, but it will not be much more than a patrol car making some additional rounds."

"A patrol car passing by the building from time to time won't be much help if someone is inside the building trying to kill Michael," Dominic said with controlled anger.

"Look, I hear what you are saying, and, believe me, I wish I could do more," Detective Jenkins responded. "If you saw the list of cases that are being worked on at my precinct alone, your head would spin. We simply don't have the manpower to assign guards unless we have real threats with real suspects. Since all we have in Michael's case are just two incidents that may or may not be related, I cannot get you 24-7 protection. If it makes you feel more comfortable, I advise you to hire a bodyguard as soon as you can."

Dominic did not look happy with that reply, but he had no justification for trying to argue with the detective.

"Of course, I expect you all to call me if you see anything suspicious." With that, the detective got up from his seat. Cynthia got up too and walked with him to the door. When she returned to the kitchen, she saw that Dominic was on his cell phone at the other end of the room.

Marti was petting the kittens with Ethan and Lexy, and it was clear that she was trying to leave. "We need to go now, Ethan. Tonight is a school night, remember?"

"Aw, Marti," protested Ethan. "We always have to leave just when things start to get interesting!"

Dominic ended his call and walked back to the group at the table. "My buddy from the FBI is going to see what he can do for us. In the meantime, I will call around and get you a bodyguard."

"Thanks, Dominic," Michael said. "I really appreciate it." Michael got up and walked all of his guests to the door. Everyone left except Cynthia and Trent, who stayed a bit longer as they were pretty concerned about their friend.

"You'll be all right, Michael. I mean that." Cynthia forced a smile on her face. "See you back at the ranch tomorrow," Cynthia joked as she walked out the door.

"Yeah, see you tomorrow," Trent said. He started to leave but stopped and turned back around. "Michael, I'm really sorry about all of this. It is bad enough to have been in an accident, but worse to know that it was deliberate. This is kind of scary, really."

"I know what you mean, Trent. I haven't been scared like this in a long time."

CHAPTER 24

The next day, Thursday, passed without incident. While Michael was grateful that nothing happened, he found himself suspecting everyone and jumping at every sound. Even getting a simple cup of coffee was stressful. He found himself observing (and trying to remember) everyone in line with him at the coffee cafe. He scanned the room for any suspicious characters while still keeping an eye on the door for any new patrons. Any strangers who attempted to make eye contact or speak with him were regarded with scrutiny. After only a few hours, he discovered how exhausting being scared could be. By noon, he decided that he would stop worrying and just live his life—with some caution, of course.

After a much more relaxed lunch, he called Trent to see when they could leave to go look at the new (and unfinished) construction site at the Lodge, as they had planned the day before. Trent ended up being buried in some work, so they agreed to go look on Monday. Michael filled the rest of the afternoon reviewing more client investment account reports, gathering more questions than answers about what was going on with the mysterious transactions. After a serious examination of the transactions over time, Michael still had trouble establishing a pattern; however, it appeared that the inflows of cash were attempting to replenish the mysterious and large outflows made several months ago.

He set up two meetings: one with Trent for first thing on Monday morning, then the other with the senior financial managers. Then he called his IT staff to have them review the systems logs to determine the source (user and location) of some of the transactions. By noon on Monday, he should have an idea of what everyone knew about this. Before he accused anyone at his company of theft, he needed to get all sides of the facts. Then he would bring in the authorities to send whomever it was to prison. As Michael knew all too well, companies went down for events of fraud like this with many corporate executives receiving an extensive stay in state penitentiaries. He reprimanded himself for not paying enough attention. He had focused too much on sales and public relations and had relied too much on others to monitor account activity.

By the time 6:00 p.m. rolled around, Michael needed to get out of the office. He had a couple of free hours to kill before dinner, so he called Dominic to see if they could meet at the clinic gym for a workout that evening, since they couldn't meet the next day. It was amazing how he was getting into a new rhythm with new friends and activities. "Sure thing, Michael! Just come find me when you get to the clinic." Dominic had responded. Michael smiled as he hung up the phone. He was starting to like the new direction his life was taking.

Michael walked into the clinic and, of course, was met by Rosetta and her big smile. "Hey, beautiful lady," Michael said as he bent down and gave her a kiss on the cheek. Rosetta had grown on him over the weeks at the clinic.

Rosetta blushed and laughed like a schoolgirl. "You are too much, you handsome man, you! Are you ready for your next session?"

"Not for a session. Actually, I am going to start working out with Dominic in the gym. He is going to let me train with him so I can pick up some exercise tips."

Rosetta smiled a knowing smile. "I could tell that the two of you were becoming friends. Understand this, Michael, you won't find many friends like Dominic."

Michael nodded. "I am starting to find that out, Rosetta." He winked at her and then walked down the hall toward Dominic's office. On the way, he passed Marti's office. He smiled and was about to pop in to say a quick hello when he noticed another man in there with her. From the brief seconds that it took for him to back out of her doorway and continue walking down the hallway, he could tell that the man was not talking to her as a patient. From what he had overheard of their conversation, it appeared that the man was trying to get Marti to go to the Children's Hospital Ball with him. He wasn't sure why, but that bothered him.

He found Dominic's office and knocked on the door while he walked in. Dominic was on the phone but smiled and waved him to sit down in one of the chairs in front of his desk. Dominic finished his call and smiled at Michael.

"So are you ready to get strong?"

"Sure," Michael responded. Dominic noticed that Michael seemed distracted.

"Hmm...," Dominic pondered. "Michael, what's wrong?"

"Oh, nothing," Michael said, trying to force a smile. "Let's get going."

Dominic didn't look convinced but stood up and walked over to where his gym bag was stored. He turned around and looked at Michael, who was lost in thought. Dominic crossed his arms and stared at Michael. "Okay, man, spill it."

Michael shifted nervously in his chair. "Dom, there is nothing. Really!"

"If you say so," said Dominic as he reached down and picked up his gym bag. "Oh, just wondering, when is your next appointment with Marti?"

"Next Tuesday afternoon," said Michael. "Anything wrong?"

"No. We just need to have her check out your limb to make sure that running blade is fitting appropriately. Or, we can have her take a quick look now."

"Oh, well, she is busy at the moment. Some guy was in her office with her."

"No problem. Let's stop on in," said Dominic, turning to walk to her office.

"No, Dominic. I don't think she would want us to interrupt her," Michael said.

Dominic turned to answer but then took a look at Michael's face. He stopped and set down his gym bag. "Describe the guy."

"Which guy?"

"The guy in Marti's office. Is he good-looking, tall, with blondish hair, nice clothes?"

"Well, I only saw him for about two seconds, but, yeah, that describes him," Michael said.

Dominic broke into a big smile. "You like her, don't you?" he asked.

Michael played dumb. "Who, Marti?"

"Yes, Marti. You like her."

"Well, maybe a little," Michael responded, feeling like an idiot. After all, he had had so many beautiful girlfriends in the past.

"She's not your usual type, is she? It is good to step out of your comfort zone."

"Yeah, she is different than the women I have been involved with in the past."

"Well, my friend, you will have to get in line. There are some others who like her too, like this guy," Dominic pointed in the direction of Marti's office. "Sven Peterson."

Michael looked a bit uneasy and asked, "Does Marti like this Sven Peterson?"

"You mean *Dr.* Sven Peterson. He is a pretty well-known cosmetic surgeon in this town. He has been trying to get Marti to go out with him for some time, but she always turns him down."

Michael felt relieved hearing this news. "Really?"

"Yes, really," Dominic said, laughing.

"You are enjoying this," Michael said, laughing now too.

"You bet I am!" Then Dominic looked a little more serious and continued, "She doesn't know it yet, but she likes you too."

Michael stared at Dominic. "You think so?"

"Yeah," Dominic answered. "I'm good at this stuff. But let me warn you: if you hurt her in any way, you will answer first to me. Then you will have to deal with her two very large brothers. I know your track record with females. Normally I would be warning her against you, but I think, somehow, that you have changed since your accident. And for the better, I might add. But think twice about being with her if you are just going to use her like your other women."

Michael swallowed audibly at Dominic's warning. "Spoken like a true friend, both to her and me."

"Okay. Enough said. Let's go to the gym." Dominic smiled, picked up his bag, and walked with Michael to the gym.

After putting in almost two hours of cardio and weights, Dominic called Michael over to the mats to begin cooling down and stretching. "So, Champ, how did that feel?"

"Pretty good!" Michael answered, amazed at Dominic's stamina but also grateful that his own was improving. He sat down on the floor and began stretching his hamstrings. "Thank you for letting me do this with you. In fact, thanks for everything that you and Marti have done for me. I have never had friends like you before."

Dominic smiled. "You are welcome." He paused for a moment before continuing, "You have never had friends like us before because you look in all of the wrong places. What is it, do you suppose, that is different about us?"

"You genuinely care about people. And you aren't looking for anything in return."

"Well, that is the end result. I am talking about the *key* difference, Michael."

"Okay, I give up. What is it?"

"Jesus," Dominic answered.

Michael faked a weak smile. "I wondered if you were going to bring this up. I noticed Marti's cross necklace and the Scripture verses posted in your offices. But honestly, does believing in Jesus make you care so much about people? Because it had the opposite result with me. I used to believe in God, Jesus—all that religious stuff—but then everything in my life went horribly wrong." Michael's eyes held bitterness as he continued, "How can I believe in God after my entire family was killed, taken away from me, when I was just a kid? My life went down the toilet at that moment! Where was Jesus when they were burning in the explosion following the crash? Where was he when I was left to grow up alone in a multitude of foster homes? Dominic, both of my parents really believed in Jesus, but then they both died young, so tell me what good it did them!"

"So you think there is a connection between believing in God and all the bad things that happened to you?"

"Either a connection or it is simply that God didn't help or care when I needed him most! If He loved me, then why did He let them die? Afterward, everyone kept telling me to 'trust God.'" He shook his head. "Trust God! If only I had a dollar for everyone who told me that empty line. It was when I decided to put my trust in *myself* that everything started to change for the better."

"In terms of material wealth, you mean."

"Of course! And in terms of happiness too."

"Happiness? You just told me that you never had friends like me and Marti, friends who care about other people. Michael, you are successful by the standards of the world, my friend, but you are anything but happy."

"So, by believing in Jesus, I will find my missing happiness? Answer this: besides destroying my life at the age of twelve, what did Jesus ever do for me?"

"He DIED for you!" Dominic replied.

"Two thousand years ago! That isn't doing very much for me right now!"

Dominic laughed. "It is doing EVERYTHING for you right now—especially right now! He died to pay for all of your sins, Michael. Sins that you would not commit for another two thousand years!"

"Oh, so that I won't burn for eternity in hell, right?" Michael laughed, waving his hands in the air.

"That isn't funny, Michael," Dominic answered. "Eternity without God means spending forever without love, hope, or happiness of any sort. It means complete separation from everything and everyone you care about. This is serious stuff. Jesus took *your* place. Truthfully, he took the place and carried the sins of everyone—so that we could spend eternity with God in heaven. Answer me this: if you really loved someone, would you give *your* life to save *theirs*?" Michael immediately thought of his parents, his sister Lexy, Marti, and Dominic. "What about your family, Michael? From your pain, I can tell that you really loved them. Think about this—would you have taken their place in the crash if you could?"

"Of course I would," he answered solemnly.

"That is exactly how Jesus felt about *you*, about *all of us*. Let me quote Scripture for you: 'Greater love has no one than this: to lay down one's life for one's friends.' (John 15:13 NIV). Do you understand what that means? Real love is about living to serve others—not yourself. The purpose of life is to live like Jesus lived—loving and helping others. Michael, the whole world is desperately seeking love, but they are trying to find it by serving themselves through wealth, power, fame, and addictions to everything under the sun. With Jesus, none of that worldly stuff matters anymore. Death is no longer the end and something to be feared. The world is just a stepping-stone to be with Jesus and the Father forever. If your family were believers in Jesus, that means that you will see them again in heaven."

Michael looked at Dominic with disbelief.

"Michael, Jesus saved me. You already know that my leg was blown off in a roadside bomb in Iraq, but that is only part of the story. One of my buddies in my platoon saw the IED and pushed me out of the way before it exploded. I was one of two survivors in the incident. What I will never understand is why my friend saved my life but not his own. When I came back Stateside, I was dealing not only with my leg injury and PTSD but also what is called survivor's guilt. I kept questioning why I was still alive while my buddy was dead. I had no answers, just an unbelievable amount of guilt." Dominic moved closer to Michael, sitting on the floor beside him.

"I became impossible to live with as I would explode in anger at anyone, especially those trying to help me," Dominic continued. "I was completely empty inside except for feelings of anger and guilt, and I was using painkillers and alcohol to get through each day. After a short while, I had a daily battle not to pull the trigger on my loaded gun and end it all. It wasn't until I came here for physical therapy and met Marti that I found my life and my purpose (or, really, God's purpose) for my life. She introduced me to Jesus—His love, His forgiveness, and His peace—and that changed everything. So, you see, while I could continue to be angry about my leg and my horrible memories of the war, I am *choosing* every day to honor Jesus and the memory of my buddy by the way I live my life." He paused. "Michael, whom are you honoring by the way you live?"

Michael struggled to find any words. There was no way to deny that, up to this point, he had only been living to honor himself. So, instead, he went back to his old argument, the one that stuffed God back into the box in which he belonged. "But I still don't understand why God allowed them to die! A loving God would not let that happen!"

"Michael, you can also ask why God allowed the many *good* things that happened in your life. There is no answer that will completely explain 'why,' and, frankly, the answer will be beyond our capacity to understand. After God gave us life, He also gave us the most incredible gift: the free will to live our lives however we choose—for better or for worse, even accepting or rejecting Him. Does that sound like an evil, tyrannical God to you? I think you already know that good and bad things are going to happen to everyone. However, God, with all of his wisdom and power, loves us enough to allow us to *choose* our own destiny. Think about that! It should be no mystery to anyone that we are all going to die someday. With this understanding, shouldn't we be treasuring each day with the people we love instead of being angry with God when something bad happens?"

While Michael heard all of this, he decided to launch his final argument—the nuclear missile. "You keep telling me how 'loving' God is, so answer this: Would a loving God *really* send his children to hell for all eternity? Is that love? Would you, Dominic, ever send your own precious child to a dark, tortuous world forever because he was naughty?"

Dominic smiled at Michael and was silent for a moment. "Let me explain it this way: Should Adolph Hitler and Mother Teresa just end up in the same place? The answer is obviously no. But with God's loving grace through Jesus, they can. All you have to do is accept Jesus as your savior, and your sins, no matter how terrible, are wiped clean. He loves you that much."

Wow. Michael had never thought of Jesus in these terms before. *Is it possible that I have been thinking about God all wrong?* he thought.

"Now I would like something in return," Dominic said with a smile.

Uh-oh, Michael thought. *Dominic's smile is too big right now.* "Okay." He gulped. "What would you like?"

"Church. You are coming to church with me on Sunday." Michael tried to keep his facial features steady as he processed this request. Other than the occasional wedding, he couldn't remember the last time he had been to a church service. "Michael, I promise that no one will harm you there!" Dominic laughed. "But seriously, you have been asking me *why* I am the way that I am, so the best way is for me to show you."

Chapter 25

Friday was a busy day for Michael. Trent was out of the office that day, so Michael had to handle the myriad of internal office issues as well as his usual sales and marketing side of the business. It was well after lunchtime before he cleared off the critical items from his to-do list. Now he could focus on his concern with the company expenses and the mysterious transactions. He checked his email again to discover that Melissa had not yet sent him the estimated projection of business losses as a result of Rensalant's construction disruption. He needed to get those numbers over to his attorney to file as part of the lawsuit. He sent Melissa another reminder email and then called her. No answer. He then called Cynthia at her desk.

"Hey, Michael," Cynthia answered. "What do you need?"

"Hi, Cynthia. I need you to track down Melissa. She was supposed to send me some projections today, but I haven't heard anything from her. And she isn't answering her phone."

"I'm on it," Cynthia answered. "Anything else?"

"Well, I was wondering something. This is kind of a female-etiquette question."

Cynthia was curious now. "Okay. I will give it my best shot."

"Should I give flowers or a corsage to a woman who is only accompanying me to an event as a *favor*? Meaning: it isn't a date or anything."

"Hmm… That depends upon the woman and how you think she will interpret the gesture. Does this woman really like flowers, or do you just feel obligated to get her something because she is helping you out?"

"The latter. I want to show her my appreciation."

"Then don't get her the flowers. It will only make her feel awkward because she will figure out that you only brought them out of obligation. Just make sure that she has a great time accompanying you and tell her 'thank you'—several times during the evening."

"Okay, Cynthia, thanks. I appreciate the advice."

"No problem, Michael. Oh, why don't you have Marti bring Ethan over to your apartment before you all leave, and I can watch him there? He can hang out with Jackie and the kittens."

Michael was dumbfounded. "How did you know I was taking Marti?"

"I am all-seeing, all-knowing," laughed Cynthia. "No, I'm kidding. Marti asked me yesterday if I would watch Ethan for her. Her usual babysitter backed out at the last minute."

Michael shook his head, laughing. "Okay. I'll call her and tell her to bring Ethan to my apartment." He had just hung up the phone when it rang again. "Michael Garcia speaking."

"Mr. Garcia? This is Joe Panetta down in IT. I've been investigating the transactions that you sent over here, and I found something strange. They were created by a strange user account—one that does not belong to any employees in the company."

"A strange user account? Are you saying that someone is hacking into our system and making transactions?"

"Yes, Mr. Garcia, that is what I believe is happening. I am getting close to tracking down the exact PC system address from which the transactions were made. Once I've done that, I should be able to tell if it is someone inside our network, or from the outside."

"Thanks, Joe. This is very disturbing news. Please keep me posted on what you discover. Sounds like we need to put in some serious system checks and controls to monitor this and alert us going forward. Let me know if you need anything from me to get started on this."

"I'll let you know, Mr. Garcia. And I am sorry that we didn't have this monitoring already established. I feel like I've let you down, sir."

"It is okay, Joe. I think we have all learned a lesson from this." Michael hung up the phone, breathing uneasily from the news.

Someone was making unauthorized transactions in the client investment system, possibly stealing money from clients as well as exposing the entire company to a host of fraudulent activity. After sharing this news with the financial managers and tasking them to dig to find the extent of the damage, his next phone calls were to report this piece of information to both his attorney and to Detective Jenkins. Upon reflection, it appeared to Michael that these fraudulent transactions might not be an isolated incident. It was very likely that whoever was responsible for the transactions was also trying to kill him.

Chapter 26

Michael was still disturbed by the systems discovery that afternoon and was having trouble being cheerful when Cynthia arrived at the apartment. He was still buttoning his tuxedo jacket when he let her in. After sharing the news with her about the potential criminal activity in the client investment system, Cynthia became visibly worried.

"I'm glad you told Detective Jenkins about this," Cynthia stated. "But we may need to have Dominic tell his FBI friend too. This could be bigger than you know. Fraud is a big deal. People go to prison for things like this."

"I know. I called him about an hour ago. He was going to pass on that information. Did you ever hear back from Melissa?"

"No, I didn't. I called around to see if anyone knew where she was. Even stranger is that no one has seen her in the office since Wednesday. I'm starting to get worried, Michael. This isn't like her."

Just then, the doorbell rang. Michael opened the door and let in Dominic and his fiancée, Keisha. Dominic wore a stylish dark suit that was cut to fit his athletic physique. He wore a silk tie that matched Keisha's beautiful teal-colored dress. Looking at Keisha, Michael remembered Dominic's words about Keisha being a beautiful and jealous woman and laughed to himself. Dominic apparently had that backward. Anyone looking at Keisha would know that it should be Dominic who would be the jealous partner in that relationship. Dominic introduced Keisha to both Cynthia and Michael.

"You are a social worker, Keisha. That is outstanding!" said Cynthia, taking her arm and leading her into the living room.

"Thanks," answered Keisha. "Actually, I am Ethan's social worker. I am helping Marti with whatever she needs to get Ethan on track. The good news is that Ethan is doing great under Marti's care."

"I am not surprised at all to hear that," answered Cynthia.

Back in the hallway, Michael decided to fill Dominic in on the news about Melissa. "It could be nothing, but she isn't answering her office phone, home phone, or her cell. Nor is she responding to emails. Trent is out of town at the moment, so he won't be of any help with this."

Dominic took in that information. "Let me know if you still haven't heard from her by Monday morning. While it may be nothing, there are too many strange events happening around you lately that we need to check into everything. If you feel like you should report this to the police, I would encourage you to do so."

Michael was still processing this, trying to decide if he should call the police and report Melissa's disappearance, when the doorbell rang again. He opened the door to let in Marti and Ethan. Ethan said a quick hello to Michael but then shot past him to find Jackie (Lexy) and the kittens.

Marti smiled in response to Ethan's quick departure. "Sorry about that. He has been looking forward to this all day!"

Michael laughed. "Well, I certainly agree that Jackie and the kittens are more appealing than I am."

Marti laughed at that. "Well, if it makes you feel any better, you look very nice. Exactly like the magazine and newspaper covers of you that I am used to seeing." She then pulled out her iPhone from her clutch purse and continued, "Please don't hate me for this, but my friends are relentless. I have been requested to take a picture of you right now and then send it to them. Are you okay with that?"

Michael smiled and shook his head in disbelief. "Believe it or not, I never wanted all of this celebrity attention with the magazines and the paparazzi. My only goal was to promote my business." He took the iPhone from her hand and stood right next to her, taking one picture with them both smiling and facing the camera. Then, without telling her, he took a second picture, but this time with him giving her a kiss on the cheek.

Eyes wide, Marti turned to look at him, her cheeks burning, but she smiled. "Well, my guess is that they will certainly like that one!"

Michael didn't move for a second but just stared at her. Her strawberry-blond hair was out of its normal ponytail and hung in soft curls around her shoulders. She wore makeup tonight—nothing heavy, but it brought out the sea-green color of her eyes. While she was not as striking as the supermodels of his past, she was beautiful. Strange, he thought. She could be wearing nothing but a garbage bag and sporting a multicolored mohawk, and she would be beautiful to him. Her beauty originated deep in her eyes, radiating her intelligence and manifesting through her works of pure kindness toward others. He blinked and returned to the moment. "You should send those to your friends now. Then they might leave you alone for the rest of the evening."

"Yes, you are right! Although, knowing a couple of them, they may try to request different poses. I think I will set my phone to Do Not Disturb and then tell them tomorrow that I couldn't hear it when they were texting and calling."

Michael smiled and led both of them down the hall and into the living room to have a quick toast with the others before they left for the Children's Ball. Cynthia was happy to play hostess, so she brought out the tray of champagne flutes and then made a show of popping the cork when she opened the bottle. Michael didn't want anyone to be left out, so he asked Mrs. Flaherty (Maria) and Gus to also share in a glass with him. For Ethan and Jackie (Lexy), there were some flutes filled with chilled sparkling grape juice.

Michael held up his glass when everyone was ready, their drinks in hand. He gave a toast, but mostly, he wanted them to know how much they meant to him. "To my friends, old and new, I want to give you my sincere gratitude for putting up with me over the last few months. To you, Cynthia, please extend this back for as many years as you feel are necessary." The group laughed, and he continued, "I know that I was a pain at times. You have all opened my eyes to start to see what it means to live, not just to be alive. From each of you, I think I am starting to learn that life isn't about living for just yourself—it is about helping others." He paused and then continued, "And from your examples of how to live, I am rethinking everything in my life including my beliefs about God."

When the group erupted in joyous shouts, he had to hold up his hands to quiet them long enough so that he could finish. "No promises," he continued, smiling. "But at least I am open to going to church this Sunday. So, again, to everyone, I say thank you. Cheers!"

"Cheers!" answered the whole group in staggered unison, clinking glasses with one another. Dominic chimed in with a big "AMEN!" and almost knocked Michael over with his exuberant slap on the back.

Maria had to hold back a sob as she listened to her son's words. She wished that Paul were here to hear this for himself, but she would call him as soon as possible and tell him about it. While Michael still had a way to go on the path toward heaven, he was making a start. She remembered how lost and bitter he was when she arrived here months ago. Now it appeared that he was changing. She just needed to help him to accept Jesus and put his trust in God now; otherwise all of this progress could slip backward.

Gus smiled and winked at Maria. She knew that he was having similar thoughts. Paul was coming over later to join them, and they were going to discuss the next steps.

After about a half hour, the two couples left for the Children's Ball. Dominic and Keisha waved goodbye in the parking garage as they walked to their car that was parked on a different level.

Marti and Michael continued walking to their car. It was then that Marti noticed that Michael was carrying a large bag. "What is in there?" she asked.

Michael smiled. "You'll see." As they turned the corner in the garage, there was Michael's new Porsche. After helping her into the passenger's side, he closed the door and walked around to the driver's side. He slid into the leather seat, put his hands on the smooth leather of the steering wheel, and closed his eyes for just a moment, lost in the euphoria from being in his new car.

"Excuse me." Marti cleared her throat, interrupting his moment of bliss. "Do you need another minute, or can we get started now?"

Michael laughed as he started the engine and then began his normal pattern of adjusting everything to his driving requirements:

mirrors, seat, radio, etc. He backed out of the parking spot and drove the car out of the parking garage and onto the street.

When they arrived at the ball, Michael parked the car himself in a garage; they did not use the valet service. He then grabbed the large bag from the back and then sat back down in the driver's seat. He smiled at Marti and then took an extra moment to pull off his normal prosthetic limb and switch it out with his running blade that he pulled out of the bag. He then got out of the car, walked around to her side, and opened her door to let Marti take a look at him.

"Well, what do you think?"

Marti smiled at the sight. "Actually, it looks good with your tux. Kind of sporty. Funny, but I never would have put those two together before."

"If I have to be an amputee, then I will go in style, by *my own* set of rules," Michael proclaimed.

"That is the secret, Michael," Marti said, cheering him on. "By Jove! I think *he's* got it!"

Michael laughed and then turned a bit serious. "Marti, I want to give you the choice for our entrance. Do you want me to hold your hand or arm when we walk in? Alternatively, we could just walk in side by side, if you feel more comfortable with that. But know this, Marti—whatever we do, the paparazzi will blow it out of proportion."

Marti stood for a moment, thinking. "In that case, let's give them something to write about!" She grabbed his hand and started walking.

CHAPTER 27

Hundreds of flashes of light from the cameras blinded Marti while the deafening screams from the stampede of people were pressing on her, fighting for her attention. All sorts of questions and comments were being thrown at them as Michael pulled her through the tight tunnel of blinding lights and rude, shouting people. Every second or two, another microphone was shoved in her face, barely missing her teeth, nose, or other appendage. In spite of the horror, she had to give the reporters credit for one thing—they knew who she was. They were yelling and calling her by name. She glanced at Michael and admired how calm he was. It was obvious that he was used to this and able to navigate the crowd very well. He smiled, waved at the screaming masses, pulled on her hand, and continued walking. When they were about halfway through the red-carpeted gauntlet, he looked over at her, winked, and squeezed her hand in a gesture of solidarity. That was what she needed, as it calmed her down a bit. What surprised her most, however, was the shocking depth of the personal questions being hurled at both them.

"How long have you two been dating?"

"Mr. Garcia, when did you decide to forgo supermodels to instead have a relationship with your doctor?"

"Do you normally date your patients, Dr. Richardson?"

"Hey, Doc, how does it feel to, uh, 'make it' with an amputee?"

At that last question, Marti lost it. She pulled back hard on Michael's hand and charged at the reporter, a female. Marti screamed her response into the waiting microphone, "I'm amazed that you could even formulate that question, being a *brain* amputee yourself!"

Michael wasted no time in pulling Marti away from the reporter amid the collective roar of laughter washing over them. When she started to yank back on him again, ready to go back for more, he picked her up by her waist and moved her in front of him. "Keep walking, Marti," he said into her ear. "Don't give them any more meat to chew on." With that, he nudged her to get her moving again. As she complied and started walking again, he whispered in her ear, "Nice retort, Marti. And you did publicly embarrass her, which is always fun."

Marti smiled a little in response, but, as she calmed down, she couldn't believe how she lost her temper like that.

After what seemed an eternity, they made it to the entrance. Michael gave both of their names to the host, as this was an invitation-only event. Walking in, it was almost as loud inside the ballroom as it was outside with the crowd. There were hundreds of people inside, and the band was doing its best to overpower the roar of conversation by playing a cover of Earth, Wind & Fire's "September." Marti and Michael were straining to find their friends through the crush of people waiting to visit the various wet bars situated every few feet. Looking up, Marti marveled at the long purple and gold drapes streaming downward from the shimmering crystal chandelier hung high in the center of the room. Admiring the decorations, she felt Michael's hands grab her shoulder to keep her from crashing into a group of people dancing off to the side of the overcrowded dance floor. After slowly making their way halfway into the room, they could see Dominic and Keisha waving them over to join them at their tall bar table.

Michael scanned the room to find the shortest and less congested path, navigating around dancing couples, clusters of people talking, and the many bar tables situated every few feet. As they made their way over, Michael deftly snagged two full champagne flutes from a passing waiter. He tugged on Marti's arm to stop her and have a quick moment with her. Then he handed her a glass and clinked his glass with hers. "Here is to your survival of the ever-hungry beast: the paparazzi."

Marti smiled and took a sip. The crisp, bubbly sensation tickled her tongue, magically washing away the muck from the previous moment outside. "It is weird, Michael, but a moment ago, I felt like I needed a shower after that!"

Michael tossed a knowing smile at her. Then he paused for a second, looking at her intently, protectively. "No, Marti, not you. Don't let them make you feel dirty or cheap just because they are. You are too good a person to be soiled by the likes of them."

Marti was speechless at that. As she stumbled for words, Dominic and Keisha walked up to join them.

"You made it! And without the Groucho Marks glasses too!" Dominic laughed. "I guess there won't be too much for them to write about in the magazines and newspapers after all! Let's drink to that!"

In response, Marti choked loudly on her sip of champagne. Michael, handing her a napkin, answered for her, "Well, we can't promise that." Michael looked at Keisha a bit nervously and said, "I am sorry, but I'll let Dominic fill you in with the details." Then he leaned over and whispered the tale into Dominic's ear. After a few seconds, Dominic threw his head back and roared with laughter. Marti cringed, trying to hide behind her champagne glass. Michael, laughing, noticed Marti's discomfort and rescued her by taking her hand. "Let's dance, Marti." A slow song had started, so he led her near the dance floor and put both of their champagne glasses on a nearby table. He guided her out onto the floor, wrapped his arm around her waist, and they started dancing. After a few minutes of slightly awkward silence, he looked down at her and smiled. "By the way, thanks."

Marti looked up, confused. "For what, Michael?"

"For defending me against that nasty reporter. Believe me, Susan Jakes is one of the slimiest of the bunch."

Marti laughed. "You're welcome, I guess. I just feel so foolish for losing my temper."

Michael mused for a minute. "Being the medical professional that you are, I recommend that you consider them in a different, less threatening fashion. Think of them instead as potential science experiments in some laboratory, sitting in petri dishes."

"Like bacteria or some kind of mold, perhaps?" laughed Marti.

"Exactly."

After a few more minutes, the song ended. Next, the hostess made the announcement for the opening of the dinner buffet lines.

The band began to play mellow dinner music, so Michael walked her back to the tall table with their waiting champagne glasses. He was about to take a sip when he noticed someone familiar at the table next to theirs. He looked again, and yes! It was Rensalant. He looked at Marti and seriously debated with himself about leaving her and going over to speak with him. It was, after all, a charity event. But on the other hand, it wasn't every day that he was face-to-face with the person who has been avoiding him while simultaneously sabotaging a part of his business. He decided that he had to take the opportunity. He looked at Marti and said, "Would you be angry with me if I spoke to the man at the table next to ours? It won't be a pleasant conversation, so I advise you to not come with me. Unfortunately, he has created trouble for my company and also refuses to answer my phone calls."

Marti looked a little worried. "Will you need any help? I could have Dominic stand nearby to help you, should you need it."

"I think I can handle this myself. However, I am happy to take any help I can get." Michael said that last part really to get Marti away from the confrontation that was about to occur. Michael waited for Marti to walk away before he turned and started toward Rensalant. As he approached the table, he didn't even try to smile; instead, he displayed polite hostility. "Hello, Rensalant. Enjoying yourself tonight?"

Rensalant looked up from his cell phone, and Michael saw the moment when recognition hit. Rensalant's eyes narrowed when he answered, "Hello, Garcia. Yes, I *was* enjoying myself."

The comment was not lost on Michael. "Glad to hear it. So how is business?"

Rensalant looked incredulous. He lowered his voice, showing the depth of his anger. "How is business? Are you kidding? You are trying to ruin me, and you have the nerve to ask me how *my* business is doing?"

Michael couldn't believe the man's audacity. It was all he could do to control his temper. "Ruin *you*? Do you realize the impact your breach of contract is going to have on my business this year? Do you know how many huge events that we already have lined up but can't host because your construction work isn't anywhere close to being finished!"

Rensalant became visibly enraged with that statement. "*My* breach of contract? Is that how your attorney is interpreting it? You canceled a multimillion-dollar contract right after a portion of the work had been completed and the materials delivered on site! How else do you think I am going to respond?"

Michael was about to answer him when he stopped. *What? What did Rensalant say?* His mind was racing—nothing was making sense. He put his hand up and calmly said, "Hold on a minute, Rensalant. You just said that *I* canceled the construction contract. Is that right?"

Rensalant was still enraged. "Yes! Dammit, Garcia, what the hell did you think I said?"

Michael ran his hand through his hair, thinking intensely. Then he looked up at Rensalant and calmly said, "Something is wrong here—"

"You better believe something is wrong here!" Rensalant screamed, interrupting Michael.

"No, hang on. Please bear with me on this, okay? Do you remember *when* I sent you the cancellation?"

Rensalant thought for a moment. "Let's see, it was a while ago." He kept thinking and then he remembered. "Yes, it was back in February, toward the beginning of the month."

Michael's heart sank. "Beginning of February? You are sure?"

"Positive," Rensalant said. "I can send you the document on Monday, but you are going to see it anyway along with our lawsuit."

"And it had my signature on it?" Michael asked.

"Yeah, yeah. Of course it did!"

"I never signed that document, Rensalant," Michael said.

"What do you mean you never signed it?" Rensalant yelled, face turning red.

Michael pointed down at his running blade. "I had my accident at the end of January. There is no way I signed or even authorized that cancellation notice. I was not capable of doing anything related to work until the beginning of April."

HELP AMONG US

Rensalant's eyes grew large. It took a minute for Michael's words to sink in. "Are you saying that you never canceled the contract?"

"That's right, Rensalant. I never did. All this time I thought that you were delaying the construction while still charging me for outrageous expenses. That is why I gave up trying to call you and finally decided to sue you."

Rensalant was clearly shocked. "My attorney advised me not to speak to you. That is why I never returned your calls. Michael, I am really sorry. I had no idea."

Michael nodded. "Me too. And to think that I was ready to sue you for everything you would ever earn." Michael composed himself and looked intently at Rensalant. "Can I call you on Monday and discuss this? We can have both of our attorneys present if it makes you more comfortable. In the meantime, I will find out who sent the cancellation notice." Rensalant seemed much happier at that point. "I look forward to working with you again."

"Me too." Michael left Rensalant and went in search of Marti and Dominic. This was absolutely crazy—someone was trying to kill him while stealing money from his company and destroying his business at the Garcia Lodge. Michael was now certain that this was someone inside the company. But who, and why?

"Hey, are you all right?" Dominic asked. Michael shook his head and realized that Dominic had asked him that question twice already.

"No, Dom, I'm not," Michael answered, still in a daze. "I'm trying to make sense of something. I just learned that someone within my company deliberately canceled a major construction contract without my authorization. I nearly got sued for it. On top of that, I have been receiving and even paying invoices for enormous construction expenses that now, apparently, were falsified." Michael looked right at Dominic. "Whoever did this has access to my office and my files."

"I'm afraid I have some more bad news, Michael," Dominic said. "I just got off the phone with my FBI buddy. Apparently, they are getting ready to investigate you for potential money laundering."

"What?" Michael asked, completely shocked.

"Yes. Someone representing your company has been opening up bank accounts all over town and making some interesting—meaning large—cash deposits and withdrawals from them."

Michael became visibly angry. "Well, that explains the mysterious transactions that I am unable to account for." He raked his hand through his hair. "I am through being a victim here. I am going to get to the bottom of this now!"

Marti put her hand on Michael's arm. "Michael, what do you intend to do?"

Michael reached for his cell phone while answering. "Well, for starters—" He paused suddenly, looking at his phone. Melissa Butano had left two messages; the most recent was fifteen minutes ago. Michael looked up at Marti and Dominic. "One second, Melissa Butano called me. I need to see how she is." She only left one message:

"Michael, it's Melissa. I need to see you as soon as possible." Her voice sounded desperate, frightened. *"There is so much going on that you don't know about. Some dangerous stuff, Michael, and I'm really scared. All I can say is that I am sorry. I didn't know what I was getting into. Please meet me at the Lodge as soon as you can, and I will explain. I don't have much time because I have to leave town. I am taking the girls with me. They are hiding out at my apartment. Please help them if anything happens to me! Promise me, Michael, that you will help them! I will wait for you, all night if necessary. I have to show you what is going on so you will believe me. But whatever you do,* DO NOT CALL THE POLICE! *I mean this, Michael!"*

"What the hell?" Michael thought after listening to her message. He handed over his cell phone so that Dominic and Marti could hear the message.

"I'm forwarding this to Reynolds, my FBI friend," Dominic said as he began typing on Michael's phone. "He needs to hear this. At a minimum, it will help prove your innocence. But it sounds like some of your people are into some pretty serious activity, Michael."

"Who are the 'girls' that Melissa is talking about? Do you know anything about them?" Marti asked.

Michael shook his head. "Not at all, Marti. Dear God, I have absolutely no idea of anything right now. But it appears that I must to go to the Lodge right now and talk to Melissa."

Dominic shook his head and grabbed Michael's arm. "This sounds like a possible trap to me, Michael. My recommendation is to call the police and have them check it out."

Michael shook his head again. "Can't do that, Dominic. Didn't you hear her? She specifically warned me not to bring in the police. It sounds like there is more than just her life at risk right now. I can't believe how desperate she sounded. I've known Melissa a long time, and there is one thing that I am sure of—she is a good person. She is not someone who would lure me into a trap."

Dominic stared hard at Michael for a moment. Then he finally spoke, "Michael, against my better judgment, I will not call the police. However, I will tell Reynolds about this now. That way, we can get some help quickly if we need it."

"We? What do you mean *we*?" Michael asked, eyes narrowing at Dominic.

"We," Marti answered. "As in Dominic, you, and me. We are going with you to the Lodge."

"Oh no, you are not!" Michael stated vehemently, glaring at Marti. "I can't put anyone else at risk!"

"If you go alone to see Melissa, my instincts tell me that you won't be coming back, Michael," Dominic responded. "With two more of us there with you, we can call for help if needed and even assist if there is a medical emergency. I'm serious about this, Michael."

"Michael," Marti interjected, "you must admit that the odds are better with three people instead of just one," Marti said. "Plus, in a fight, both Dominic and I are pretty good at bringing people down. We both know where the key pressure points on the body are located as well as where to hit someone to knock them out or even kill them."

"That doesn't change my mind to put my friends in danger," Michael answered.

"We will be careful, Michael," Marti answered, putting her hand on his arm. "Let us help you. It is still better to go in there with more people than just yourself."

Michael looked back and forth between Marti and Dominic, mentally weighing the entire conversation. Their arguments made sense, although he didn't like the idea of putting his friends at risk, especially Marti. But now that he was thinking about it, Dominic was a trained soldier who had seen combat; the chances of survival were greatly improved with Dominic there. Although he couldn't believe that they were talking him into this, he had to admit that they were right. Additionally, Dominic could contact the FBI should anything look suspicious. Finally, he nodded his head in resignation. "Okay. I can't believe I am saying this, but okay. And only the two of you! Keisha takes your car and goes home, Dominic. Having you and Marti on my conscience is already more than I can bear—I don't want to be responsible if anything happens to Keisha too."

"Keisha? Keisha is definitely not going with us!" Dominic said protectively.

"Keisha is fully capable of making her own decisions, thank you very much!" Keisha stated firmly. "However, I think I would be more useful if I am at home and can make any emergency calls if you need any. I have some resources I can quickly bring in, if necessary."

"Thanks, Keisha. I appreciate it," Michael answered. "From the desperate way Melissa sounded on the phone, I am recommending that she speak to someone when this is all over." He turned to Dominic. "Meet us outside at my car." He grabbed Marti's hand. "Marti, we are going out the back entrance to avoid some of the crowd."

"Give me ten minutes," Dominic answered. He and Keisha went to the coatroom to get their coats and then walked out the back entrance to get to their car.

Michael and Marti slowly made their way to the back entrance. Not an easy task because people kept coming up to talk with them. Michael had forgotten how many business associates would be there; he hadn't seen really any of them since the accident. Marti couldn't take two steps without seeing fellow therapists, doctors, famous celebrities, and charity ball volunteers. After explaining numerous times that they needed to leave, they finally made it out of the back entrance and into the alleyway. Michael started to walk to the garage when he suddenly stopped and grabbed Marti's arm. He turned her so that he could speak to her in this rare moment of solitude. He looked down at the ground for a second and then finally looked into her eyes. "I'm so sorry, Marti," Michael said. "This is not how I planned to spend this evening, especially with you. And now it seems that I've completely ruined the night and the ball for you now."

From the pained expression on his face, Marti could tell that he was really troubled by everything. She smiled up at him and took his hand. "Believe it or not, I've had a great time this evening with you."

"You liar!" Michael laughed, looking into her eyes.

Marti laughed back, then stood up on her tiptoes and pressed a quick kiss to his cheek. She immediately blushed and was a bit surprised at herself; she didn't even realize what she was doing until it was done.

Michael smiled back at her, feeling her kiss melt into his being. Funny, he thought, how her little kiss affected his heart more than any other ever had.

Before they could think much more about it, Michael's cell phone rang. They both jumped at the sudden interruption. "Hello?" he answered, fumbling to get the phone out of his jacket pocket. After a moment, he responded. "Sorry, man! We had trouble getting out of the building. We are walking to the car now." At that, Michael took Marti's hand, and they both continued walking to the garage.

Michael steered the Porsche into the entrance of the Garcia Lodge. The place was mostly empty, as it should be, considering there were no major events scheduled for that weekend. He drove to the main building, where Melissa worked, but all of the lights were off, and the parking lot was completely empty. *That is strange*, he thought, considering that Melissa was supposed to be there. He drove around to the back and still didn't see anyone.

"I'm confused," Michael announced to Dominic and Marti as he continued to circle around the various Lodge buildings. "I don't know where she is." He tried to call her for the fourth or fifth time (he lost count), but she did not pick up. He decided that, since he was here, he might as well check out the new construction area. He drove a little ways to get to the back of the Lodge property where all of the new buildings were being constructed. As he turned the corner, he saw some cars and a truck in the parking lot down the road. Even more bizarre, there were lights on in the supposedly unfinished building. He stopped deliberately, to avoid being seen, keeping them a safe distance away from the building.

"Um, Michael," Dominic pondered aloud, "is it just me, or is it normal to see cars parked late on a Friday night in front of a building that isn't supposed to be anywhere close to being finished yet?"

"Even stranger, Dominic, is that fact that Melissa's car is parked at the end of the row, over there. I know her Cadillac anywhere."

Dominic shook his head again. "Michael, I don't think I need to tell you that this has all of the signs of a trap."

"I know, Dominic. But I can't just leave Melissa to fend for herself. It sounds like she is in some serious trouble."

"Yes. The kind of trouble that has tried to kill you, Michael, twice already."

"I am aware of that, Dominic."

Dominic sighed loudly, shaking his head for probably the sixtieth time that evening. "One more chance, Michael," he said. "I'm giving you one more chance to call the police, *now*, before we all get stupid and run willingly into that trap."

"No, Dominic. Melissa told me not to. I can't do it."

Dominic gave up. "Well, let's start by turning off your headlights. We don't want to announce our presence. Next, we need to huddle up and make a plan." Dominic took charge, and together they concocted a basic strategy to get inside. Then Dominic went over a few survival tips of how to stay alive when going into an unknown building. Afterward, Michael started to get out of the car.

"Wait," Dominic said. "Sit back down and give me your hand."

"What?" Michael asked. He sat back down in complete confusion and lifted up his hand toward Dominic.

Dominic stared intently at Michael. "Man, you don't go running into danger without asking for a little help first."

Marti, sitting in the back seat, grabbed Michael's right hand and Dominic's left. "Ready, Dominic."

Dominic closed his eyes. Michael looked at Marti, who had also closed her eyes. Feeling extremely uncomfortable, Michael kept his eyes open but put his head down. He honestly could not remember the last time he prayed. It had to have been years ago at church with his family or at the dinner table.

"Holy Spirit, please come into our midst," Dominic began. "Dear Lord, please protect and guide us as we go into the unknown to help Melissa. Grant us the wisdom to determine how best to help her and the courage to do what is necessary. If we should fall today, oh God, please grant us your mercy and welcome us into your kingdom. We ask this in the name of Jesus, our Savior. Amen."

"Amen," Marti repeated, squeezing both Dominic's and Michael's hands.

"Amen," Michael also repeated, rather awkwardly. While he was a bit uneasy about praying in front of other people and also inside a car, it felt good. Maybe this was a beginning. Maybe he would give God a chance.

"That didn't hurt too much now, did it?" Dominic said to Michael with a little smile.

"Do you always pray before doing something potentially dangerous?" Michael asked.

"I pray every day, Michael, but *especially* when I am doing something dangerous," Dominic answered. "You should have heard how many prayers we all said in Iraq—before each mission, during each mission, and afterward. People who never prayed in their lives got down on their knees to ask God for help. It really helps, Michael. You should try it."

"Yeah." He nodded. "I just haven't had much luck with prayer in the past."

"Prayer isn't so much about asking God to give you what you want, but rather about asking for His guidance to help you do what He needs you to do," Marti said softly. "God has a plan for everyone's life, Michael. The hard part is that sometimes we don't want to accept that plan."

"I am honestly not trying to sound rude, but if I live my life according to God's plan and not my own, that sounds like I am not making my own decisions. Someone else is pulling all of the strings."

"Living God's plan doesn't mean you have zero control of your own life, Michael," Marti explained. "Actually, you are free to accept or reject that plan. Instead, it is about choosing to live for someone besides yourself. In fact, Michael, you are already doing that."

"What do you mean?" Michael said.

"Michael," Marti answered, "right now, in fact. You are about to go into a possibly dangerous situation to help Melissa. Most people would choose to be back at the charity ball, enjoying themselves."

Michael reflected on that for a moment. "That is what you both do all the time, isn't it? You live for others. You both have devoted your entire lives to helping other people."

Dominic smiled. "That is the general idea, Michael. Well, time to go be heroes or idiots. Hopefully not the latter," he said, opening his door. When they were all outside of the car, he gave one last piece of advice. "All jokes aside now. Remember: stay quiet, and DON'T try anything crazy. I will follow you both and watch our backs."

Chapter 28

After circling the grounds and the building on foot, keeping well away from the lights, they found a back entrance. To their amazement, the door was unlocked. Dominic was simultaneously glad and alarmed. They slowly entered the building and began making their way down the hall. The hallway was dark and completely unfinished with concrete floors and only the wood from the building frames for walls. Fortunately, there was some moonlight coming in through the few finished windows that enabled them to see where they were going. They silently passed a few doors, all locked. They kept going down the hall until they came to a large steel door. Michael carefully turned the knob, and, to their collective surprise, the door opened. The group carefully went through the door—Michael first, then Marti, and finally Dominic, watching their backs.

Inside the room, the group could see a bit more, as there was some light coming in from behind the closed door on the far end. Enormous shelving units lined the walls and were formed into long rows in the middle of the room. Large, oversized packages were stacked high on the shelves. There appeared to be literally hundreds of these packages. Dominic and Michael looked at each other and then walked up to one of the shelves. Dominic took position to watch the doors and then gestured to Michael and Marti to check out one of the packages. Michael tried to rip open one of them, but there was too much packing tape wrapped around it. Dominic pulled out his pocketknife and handed it to Michael. Michael carefully cut into one of the package ends, and a white powder came gushing out. Dominic licked his finger and then picked up a few grains of the powder and tasted it. He then wiped it off onto the back of his hand. By his expression, Marti and Michael both knew instantly that this room was storing some kind of illegal drugs, probably heroin or cocaine.

Michael wandered over to the other side of the room to check out the strange-looking crates that were stacked up to the ceiling. Marti and Dominic followed behind and almost tripped over a large crate lid that was on the floor. Walking over to the open crate, the group looked inside, moving the straw around to see what was contained inside.

"Holy crap," whispered Michael as he viewed the rifles carefully packed inside the crate.

"Not holy, but I agree with the 'crap' part of your statement," Dominic whispered back. "Well, I guess we found the 'trouble' that Melissa was referring to in her message. Michael, this is serious stuff. Whoever put this stuff here will be guarding it well. I suggest we leave now and call the police."

Michael nodded in agreement and took Marti's hand. As they started to make their way back to the door from where they entered the room, they suddenly heard some shouting. It was coming from the other door, the one with the light streaming behind it. It was growing louder and then they heard a loud crash on the other side. Dominic motioned for the group to hide in the dark corner of the room behind some shelves. He reached into his suit jacket and pulled out his concealed pistol from his shoulder holster. Immediately, the door was kicked open, and a young woman, with her hands bound behind her, was shoved forcefully onto the floor. Two men followed her into the room; one had a pistol aimed right at her head. The other kicked her hard in the stomach. The woman gasped aloud in pain and tried to protect herself by pulling her knees in close to her stomach. Both men appeared to be in their early twenties and were dressed in baggy jeans and sleeveless T-shirts. All exposed skin seemed to be covered in tattoos, including their faces. One of the men wore a red bandanna tied around his head. From their appearance, they looked like they were members of some kind of gang.

Michael mouthed "Melissa" to Dominic and Marti to let them know that they found her. They watched in horror as they witnessed Melissa pleading for her life.

HELP AMONG US

"Please! Please don't kill me!" Melissa screamed to the men, legs sprawling on the floor, unable to use her bound hands. "I promise I won't tell anyone about this! I just want to leave town."

The man with the gun laughed at Melissa's response and translated her comment for his companion, deliberately mocking her by using a high, squeaky voice. "*La puta dice que no va a decirle a nadie sobre esto.*"

Both men laughed out loud at this. The man with the gun decided to have some more fun with her. "You right, you *puta*, whore. You tell no one *porque* you dead!" He then translated this into Spanish for his companion's benefit, and both men laughed out loud again.

Before Dominic could even respond with his weapon, the man with the gun took aim and fired at Melissa just as a piece of debris simultaneously fell from the ceiling above, hitting him on the arm holding the gun. The loud blast from the gun exploded through the room. While Marti was reacting to the horror with a choked scream, Dominic stood up and fired his gun, shooting the armed gangster in the chest. The other gangster, unarmed, tried to run back through the door. Dominic fired his gun again, this time deliberately shooting him in the leg to wound but not to kill him. The unarmed man dropped to the floor, writhing in obvious pain.

Michael grabbed Marti, who was trying to run toward Melissa. "Wait!" he whispered to her. "We need to see if there are any others."

Dominic carefully crept over toward the doorway and stood on one side of it, gun poised for action. He waited for a moment and listened. While he waited, he studied the two gangsters who were now lying on the ground. From their inactivity, it appeared that one of them was dead and the other was severely wounded. Feeling that they no longer posed a threat, he decided to check out the other room. Slowly he took a peek through the doorway and looked in. He didn't see anyone. Inside, there was a table with two chairs. On top of the table, he saw two glasses and what was left of some food. From the look of everything, it appeared that there were only two gangsters here at the moment.

Suddenly, the unarmed gangster spoke to his buddy, "*Usa tu cuchillo!*"

Michael, hearing this, yelled a warning to Dominic, "Dom, he's got a knife!"

Dominic turned just in time to see the previously armed gangster pulling a knife out of his jeans. Dominic fired his gun again, and this time the shot was fatal.

Marti determined that this was the sign for her to go to Melissa to check her condition, so she carefully crept over and began a cursory examination.

Michael walked over to the unarmed gangster who was lying on the ground, injured in the thigh but alive. "Do you speak English?" he asked the man.

"*No entiendo tu estúpida Inglés!*" (I don't understand your stupid English) answered the gangster between labored breaths.

Michael laughed darkly in response and then retorted back, "*Estúpido, ¿eh? Yo no soy el que está sangrando en el suelo en este momento.*" (Stupid, huh? I am not the one bleeding on the ground right now.) When the gangster did not respond to this, Michael asked him another question, "*¿Hay alguien más aquí?*"

The gangster responded with a comment describing something nasty that Michael could do to himself.

"Wow, man. You speak Spanish?" Dominic asked.

Michael answered without losing eye contact with the gangster. "Yes. My mother's family was from Mexico."

"What are you saying to him?"

"I'm trying to get him to tell us if there is anyone else here. So far, he is being uncooperative, to say the least."

"I am not positive, Michael, but I don't think anyone else is here right now. This guy"—Dominic gestured to the wounded gangster—"would be shouting out for help if there were. Right now I need you to call the police and get an ambulance here ASAP while I stand guard."

Michael agreed and pulled out his cell phone. After a few minutes on the phone with 911, he hung up and announced that the police and an ambulance were on the way.

Marti, who had been checking Melissa's pulse and other vitals, looked up at Michael and Dominic. "She is alive," Marti announced. "Thanks to Dominic's quick response, that thug only got off one shot. And, lucky for her, his aim wasn't very good. It is only a shoulder wound, but she is losing a lot of blood. If we can get her to a hospital soon, she might make it." Marti stood up, reached under her dress, and removed her half-slip. She then bunched it up for use as a makeshift bandage. "We need to apply pressure to try to slow down the bleeding. Also, we need to keep her warm."

Michael removed his tuxedo jacket. "We can use this, Marti."

Marti looked at it with amazement. "Are you sure, Michael? That must have cost a lot of money!"

Michael rolled his eyes. "Melissa is a good friend of mine. She is worth more than any jacket."

Marti smiled at Michael and took the jacket. She wrapped it around Melissa to keep her warm while still applying pressure to the wound.

Dominic pulled out his cell phone while still holding onto his gun. It was time to get help from his FBI buddy. "Hey, Reynolds? It's Dominic. This situation with Michael Garcia just got serious. Write down this address, and meet me here as soon as you can." Dominic briefly filled Reynolds in on the details and then hung up.

Dominic walked over to Michael and Marti. "This is important. Reynolds just advised me to keep Melissa's identity quiet. He is going to call the police and have them admit her into the hospital as a Jane Doe for her protection. From the nature of the 'merchandise' in this storeroom here, it appears that we have stumbled into the nest of a gang, most likely a drug cartel. If they find out where she is, they will go to the hospital and finish the job."

Just at that moment, Melissa tried to speak. Marti called out, "Michael, you need to get over here. Melissa is trying to tell us something."

Michael dropped to the ground and put his head near Melissa's. "Melissa! It's Michael. Can you hear me?"

Melissa briefly opened her eyes. Her breath was ragged, but she spoke, "Mi-Michael. Girls…Please…get…them…"

"Melissa, what girls? Where are they?"

"My…apartment…Hiding…Get…them…" After that effort, Melissa went unconscious again.

Marti and Michael looked at each other. "When we are done here, we will go to Melissa's apartment," Michael said. "Oh no! I don't know where her keys are! We need to look around and find her purse—"

Before Michael could put any more effort into this, Marti stopped him. "Don't forget, Michael, we have Ethan. There isn't a lock that he cannot pick."

Michael looked both relieved and horrified. "Oh, right! I forgot about Ethan's talents."

Just then, the loud roar of sirens filled the air. "Well, team, looks like the cavalry has arrived," announced Dominic.

The EMS team immediately went to work to get Melissa somewhat stabilized, then put her into the ambulance and left. Per the instructions of the FBI, the group did not reveal Melissa's identity, and she was admitted as Jane Doe. Reynolds arrived shortly after the police and then began asking more questions and taking careful notes on the items stored in the building. As it turned out, there were more rooms of "merchandise" in that building. The unfinished construction area of the Garcia Lodge had been turned into an illegal drug and weapons superstore. From the tattoos on the arms and backs of the two gang members and other items found in the building, Reynolds announced to the group that this was indeed a storehouse of one of the most dangerous drug cartels in Mexico.

The group left the police to do their work in the building. Everyone drove back to Michael's penthouse to debrief the others and decide next steps. Maria kept everyone awake by supplying endless cups of hot coffee. Sitting around the kitchen table were Mrs. Flaherty (Maria), Dr. Sherman (Paul), Gus, Cynthia, Keisha, Reynolds, Detective Jenkins, Dominic, Marti, and Michael. Lexy and Ethan were sitting at the kitchen island, on tall chairs. They were each holding a kitten, playing a card game, and listening.

"My team in the FBI has been tracking this cartel's movements in the US for a couple of years now," Reynolds explained. "We knew that they were active in the Chicago area and had built a complete supply and distribution chain of narcotics all the way here from the Mexican border. We just needed to know where their HQ was located before we moved in. This discovery certainly brings us closer. The best part of this evening is the potential intelligence that we can gather from the gang member we now have in custody, thanks to all of you."

Reynolds then questioned Michael for several minutes. "Is there anyone else in your company who might have been working alongside Melissa in this? While it is possible that she worked alone with this drug cartel, I don't think that is likely."

Michael racked his brain. "Wow. The only person that Melissa would trust enough with something like this would be Trent Wentworth. However, he is absolutely not the kind of person who would be mixed up in something like this."

Cynthia looked at Michael and gently asked, "Are you so sure? Before tonight, would you have ever suspected Melissa of something like this?"

Michael raked his hand through his hair and closed his eyes, obviously in emotional pain. "No, Cynthia, I would never have thought it possible that Melissa could be involved in something like this."

"Then, sadly, we can't rule anyone out, Michael, even Trent," Cynthia responded. "I think it is best to not mention anything about Melissa and what happened tonight at the Lodge with Trent or anyone—just in case."

"I guess you are right. But first we need to go to Melissa's apartment and find the girls that she was asking about."

"I will accompany you on that," Detective Jenkins said.

"Update me on whatever you find. I will also need to question the girls to learn what they know," responded Reynolds.

"Absolutely," Jenkins answered.

"Thanks, Detective Jenkins," said Michael. "I was going to request that you come along with us to Melissa's apartment."

Michael turned to Dr. Sherman. "Dr. Sherman, can you be available later for medical assistance should these girls need some help? Obviously, we will take them to the hospital if it is serious, but otherwise they may still require some care."

"No problem, Michael. I can be back over here at any time."

"Keisha," Marti said, "be ready in case we need to get some help for these girls."

Keisha nodded. "Absolutely. My cell phone will be on my pillow. Keep me posted.

After that, the group disbanded. Michael walked Keisha, Dominic, and Reynolds to the door. "Thanks, everyone. And especially you, Dominic. You saved Melissa's life, but I think that you also saved both Marti and me too. If you hadn't been there, we may not have made it out alive."

"That is what friends are for." Dominic smiled. "But next time, Michael, we are *not* running into a building without calling the police first!"

"That is a promise, Dominic!" Michael smiled.

Michael walked back into the kitchen. "Okay, Marti, Ethan, and Detective Jenkins. I think it is time to go to Melissa's apartment." Marti and Ethan said good night to Jackie (Lexy), Cynthia, Gus, and Mrs. Flaherty (Maria).

CHAPTER 29

As the group of humans finally left the apartment, the guardians held a quick meeting. Cynthia went to the door to let Paul back in. She and Paul rejoined the others at the table.

"That was outstanding work tonight, Gus!" Cynthia said. "We were watching you through the transporter monitor tonight, and we just replayed it for Lexy so she could see what happened. I can't believe how you were able to throw that big piece of broken ceiling timber with enough force to hit that gangster's gun! That definitely reduced the severity of Melissa's wound. And while he was firing it too!" Maria and Paul joined Cynthia in congratulating Gus on the great work that night. Gus had to work alone that night, as the others could not leave Ethan without arousing too much suspicion.

"Thanks, but I had some help with that!" Gus laughed. "I was praying hard for assistance in steadying my aim! I'm relieved the bullet only hit her shoulder."

"Gus," Paul started, "the demons surrounding those two gang members—I've never seen anything like them before. They actually had some different coloring—harsh red swirls mixing in with the usual thick darkness. Even through the monitor, I could tell that they resonated pure evil. It was so creepy to watch them lean in and whisper thoughts and ideas to the gang members."

Gus nodded his agreement. "Those particular demons are extremely powerful and specialize in convincing humans to perpetrate the most horrible kinds of acts such as murder, torture, and rape. But remember, demons only plant these evil thoughts in the minds of the humans. It is up to the human to decide to listen and act upon them. Unfortunately, those two humans were only too willing to listen."

"What was also disturbing, Gus, were the auras coming off of those gang members. I have never seen such darkness surrounding anyone before!" exclaimed Paul. "I could actually *see* the evil encircling them, even pouring out of them."

"In human form, you cannot see the evil in a person, but you can certainly feel it. Now that you are no longer human, you can literally see that evil is a living thing, a power. Once a human welcomes it in, it is a real challenge to remove as it completely surrounds and effectively traps the soul."

"Gus, who were those other people? The two that were helping you?" asked Lexy. "Their inner lights were so bright!"

"A couple of my angel friends," answered Gus. "They left right after the gun fight."

"Angels! Really?" squeaked Lexy, then, in a more serious tone, she continued, "I'm confused. So why did the bullet still hit her? If you had angels helping you, the bullet should have missed her."

"My fault. But actually, it was much harder than it looked. You see, I was not only trying to stop the gunman but also the demons surrounding him too. Believe me, they were not willing to let me foil their plans. I kept trying to get closer to the gang member before he fired, but the demons were shielding him. That is when I prayed for assistance, and my friends quickly arrived. It took both angels to push back the demons so that I could finally do something useful."

"Wow! Angels," exclaimed Lexy. "Can I meet them sometime?"

"I think I can arrange a meeting the next time one is here." Gus smiled.

"Prayer definitely helped a few times tonight," Maria said. "It was a good thing that Dominic and Marti prayed before they all went into the building." She paused for a second, then added, "I even heard a small half-hearted prayer from Michael! It made me so happy."

"It was quite fortuitous that they prayed first," replied Gus. "We would not have been able to track their location so quickly otherwise. Transporting to their location still takes time, even with our devices."

"Why can't guardians know where their subjects are at all times?" Lexy asked. "Shouldn't we be able to just 'know' everything that the humans do?"

HELP AMONG US

Gus laughed. "Only God has that power, Lexy. Guardians, angels, and other heavenly beings have to rely on other tools, like prayer, to locate our subjects. The really unfortunate part about being a guardian is the necessity to sometimes stay out of sight while we help our subject. As demonstrated tonight, it gets even more tricky when you have trouble locating them at times."

"Right," said Lexy. "When they prayed, we were able to see this really big light."

"Correct, Lexy," said Gus. "Prayer creates another kind of aura, an illumination, around the praying person or people that can be seen all the way to heaven. Here on earth, we guardians can track the exact location of the prayer aura on our devices." Gus held up what looked like an iPhone but with more gadgets on it.

"What about when we pray?" Lexy asked. "I see an aura around us whenever we pray too."

"Prayer auras are created whenever anyone, human or not, is praying. In fact, that is how my angel friends found me tonight when I called out for help with the demons and for steadying my aim."

"Are there other uses for prayer auras?" asked Paul.

"Many," answered Gus. "The prayer aura opens up channels for communication with God. And the more people join together in prayer, the bigger and brighter the illumination becomes. No prayer goes unanswered, and no prayer becomes garbled in transmission," Gus stated. "Now onto our task at hand. We need to figure out what is happening and the best next steps to help keep Michael alive and on track."

CHAPTER 30

Ethan stood back in pride, admiring his work as Detective Jenkins and two other officers, guns drawn, cautiously entered Melissa's now-unlocked apartment. While Detective Jenkins had ordered a locksmith to come to the apartment, Ethan had once again proved himself useful by quickly picking the lock. Detective Jenkins smiled, shook his head, and made a mental note to keep an eye on Ethan from now on. Ethan and the others had to wait outside of the apartment with their backs to the wall in case there were any "surprises" inside the apartment. After a few moments, Detective Jenkins returned.

"The apartment is safe for you all to enter. However, does anyone here speak Spanish?" he asked. "We found the girls hiding under the bed, but it doesn't appear that they understand what we are saying."

Both Michael and Ethan answered yes simultaneously. They looked at each other in surprise.

Ethan shrugged. "Hey, you learn many things living on the streets."

"Okay, then. Let's give this our best shot," said Michael.

Detective Jenkins led the way through the beautifully decorated living room and into Melissa's large bedroom. The other two officers were standing guard by the bedroom door. Detective Jenkins walked over, bent down, and pointed under the high king-size four-poster bed. The head of the bed was pushed up against the wall. He spoke gently to the group, "They are under here. I think that they are very scared right now."

Michael approached the large four-poster bed, then bent down to look under it. He began to gently speak in Spanish, introducing himself and the others. He then told them that the police were with them and that they were safe now. When he tried to bend down to extend a hand to them, he could hear the girls breathing harder and trying to back as far away from him as possible. He told them that Melissa had been shot but was now safe at a hospital. Unfortunately, that news appeared to make them even more afraid, as they heard one of the girls gasped in horror. Michael stood back up and turned to the group. "I am not making any progress. They seem terrified at the moment."

Ethan sat down on the wooden floor next to the head of the bed. He pulled out a chocolate bar from his jacket pocket and slowly unpeeled the wrapper. The bed was elevated high off of the ground so that he could sit on the floor and see the girls underneath the bed at the same time. It was true; they were terrified. They had pushed themselves up against the wall at the head of the bed, and it appeared that they were trying to press themselves even harder against it. He smiled at them, waved, and took a bite of the bar. He made a big show of enjoying the chocolaty goodness.

"What is he doing?" Michael whispered to Marti.

"I'm not sure. I'm trying to decide if he is really clever or simply being rude," Marti whispered back.

When Ethan loudly groaned his delight with the chocolate, Marti started to step forward to stop him. Michael pulled her back. "Give him another minute. Let's see what happens."

Ethan then started speaking in Spanish. "Hi! My name is Ethan. I'm twelve. How old are you all?"

From under the bed, a very young girl's voice answered in Spanish. Then a much older girl's voice spoke out, scolding her.

"What just happened?" Marti whispered to Michael.

"First Ethan introduced himself to the girls and told them that he is twelve years old. Then the first voice we heard said that she is five years old. The second voice, however, told her to not to talk to us."

"Five years old! Oh my gosh, Michael!" Marti whispered in horror.

Michael grabbed her hand and nodded.

Ethan continued speaking to the girls in Spanish, while Michael softly translated for the group. Ethan began telling them that he used to be poor and lived on the streets but now lives in a nice apartment, like this one. He then told them that the person who rescued him from both the streets and a dangerous gang was here. He pointed to Marti when he told them about her.

Suddenly, the little girl voice spoke out. Again, the older voice scolded her into silence once more.

Michael translated to the group that the little girl had reacted to the news that Ethan had been rescued from a dangerous gang. In fact, Michael explained, she had said, "We were rescued from a bad gang. Melissa rescued us!"

Ethan continued to speak, telling them that Melissa could not help them anymore because she had to go to the hospital. He then told them that Melissa had asked him to come here and take them to Marti's house until she gets better. He told them about all of the things that they would do while waiting for Melissa to return; he told them about the kittens, Marti's big clinic, and all of the parks that they could go to.

While Michael was translating, he could tell that the girls appeared to be relaxing since their loud breathing had quieted down. Suddenly, a small hand appeared from under the bed. Ethan placed a big piece of the chocolate into the palm. Then the hand disappeared back under the bed. A few seconds later, it returned again. Ethan smiled and placed the rest of the chocolate bar in the hand.

"Smart boy," Marti said as she walked over and sat down next to Ethan. Since she was taller, she had to lie down on her side to see under the bed. "Translate for me, Ethan."

Marti looked under the bed. While it was somewhat dark under the bed, there was enough light to see both girls. The littlest girl was curled up next to the bigger girl and was eagerly eating the chocolate bar. The older girl looked about sixteen or seventeen and was nervously watching Marti while trying to protect the smaller girl. Marti smiled and said hi. She told them who she was and that she had, in fact, saved Ethan from a dangerous street gang. Then she told them that they were safe and that they were leaving to go to her apartment.

After Ethan had finished translating, at last, the older girl spoke. She asked if they could see Melissa. Marti told her that they could, perhaps in a couple of days, when Melissa was feeling better. Marti then told them that she knew that they were scared but that they had to leave the apartment because the men who hurt Melissa might come here. This news finally got the older girl's attention. Both girls finally came out from under the bed at that point.

From their ragged appearance, it was obvious that they had been wearing the same clothes for a very long time. Both girls were pretty thin, their hair was in disarray, and they had patches of dirt on their faces and on exposed parts of their body. The older girl looked thoroughly exhausted, but she held her head high as she stood in front of the group. The little girl looked a bit scared, but then she smiled a little at Ethan. She pointed at her teeth to proudly show him that she just lost a tooth.

Michael smiled at this innocent gesture, while his heart was breaking for what these girls must be living through.

The older girl possessively stepped in front of the little girl and held her hand. "Me Ingles is not so good now," she tried to explain in English. "We are run from very dangerous men."

Michael introduced himself and gently told her that he would translate for her. She nodded and continued in Spanish. Michael let her speak for a few minutes before he translated for the group.

"Her name is Ynez, and she comes from Honduras. She is seventeen years old. She left Honduras *accidentally*, if you can imagine this. She was kidnapped in her attempt to prevent her boyfriend from coming here, to America. Her goal was to stop him from joining and leaving with the drug cartel that had taken over their village.

"About two years ago, the drug cartel had become very powerful in her village and had begun to terrorize everyone. Businesses were being extorted, girls were being raped, and the police were either paid off or murdered, so there was no one to help. It seemed that the only ways to survive were to either join or pay money to the cartel. After a while, most of the older boys and young men had voluntarily joined or were being pressured to join."

Ynez continued with her story for a few more minutes while Michael listened. Michael then translated the next portion of her story. "Unfortunately, her boyfriend, Eduardo, was not strong enough to stand up against the pressure. He is nineteen and was a serious student at the small college near their village. He had dreams of being a doctor one day. Eduardo's parents both died when he was young, so he was raised by his grandmother. Both Ynez and Eduardo's grandmother begged him not to join the cartel, but the pressure became too intense. Every day the cartel gangs would roam the streets and schools, harassing him and others by knocking them down, taking their money, and burning their textbooks. They even burned down a few of the school buildings, killing some students and teachers. They were relentless. You see," Michael explained, "the cartels always need more recruits, as there is a fairly high rate of member 'turnover,' especially in the lower ranks."

Ynez spoke for a few more minutes. While the fatigue was evident in her face, her eyes were dazzling like crystals as she told her story.

Michael began to translate again, but Marti could tell that he was clearly disturbed by what he had just heard. "After Eduardo finally relented, dropping out of school and joining the cartel, Ynez decided to try one last time to stop him from leaving the country with them. She was afraid that she would never see him again. Eduardo had no idea that she had followed him into the cartel hideout that day. When the gang was busy loading the trucks with drugs, guns, supplies, and dozens of people who had paid to travel north to cross into America, she found Eduardo and tried to talk to him. Almost immediately she realized that she had made a terrible mistake by going there that day. The cartel members instantly surrounded her, grabbed her by the neck, and held a gun to her head. Eduardo, without speaking, shook his head to signal to her to be silent and say nothing about their relationship." Michael paused for a moment, swallowed, and then added, "Eduardo could not let the gang know that Ynez was his girlfriend. Apparently, it is a gang custom to 'share' your girlfriend with all of the cartel members." Marti, feeling sick from the story, put her hand over her mouth to stifle a gasp.

Ynez spoke some more while Michael's face reflected the pain from her story.

"The next thing that Ynez knew," Michael began again, "she felt a tremendous pain in the back of her head. Someone in the gang had hit her from behind with a rifle, and she went unconscious. She woke up several hours later, gagged, tied up, sick, and stuffed in a corner of a crowded truck that was en route to the border. It was then that she learned that she was being trafficked into the sex slavery trade."

Marti closed her eyes and tried to stifle the next gasp that escaped her.

"Eduardo did his best to try to shield her from some of the worst, but unfortunately, she has suffered."

Ynez then gestured to the little girl and spoke for several minutes. While waiting for the translation, Marti opened her eyes and just stared at Ynez. She found herself simultaneously weeping internally for Ynez while also admiring her strength.

Michael then pointed at the little girl and translated Ynez's words. "This is Sofia who is five years old. She is from Guatemala. Her mother paid the drug cartel a lot of money to smuggle both herself and Sofia to America. Unfortunately, when they arrived here a few months ago, the drug cartel demanded more money before they would finally let them go. When Sofia's mother couldn't pay, they beat her, raped her, and then killed her. Sofia's mother had no husband and no family, so they knew that they wouldn't get any more money from her."

"Why did they kill her mother?" Marti asked.

Michael translated the question. His face grew angry when Ynez told him the answer.

"They killed her to set the example for the rest of them," Michael explained. "Essentially the message is this: pay up or you too will die like her."

Ynez spoke for another moment. Marti looked over at Sofia who was now sitting on the floor with Ethan and playing a game on his cell phone. When she and Ethan started laughing at the game, Marti's heart lurched in her chest. "Thank you, Jesus," Marti silently prayed, "that she can still laugh after everything that has happened to her and her mother." Marti realized that a tear had slipped down her cheek when it splashed down onto her hand.

Michael continued translating for the group. "Sofia doesn't understand what happened to her mother. She thinks that she is gone and might come back one day. Ynez has been protecting her ever since."

Detective Jenkins interrupted the conversation, "I'm sorry to break this up, but we really need to get these girls out of here. If the cartel figures out where Melissa took them, they may be coming here to silence them. Remember: these two girls can identify the gang members and their location."

"Can they go to my apartment for tonight?" Marti asked. I think that they need to be in a quiet surrounding for a while. And no one would think to look for them there."

Detective Jenkins thought for a moment and then nodded his consent. "Okay. But we will have some extra patrol cars watching your street tonight."

"That sounds great." To Michael she asked, "Can Dr. Sherman come over and take a quick look at them to make sure that they are all right? Please explain to them that he is a good doctor and that I will be in the room with them during his examination."

After a few more minutes of conversation, they packed up the very few items belonging to the girls, left Melissa's apartment, and took them to Marti's house.

Chapter 31

"I can't believe how quickly they both fell asleep," Marti remarked to Michael. They were standing in Marti's living room, looking at the huge makeshift bed of blankets, sofa cushions, and pillows that were being shared by Ynez, Sofia, and Ethan. The girls did not want to stay in the guest room but instead wanted to sleep on the floor in a large open space. Somehow this made them feel more secure. Also, both girls had insisted that Ethan stay in the room with them as they felt more comfortable with his presence in this unfamiliar place. The good news was that they had both bonded quickly with Ethan.

After the girls had both taken a hot shower, put on fresh clothes, and ate some hot soup, they fell immediately asleep when they lay down. Mrs. Flaherty and Cynthia had just left after bringing the food, extra clothes, towels, and other items to make the girls feel more comfortable. Ethan finally joined the girls by rolling himself in a blanket and settling on the far end of the living room.

Michael and Marti turned down the lights and then just stood together in the calm silence, watching the group sleep. Both of them were trying to process everything that had just happened in the last twelve hours. Funny, they were both still wearing the dress clothes that they had on when the evening began, but they were definitely looking pretty ragged at this point. Marti's hair was a tumbled mess, and her dress was ripped on one side. Michael's tuxedo jacket was still at the hospital with Melissa, and there was blood and dirt on his torn dress shirt. Marti did try to relax a bit, however, and had kicked off her high-heeled shoes and was standing in her stocking feet. Michael looked at her and thought that she never looked more beautiful.

He looked back at the two girls, trying to comprehend how much they had suffered. "My guess is that this is the first place that they actually feel safe in, probably in months," Michael mused. "By the way, Marti, it was really kind of you to take them in. I was going to offer my place to them, but then you jumped in."

Marti smiled. "I'm happy to help them, Michael. I honestly cannot imagine what they must have gone through all of this time."

Michael nodded. "What I wonder is what is going to happen to them now. Where will they go?"

"Great question, Michael. First the police need to finish questioning them. After that, we will need to determine where they can go and who can help them."

Just then, a momentary flash of light caught Michael's eye. Oddly, the lights of a passing car outside reflected directly on Marti's cross necklace. Michael stopped speaking for a moment and just stared at Marti, in deep thought.

"What?" Marti asked.

He shook his head, then looked back at her with a serious tint in his eyes. "I never really thought about it before, but helping someone can be really painful, gut-wrenching at times."

Marti chose that moment not to respond, just let him continue speaking what was in his heart.

"We almost died trying to rescue Melissa tonight," he continued. "Now we are sheltering complete strangers in our homes, all the while wondering what, if anything, we really can do for them in the future." He stopped speaking and looked away.

"Tell me what you are thinking," Marti gently requested.

He turned back to her, a look of pain on his face. "I don't know how to say it, really. I guess I find that helping people really *hurts* sometimes."

Marti took his hand and smiled at him. "Sometimes it does, Michael. It becomes very painful, very hopeless at times, which is why many people don't help. Or some take the less complicated route of just contributing money to a cause and then walking away."

Michael laughed, but his smile did not reach his eyes. "Sounds like me in the old days."

"Michael, *really helping someone* requires your personal involvement. If you think about it, it always *costs* you something to help someone else. That cost can be in the form of your money, your time, and even your heart."

"Yes, I guess you are right. I never thought about it in those terms. But I was always under the impression that helping others was supposed to make you feel really good."

Marti smiled. "Believe me, it does. Sometimes that feeling takes a while to arrive. The key is to stick around long enough to see the results. Right now we are in the 'stressful' stage of helping."

Michael laughed and nodded. "Stressful is right!" He stared at her for another moment. Never in his whole life had he ever met anyone as unselfish as her. Well, both she and Dominic. And in this brief time that he has been with them, they seemed to bring out the best in him, he thought. *Could I change my life and become like that? Be unselfish and live to help others?* His eyes drifted back to her cross necklace. Staring at it, he knew that this was the missing link in his life. After all, both she and Dominic really believed in God. More than that, he corrected himself; they actually *lived* their faith. Thinking harder, he remembered that his parents were also very unselfish people. They too were strong believers in Christ. He glanced down at his watch and exclaimed in horror, "Oh, wow, it's late! Four a.m.!"

Marti looked shocked. "What? Already?"

They looked at each other and laughed a little. "Well," said Michael, "I better go. I will come back in the morning to check on all of you."

"Thanks, Michael, for everything. And most especially for your help tonight," Marti replied. Then, without thinking, she stood on her tiptoes and gave him a quick kiss. Michael responded by cupping her face with his hands and returning the kiss, but much slower. Time seemed to stop as they melted into each other's embrace.

They both pulled apart when they heard Ethan snorting with laughter and pointing at them.

Marti blushed. "Well, I guess we have an audience." Michael laughed and pressed a quick kiss to her forehead.

"See you tomorrow," he said as he left the apartment.

CHAPTER 32

Michael awoke the next morning around ten. He deliberately left his blinds and curtains wide open so that the sunlight would wake him. While he did not get much sleep that night, he was eager to get back to Marti's apartment and check on everyone. Strange, while his world was falling apart in so many ways (multiple threats on his life, potential financial and legal disaster for his company, dangerous cartels operating on company premises), he found himself happy that morning. He had no explanation except for the realization that he was in love for the first time in his life. Just thinking about Marti made him smile.

He got dressed, whistling a silly tune in the process, and was talking nonsense to the kittens who were lounging in his soft-cushioned chair. He laughed at himself. He was acting like he was twelve years old. He walked down the hallway to the kitchen to grab a quick bit of breakfast before setting out. As he entered the room, he heard Cynthia's voice.

"And you are sure that they are all missing—Marti, Ethan, and both of the girls?" Cynthia asked, panic in her voice.

Michael rushed into the room. Mrs. Flaherty, Gus, and Cynthia were gathered around the telephone. It had been placed on speakerphone so that they whole group could participate in the call.

"Can you tell if they somehow left on their own? Maybe they just all went to get some breakfast somewhere," Cynthia continued.

"What?" Michael demanded. "What do you mean by *missing*?"

"Michael! We were just going to get you!" Mrs. Flaherty said. "Detective Jenkins went to Marti's apartment to pick up the girls for questioning, and he found no one home. Marti isn't answering her phone, and, even worse, it appears that her door was forced open."

"Oh my god!" Michael exclaimed. "How long ago was this?"

"Thirty-five minutes ago, Michael," Detective Jenkins's voice responded. "I have already called the feds to come over to assist us and see what clues they can find."

"I thought that there was supposed to be extra patrol on duty to watch Marti's apartment!" Michael roared. "How could this have happened?"

"We had extra cars patrolling her street all night. No suspicious activity was reported. The only break in the patrols was a fifteen-minute shift change around eight thirty this morning. We believe that is when it must have happened. I am not sure how, Michael, but we must have been followed last night when we left Melissa's apartment."

While the conversation continued for a few more minutes, Michael had to sit down to try to control his panic. Visions of Marti, Ethan, and the girls in the hands of absolute killers made him almost sick with worry. *Control*, he thought to himself, trying to slow down his breathing. *You can't help them if you panic.* Thinking hard, he tried to imagine where they would be right now. He didn't think that the cartel would take them back to the Garcia Lodge, especially since the police were now combing through the buildings. While his mind was going over the possibilities, he heard the doorbell ring.

"That's the doorbell, Detective Jenkins," Cynthia replied. "Hopefully they are both here now." She left the room and walked down the hallway to the front door. After only a moment, both Dominic and Reynolds entered the room with Cynthia.

Michael felt so relieved to see both of them.

"We are on the phone with Detective Jenkins right now," Cynthia informed them.

Reynolds spoke first. "Any updates since we last spoke, Jenkins?"

"No, nothing yet. Your crew arrived on the scene five minutes ago and are now examining the entranceway and the living room."

Michael looked over at Dominic. Not since last night when they were facing off with the gang members had Michael seen such an intense expression on Dominic's face. It was clear that he was very worried about his friends.

"I will be there as soon as I can, Jenkins," Reynolds said. "I've been with Dominic this morning, clarifying some details from last night. I know you want to talk to him too, so I can bring him with me as soon as we finish up here."

"Sounds good, Reynolds. Call me when you are on your way."

Cynthia pressed the button to hang up the phone call. She turned to Reynolds and Dominic and forced a smile. "Can I get either of you some coffee?"

"None for me," Reynolds answered.

Dominic took a moment to answer. Clearly he was still in shock from the news. His face relaxed a bit and he responded, "No, thanks, Cynthia."

After a moment of awkward silence, Michael spoke, his voice choking up with emotion. "Reynolds"—he paused, closing his eyes and swallowing—"do you think that the cartel will, uh, hurt them right away, or is there a chance that they could still be alive?"

Reynolds exhaled. "The hard truth is that if the cartel really wanted them dead, they would have murdered them right in Marti's apartment. The fact that they went through the trouble to kidnap them tells us that they are probably holding them for a grander purpose, perhaps for ransom." He paused for a moment, rubbing the back of his neck with his hand while carefully sifting his words in order to present his next point with some tact. In the end, he gave up. "I'm just going to have to say this. All of you are going to have to brace yourselves for the possibility that this could end badly. This cartel is not known for showing mercy to anyone."

Michael covered his face with his hands, trying hard to block out the images of Marti and Ethan, hands and legs tied up, lying helpless on the floor while gunmen pointed rifles right at their heads. "I'm going with you to Marti's apartment. I want to help look for clues."

"No, Michael. We already have enough people at the scene," Reynolds answered. "Dominic is coming with me so that he can answer some of Detective Jenkins's questions."

"I can't just sit here and do nothing!" Michael yelled. After a second of silence, Michael's expression softened as he examined his behavior. "Sorry," he said, running a hand through his hair. "What can I do to help?"

"I need you to do a few things for me. First, make a list of everyone you think may be involved in this. I sincerely doubt that Melissa Butano was dealing with the cartel by herself. Next, write down everything you remember about the cartel hideout at the Lodge. It may tip us off to where they have relocated now."

"Okay. I can do that. Anything else?"

"Yes. We need access to all of your company records, including your financial systems, customer databases, websites, backups, mail servers, everything. We also need to look around your personal files and those of your employees, including Ms. Butano. Sorry, Michael, but we need to check out everything going on inside your business to see how deeply the cartel had its hooks in there."

Michael nodded. "Sure, I understand. I want to know those answers too, including if any other employees were helping them." Michael then added, "Actually, I could use your help here. I need to show you some suspicious transactions I discovered in our investment database to see if you all can determine who made them. I will make a few phone calls today and have my IT group meet you at the office. Will tomorrow be soon enough?"

"Yes, that will be fine. One more thing—should anyone in the cartel contact you, do *not* try to handle them on your own. No matter what they tell you, you must contact me to determine what to do." Reynolds reached into his duffel bag, pulled out a cell phone, and placed it on the table in front of Michael. "This is a prepaid disposable cell phone that was just purchased a week ago. If you need to contact me, do not use any of your devices. The cartel most likely is surveilling all of your phones, computers, everything."

"They are that sophisticated?" Michael asked.

"How else do you think that they have evaded arrest for well over a year now?"

Michael thought about that for a second, then asked, "Well, don't you think that they are monitoring your cell phone too?"

"Of course they are!" Reynolds answered with a smile. "So absolutely don't call my real phone number. Call the number that you see taped on the bottom of that phone. That is the number of *my* new prepaid cellphone."

Michael turned over the cell phone and looked at the taped number. "Right. That makes sense."

Dominic put his hand on Michael's shoulder. "We will get them back." With more intensity, he added, "I will personally see to it."

Michael tried to smile but failed. "If those bastards hurt any of them…" He couldn't finish the sentence.

"Then let's just say, Michael," Dominic slowly replied, his expression so fierce that he almost looked like a wild animal, "that they had better pray for a miracle when I find them."

Chapter 33

Michael was still sitting at the kitchen table, making his lists for Reynolds. Truthfully, he could barely stop himself from being overcome with panic for Marti, Ethan, and the girls, so he was glad to have some mundane tasks to keep him busy. He just completed one list when the doorbell rang. He started to get up, but Cynthia motioned for him to stay seated. *Who could that be?* he wondered. Instantly, his mind began to race with fearful, unthinkable thoughts. *Are they dead? Is Reynolds coming to tell me the horrible news in person?* Time seemed to crawl as Cynthia made her way to the door. He closed his eyes, bracing himself, as an icy chill invaded his stomach and his heart hammered against his rib cage.

After what seemed like an eternity, he heard Trent's voice echoing from the hallway. Michael opened his eyes, and relief flooded into him. *Not Reynolds or Detective Jenkins.* While he was momentarily relieved, he was certainly confused as Trent was supposed to be out of town this weekend. Remembering what Reynolds told him about being careful and trusting no one, he quickly hid his lists for the FBI under a stack of magazines on the table. He then pretended to be causally reading when Trent walked into the kitchen.

"Hey there," Trent said with a smile on his face. Michael looked up at his friend. As usual, Trent looked like he just walked out of a photoshoot for a men's fashion magazine. Today he was wearing athletic shorts, expensive leather trainers, a nice T-shirt, and had his racquet ball safety glasses strung around his neck. Even his leather duffel bag matched his outfit perfectly. Curiously, however, the only out-of-place parts of Trent's attire were the dark circles under his eyes. He looked really tired. Michael knew that Trent had been working extremely hard, so that probably explained it.

"What's the outfit for, Trent?" Michael asked. "And aren't you supposed to be out of town?"

Trent laughed. "You must have forgotten about the massive racquet ball tournament this weekend." He suddenly stopped himself, obviously remembering that Michael wouldn't be able to play this year. "Oh, sorry, dude. Didn't mean to be insensitive."

Michael forced a small smile on his face and folded his hands on the table. "No worries, Trent." He paused for a moment and then added, "Actually, I hope to be playing in that tournament next year, if I can. I just need to train hard. Are you up for helping me get my game back?"

Trent laughed, rubbing the back of his head in a nervous gesture. "So you can beat me in the tournament again?" He laughed. "Of course, Michael, let's plan on that. And, if you recall, I told you on Thursday that I was *busy* all weekend—not out of town. Sorry if I wasn't clear."

Michael smiled, closing the magazine that he wasn't really reading anyway. "No problem, Trent. So what brings you here this morning? Shouldn't you be warming up at the courts?"

"Well, I would be, except for the fact that my racquet broke last night during my first game. Can you believe it? So actually I am here for a big favor. While I could spend time trying to find a replacement in time for my next match, I remembered that your racquet is almost identical to mine." He paused and looked at Michael sheepishly. "I was hoping that you would let me borrow it for the rest of the weekend, since—"

"Since I won't be using it anyway." Michael smiled and finished the sentence. "Be my guest, Trent. I hope you don't mind retrieving it yourself, however," he said, motioning toward the hallway leading to his bedroom. Michael had to force his smiles with Trent, but he knew that he needed to act naturally right now.

Trent looked instantly relieved. "Whew! Thanks, dude! I owe you!" Trent rushed off down the hallway toward Michael's room.

Cynthia came back into the kitchen and poured herself a cup of coffee. As she was adding her usual too-many spoonful of sugar, she looked over at Michael. From his pained expression, he clearly was worrying about his friends. "Can I get you some coffee? It looks like you didn't even get any breakfast this morning."

Michael looked over at Cynthia and managed a smile. "Coffee would be great, if you don't mind." He watched her retrieve a mug from the cupboard and then pour some hot coffee into it. She placed it in front of him and then returned with creamer, sugar, some spoons, and her own coffee. She started to sit down but then shook her head and sighed. She got back up, grabbed a plate, and then cut a piece of cinnamon coffee cake for him. She finally sat down after setting the plate in front of him.

"Thank you, Cynthia," Michael said. His expression grew serious as he looked at her. "Really. I mean it—thank you. I don't know how you do it, but you are always there when I need you."

Cynthia smiled back at him. "That is what friends are for, Michael. Just remember to pray for some help and guidance from above to help us find Marti, Ethan, and the girls. You may be surprised what God can do when you give Him a chance."

"I think I will, Cyn. Pray, I mean. We prayed last night before we went into the Lodge, and it definitely helped."

Cynthia's heart swelled. *He is starting to believe*, she realized. *Thank you, Jesus. Please come through for us right now so that Michael can finally see you for who you really are and change his life to follow you*, she silently prayed.

He smiled once more and picked up the fork, taking a bite of Mrs. Flaherty's wonderful coffee cake. His sense of taste immediately overpowered his emotional turmoil. *Wow*, he thought as his taste buds soared to heaven. The cake was pure ecstasy: crispy, buttery sugar cinnamon on the outside and fluffy delicate cake on the inside. Additionally, there was a delicious band of the cinnamon sugar running through the middle of the cake. Amazingly, happy memories of eating coffee cake in his childhood came flooding back. He mused how strange it was that a sound, a touch, a smell, or a flavor could bring back long-forgotten memories. Even stranger, he thought, he hadn't had or even seen a cake exactly like this since he was a boy. His eyes suddenly popped open, and he stared down at the cake on his plate. In fact, this cake was *exactly* like those he ate as a boy. *But how could that be?*

"Something wrong, Michael?" Cynthia asked with concern. "Is the cake all right?"

Michael took a moment to answer, obviously thinking hard about how to articulate his thoughts. After a moment, he finally sighed and shook his head. "This is going to sound crazy, Cynthia. But this cake"—he gently gestured to it with his fork—"is *exactly* like one that my mother used to make me."

Cynthia smiled. "Well, cinnamon coffee cakes are pretty common, Michael. And I certainly agree that Mrs. Flaherty is an excellent cook."

Michael smiled and shook his head, gesturing with his fork to the different layers in the cake. "No, Cynthia. I mean that this cake is identical in *every* way to one that my mother used to make."

As Cynthia smiled and started to shake her head in gentle disbelief, Michael continued, "Believe me, Cynthia, I can taste the difference. I rather consider myself an expert in cinnamon coffee cakes, having eaten many of them in my lifetime, but, until now, there was only *one* that ever tasted like hers." He smiled. "For a moment there, I was transported back to *her* kitchen table, with her smiling and nagging at me to eat up because I was too skinny."

Cynthia smiled at Michael and patted his hand. "Well, I agree with your mother. Eat up, Michael. You are still too skinny!"

They both laughed at that.

From outside the kitchen doorway, Maria had been listening. She hadn't meant to eavesdrop; she just didn't want to intrude on their conversation after tidying up the living room. First she almost cried when she heard Michael say that he was going to pray today. Then she mentally scolded herself for the cake blunder. In her haste to quickly make breakfast that morning, she had forgotten to purposefully reconfigure her special coffee cake recipe. However, hearing the way that Michael spoke about his memories of her and her cake, her heart almost burst with love. She felt something tickling on her cheek. She gently scratched it and immediately looked at her wet fingers in curiosity: it was a tear. This was strange—she didn't think she could cry anymore. However, these were tears of joy, not of sorrow. She would share all of this with Paul and Gus as soon as she could.

She wiped her face, put on a smile, and walked into the kitchen. "Oh, good, Michael, you are eating," she said as she walked past the table. "Do either of you need anything else?"

"No, Joanna, we are good!" Cynthia answered, taking another sip of her coffee. She paused, thoughtful for a moment, and continued, "Michael, I didn't hear Trent leave. Is everything okay with him?"

Michael looked up and finally answered when he had swallowed his mouthful. "Oh, I completely forgot about him. Actually, Cynthia, he hasn't left yet. He came here to borrow my racquetball racquet for the tournament today. But he is taking a while to find it." He stood up from the table and spoke as he left the room. "I'm going to give him a hand."

Michael walked down the hall and bumped into Trent as he was leaving Michael's room. Michael looked down to see the racquet in Trent's hand. "Oh, good, you found it! I was thinking that maybe you got lost!" he joked.

Trent laughed, "No, I just forgot where you put it, so it took me a moment." They both walked back to the kitchen.

Mrs. Flaherty forced a smile at Trent when he and Michael walked into the kitchen. She was internally reeling from the new darkness emanating from him. Something was terribly wrong with Trent. "Hi, Trent, can I offer you some breakfast or perhaps just some coffee?"

Trent looked down at the table with the delicious-looking cake. "Boy, as tempting as this looks, I am going to have to pass. I am already late for my warm-up before today's tournament games." He looked over at Michael. "I'll give you a call later to tell you how everyone did today."

"I'll walk you out, Trent," Michael said, and they both left the room and walked to the front door.

Cynthia cupped her ear and then signaled to Maria to also adjust her own hearing to be sure that they knew when Michael was coming back.

"Maria," Cynthia said seriously and very softly, "something is wrong. Did you see the darkness surrounding Trent? It has grown worse."

"How could I miss it, Cynthia? I was so horrified that it took every bit of my control to act normally and focus on what he was saying. And I could barely see anything of his inner light. So thick is the dark band surrounding it. I wonder what this means. Do you think he is involved in all of this?"

Cynthia shook her head slowly, thinking hard. "I don't know, Maria, but my gut is telling me that we need to really guard Michael. Judging by the depth of the darkness surrounding him, Trent is being guided by a very dark influence which means that he could be capable of almost anything right now."

They both stopped their conversation when they heard Michael's footsteps back down the hallway. They both expected him to enter the kitchen, but he continued on down the hallway to his room. After only a moment, Michael came back down the hall and entered the kitchen. He put on his jacket and was shoving his car keys and wallet into his pockets.

"Going somewhere?" Cynthia asked.

"Yeah," Michael answered. "Trent wants a ride to the tournament. His next game is in twenty-five minutes. Trying to find a parking space right now will be a nightmare, so I agreed to drop him off outside of the complex."

Cynthia and Maria silently communicated concern to each other.

"I don't think you should go anywhere right now," Maria blurted out after moving to block his exit from the kitchen.

Michael paused, his hand in mid-motion of grabbing his piece of cake. "Why not?" he asked, clearly confused by her behavior.

Cynthia took over, lowering her voice to prevent Trent from hearing. "Well, you…really, all of us"—she gestured to everyone in the room—"we are supposed to wait here should the police or the FBI need to speak to us."

Michael's frown disappeared. "The complex is only ten blocks away. Pending any traffic," he added, "I will only be gone a few minutes." He picked up the rest of his cake and crammed it completely into his mouth. "Bhee bhack soohn," he managed to say while waving goodbye and leaving the room.

While still trying to decide how to think about all of this, Cynthia spotted the prepaid cell phone on the table from Reynolds. She grabbed it. "Michael, wait!" she cried out, catching him in the hallway and discreetly handing it to him. She quickly stole a glance at Trent, hoping that he did not see what she had given Michael. Fortunately, he was busy adjusting his hair in the mirror next to the front door. *Thank God for vanity*, Cynthia thought to herself as she walked back to the kitchen.

"Should we have Gus follow Michael? I can call him right now," Maria asked when Cynthia reentered the kitchen. "He said for us to keep him informed anyway." Before Cynthia could answer, Lexy walked in, holding the kittens.

"Mama, I'm going to give the kittens a treat. They are feeling a bit sad at the moment."

Maria looked over at the kittens, who were now purring loudly in Lexy's arms. "Hmm, Lexy, they don't seem to be suffering too much right now."

"Well, Mama, I suppose you are right," Lexy said, gently putting the kittens down on the floor. "But they were pretty angry just a moment ago." She and the kittens went to the other side of the kitchen so that she could give them a snack. Although they were trying to be quiet, the kittens and Lexy were speaking pretty loudly with each other.

Maria smiled patiently at her daughter and then tried to resume her conversation with Cynthia. "Maybe we are concerned over nothing. After all, he will be right back."

"Who will be right back?" Lexy asked from the other side of the room.

"Michael, sweetie," Maria answered.

"Yes, he is only going a few blocks," Cynthia responded with cheerfulness that she clearly didn't feel. It was obvious that they were both trying to comfort each other.

"I don't know why, Cyn, but I am getting a bad feeling about this."

"I know just what you mean, Maria."

"However, Trent did legitimately come here to borrow the racquet, so maybe everything is okay."

"Oh, is that what he came here for?" Lexy called out from the other side of the kitchen.

"What, Lexy?" Maria asked.

"Trent, Mama. Are you sure he came here to borrow Michael's racquet?"

Maria was really not in the mood to answer a hundred questions with Lexy right now, so she mentally counted to three before answering. "Yes, dear. He is playing in a tournament this weekend, so he just came here to borrow Michael's racquet. Please, dear, I'm trying to discuss something important with Cynthia."

"Really?" Lexy responded.

Maria let out a sigh of exasperation. "Really *what*, sweetie?"

"Well, if Trent was here just to get the racquet, then he was looking in some really weird places to find it!"

"Lexy, what do you mean?" Cynthia asked, curious now.

"Well, according to the kittens, Trent spent a lot of time in Michael's room, digging through his desk drawers."

Both Maria and Cynthia's heads whipped around at that statement. "*WHAT!*" they both loudly answered in unison.

"Yes, Mama," Lexy answered, clearly impatient now herself. "That is what I've been trying to tell you!"

"Lexy, please ask the kittens to tell us exactly what Trent did in Michael's room," Cynthia requested.

Lexy translated this question to the kittens who took turns answering. After a couple of minutes, Lexy relayed their answer. "The kittens said that when Trent came into Michael's room, he quickly found the racquet in the closet."

"Lexy, are they sure?" Cynthia asked, clearly concerned.

"Oh yes," Lexy answered. "You see," she explained, "they were both sitting in Michael's desk chair, cleaning themselves after their morning snack, so they had a perfect view of everything.

"At first, they said, everything was peaceful. Trent spent some time looking at a few things on top of Michael's desk, mostly some papers and stuff. *Then*," Lexy's eyes widened and her tone changed to show emotion, "Trent started going crazy. He was rubbing his hands all over his face and making some weird sounds. The next thing that they knew, he walked over and then pushed them—really SHOVED them off of the chair! They both fell hard on the floor!" She put her hands on her hips to emphasize her outrage. "Can you believe it? He pushed the kittens onto the *floor*!"

Cynthia and Maria looked at each other, trying to hold onto their patience. Cynthia calmly spoke next. "Lexy, sweetie, can you ask the kittens what Trent did next? Where else he looked?"

Lexy's face grew angry now, and she sharply crossed her arms over her chest. "I am surprised at both of you! Trent was so *mean* to the kittens, and you don't seem to care!"

Maria touched Cynthia's arm to signal that she would handle asking Lexy the next question. Wisdom told Maria that the most efficient method to getting to the important facts would be to show some immediate sympathy for the kittens' plight. So she took a deep breath, walked over, and squatted down in front of them. Taking a moment, she thoroughly pet each one, gently scratching them behind the ears and under their chins. Exaggerating her sympathy, she cooed and coddled them: "There, there," she said. "I know that must have hurt, being pushed onto the floor." The kittens were clearly happy to receive this extra bit of attention, as they were purring with the ferocity of little freight trains. "Now, Lexy," Maria gently asked, "can you please ask the kittens what Trent did next?"

Satisfied that an adequate amount of concern was finally shown toward the kittens, Lexy translated the next question. She then replied with their answer.

"They said that Trent sat down in the chair and began looking through each of Michael's desk drawers. He was particularly interested in some of the papers in one of the folders, because he took a few of the pages. And he was *really* interested in that small piece of paper that Michael keeps hidden under his computer keyboard. You know the one that has all of his computer passwords written down? Trent took a picture of it with his cell phone."

Maria and Cynthia looked at each other with full realization that Trent was most likely involved in the business with the drug cartels. "We need to call Gus and Detective Jenkins right now," Cynthia exclaimed. "Michael shouldn't be anywhere alone with Trent." She pulled out her hand device and pressed a few buttons. A few seconds later, the device beeped a few times. Cynthia quickly typed a message and then waited for Gus's response. After a minute, she read the screen and announced that Gus, who happened to already be in his car, was now on his way. I am messaging Paul now. He needs to be here too."

"Yes, definitely!" Maria answered.

"You think that Trent has something to do with those gang members?" Lexy asked.

"We aren't 100 percent sure, Lexy, but we think so," Maria said.

Lexy shared this news with the kittens. Odd, but after Lexy told them that Trent was 'doing some bad stuff,' the kittens started meowing very loudly. As Lexy listened, her eyes widened. Both Maria and Cynthia were amazed at how animated the kittens were in their conversation with Lexy.

"Lexy, what is it?" Cynthia asked.

"Well," Lexy began, "they remember another weird time with Trent, something that happened a while ago."

"Yes?"

"Do you remember when we had to call the ambulance take Michael to the hospital? When he almost died?"

"What happened, Lexy?" Maria asked.

"The kittens just told me that they think Trent might have had something to do with it. They didn't understand what he was doing at the time because, to them, *all* humans seem to do a lot of weird things."

Cynthia, stealing a quick glance at Maria, didn't think her eyes could get any wider.

Lexy continued, "Do you remember that Trent came to see Michael that day? Well, the kittens told me that Michael left Trent alone in his room for a few minutes. It was after you brought in some sandwiches and hot coffee, Mama."

"Go on," Maria said, trying to control her facial features to not reveal the horror she was feeling.

"Well, they said that Trent went inside the drawer next to Michael's bed. You know, the one where he kept his medicine for his pain."

"Yes?"

"Well, they watched Trent grab one of the bottles and then pour out a bunch of the pills into this jar thing that he brought with him. The jar thing made a strange noise when he turned it on, but it must have crushed all of the pills into a powder. Finally, they watched Trent pour the powder into Michael's coffee along with more sugar."

"The OxyContin," Cynthia choked out, grabbing Maria's arm. Maria nodded and covered her mouth with her hand, trying to slow down her breathing.

"I am worried, Cyn. I think we should call Michael and get him back here as soon as possible," Maria urged. "We need to make up some excuse."

Cynthia nodded her agreement. "Yes, but we have to be careful not to tip off Trent about our suspicions. He has already tried to kill Michael once, that we know of."

"You think that Trent tried to *kill* Michael?" Lexy squeaked.

"It sounds like it, Lexy," Maria said.

Cynthia exhaled loudly after thinking for a moment. "Okay, here is where it gets tricky, everyone. We need to present our theories about Trent to Detective Jenkins and Reynolds, but we obviously can't tell them that our source is a couple of *kittens*," Cynthia stated. "While we are thinking of how to explain this to the authorities, I will call Michael and make up some lame excuse to bring him back now." Cynthia retrieved her "human" cell phone from her purse and dialed Michael's number. While it was ringing, she put it on speakerphone.

"Hello?" Michael answered.

"Michael!" Cynthia responded. Maria almost fainted with relief. "Have you dropped Trent off yet? We have a small emergency here that needs your attention."

"Emergency? Nothing too serious, I hope."

"Not too serious, but can you get back here ASAP? I just don't want this water leak in the kitchen to become a gushing geyser," Cynthia asked.

"Water leak? In the kitchen? I am about to drop off Trent at the racquetball club, so I will be right back."

Cynthia muted the phone for a second to allow her and Maria to release their anxiety.

"Thank God he is all right!" Maria mouthed to Cynthia.

Cynthia nodded her agreement, ended the call, and put the cell phone down on the table.

"I feel a little better now," Maria said.

"So do I," Cynthia said. "Except now we had better come up with some kind of leaky-water 'emergency' for Michael!" They all had a much-needed laugh.

Just then, the doorbell rang. "That must be Paul," Maria said as she left the kitchen and went down the hall. Her guess was confirmed as Cynthia and Lexy heard his voice as he and Maria walked back into the kitchen. Maria was quickly filling him in on all of the news.

"So Michael is on his way back here now?" Paul asked.

"Yes. We just spoke to him before you arrived."

"So his best friend and business partner, Trent, gave him the overdose?" Paul asked in astonishment.

"It appears so," Cynthia answered. "I've always known that Trent had some issues, but I never dreamed that he would be in league with a drug cartel. We need to warn Michael as soon as possible because his life is in serious danger. Two unsuccessful attempts have been made on his life. We should not fool ourselves about the outcome of the next attempt. We also need to somehow pass this latest discovery on to Dominic and the police, because they need to ramp up their security over Michael."

"Where is Michael now?" Paul asked.

"He is with Trent, dropping him off at the racquetball club but will be right back."

"Okay, this is news that is better said face-to-face and not in front of Trent. We just need to think of a creative way to present this to him and everyone else without sounding like we are completely insane."

"Let's quickly brainstorm. Call Gus and get him on speakerphone. He always has good ideas. We just need to pray hard to the Holy Spirit to protect Michael, as we have no idea what will happen next."

Chapter 34

Marti opened her eyes, blinking a few times to adjust her vision to the dim light. She had fallen asleep sitting upright on the dirty ground, with her back pressed up against the damp yet dusty brick wall. She rubbed her right cheek and mouth on her shoulder to remove some of the dirt and cobwebs that she had collected while sleeping with her head resting against a large rusty old drainage pipe. Looking around, from the best that she could determine, she was in an old, abandoned warehouse with massive brick walls and a ceiling made of glass. A thick layer of dust and grit covered everything, including the walls and floor, but judging by the sizable dirt pile in the far corner, it appeared that an effort had been made to sweep some of it off to the side of the large room. Unfortunately, the general filth in the place extended even to the glass ceiling, blocking out some of the sunlight. But maybe that was a good thing since it was already very warm in the building, and the ceiling fans that were spinning at full blast were only succeeding in blowing around the dirt and hot air directly in her path.

While she slept, she had purposefully wrapped her arms tightly around Ethan so that she would know if he were taken away. Her second motive in doing this was to give him some comfort while being locked up in this horrible place. She looked down at him, and, thankfully, he was still sleeping across her lap. She dared not move too much because Ynez was leaning against her left side and was cradling Sofia in her lap. Both girls were asleep, their fatigue born from the terror of the past few hours. Marti silently watched them, observing that, for the moment, they all looked peaceful—if only in their dreams. While she knew she should get whatever rest she could, she thought her time was better spent trying to figure a way out of their situation.

As she looked around, she could see only two exits in the large room. One led into the rest of the warehouse; the other opened directly to the outside. Each door had armed cartel members standing guard, so getting out would be a challenge. On the far wall was a doorless room with a toilet, sink, and an open shower. (Unfortunately, the room contained no windows—she already observed that on her *one* permitted visit.) While there were numerous massive windows framing the entire room, they were all positioned high from the ground, probably thirty feet up. The glass ceiling was close to forty feet up or more. Escape from this place would not be easy.

She and her little group were not the only people in the room. There were about twenty to thirty others who appeared to have been there for a while, as they had created some makeshift beds from some sleeping bags and large blankets. There were a few boys, but mostly the other people were comprised of young women and children. From the clustering of the beds, she could tell that several of the people had apparently banded together in their misery. Looking around, she noticed one little girl staring at her, so Marti attempted to smile at her. The little girl immediately turned her head away and nestled closer against the young woman with whom she sat. Marti initially guessed that this must be the girl's mother, but nothing could be assumed in a place like this. The general mood of the place was fearful, with little to no talking among the people. Whenever they did speak, it was always in Spanish.

As Marti momentarily gave up any plans of immediate escape, she returned her thoughts to her group and herself. She needed to scratch the back of her leg, but this was made difficult not only because of Ethan lying across her lap but because of the thick plastic ties binding her wrists and also her ankles together. Being forced to do nothing but sit in silence, she was prevented from having any distractions from the pain she felt in numerous body parts. To begin with, her face still throbbed, mostly below her left eye, where the gang member had struck her with the butt of his rifle during the capture at her apartment. Her neck and back ached from being repeatedly slammed against the pole to which she had been tied during the bumpy ride over in the van. She badly needed some water, as her throat hurt every time she swallowed. Since it had been hours since the last time anyone offered them anything, she began to wonder when next they would eat, drink, or even use the bathroom. Gauging from the amount of the light coming in through the windows, she guessed that it was around four or five in the afternoon. She sighed in silent frustration as she realized that almost a full day had passed in captivity. She closed her eyes and wondered if Michael and Dominic had any idea what had happened to them. She then had a momentary panic attack, wondering if they too were also in trouble.

Reflecting on the day, she still could not believe that the cartel had found the girls in her condo. She spent the last few hours trying to determine exactly how the cartel had tracked them down, but could come up with nothing. She had absolutely no ties to Melissa Butano, so how did they know to go to *her* residence? Nothing made sense. She was also angry with herself for not being more careful. In hindsight, she should have called the police to escort her to the donut shop that morning, but she really didn't believe that they were in any danger. She was still not sure how, considering that the police were monitoring the street, but the gang members must have been lying in wait for her because the moment she stepped outside of her condo, she was grabbed from behind the head and shoved back inside. While she, Ethan, and the girls all put up a pretty pathetic struggle, it ended when the rifle came down on her face. Amazingly, Marti thought, the worst part of it was the absolute terror on Sofia's face when she saw the cartel members. Marti clenched her jaw at the memory; Sofia was so scared that she couldn't even scream. No child should ever be scared like that, Marti thought angrily to herself.

Sadly, no one seemed to notice when the cartel hustled them out of her condo and into the waiting windowless minivan. Once inside the minivan, they were all gagged and had their wrists and ankles bound with long zip ties. From viewing the inside of the van, it appeared that it was used extensively for the purpose of transporting unwilling passengers. They were all seated on the dirty floor and securely tied, with their backs to the numerous steel posts that had been welded vertically onto the floor and ceiling of the bare van. With nothing but a hard metal pole to cushion her, Marti's head and back were slammed against the post with every turn and bump of the van as it drove down the road. After about forty-five minutes into the bumpy ride to hell, the van finally stopped. From there, they were untied from their posts in the van and then forcibly led at gunpoint into the old abandoned warehouse.

Marti's ankles still throbbed from trying to walk the long distance while still bound by the plastic ties. It wasn't just painful; it was difficult and slow as the tight plastic ankle ties only allowed for tiny steps. Not surprisingly, each one of them fell a few times, resulting in a swift kick to whichever body part was the most advantageous for the cartel member to reach. Trying to get up with bound wrists and ankles while being repeatedly kicked was close to impossible, but each one of them somehow managed the task. After what seemed like the longest walk of her life, they finally reached the room that they were presently in.

To her amazement, they were not separated upon arrival, as she fully expected them to be. Instead, they were all allowed to be confined together and even rest for a few hours. However, Marti had no doubts that eventually some form of revenge would be exacted upon both Sofia and Ynez because they would need to serve as an example for anyone else attempting to escape the cartel. She just prayed that somehow, someway, help would arrive before that happened.

Marti was immediately stirred from her thoughts by the activity in the room. Without a word being spoken, the group of people seemed to know that it was mealtime, because they started to line up near the large table set up on the opposite side of the room. As with everything in that place, the table was flanked with armed cartel members directing the procession of people. A moment later, the door opened, and several older women and teenage boys came in carrying some large buckets and a few trays of food. They were escorted by a couple of armed cartel guards. A few kids came in later, pushing a metal shopping cart loaded with paper plates, some plastic cutlery, and large dispensers holding some kind of beverage.

The noise woke up Ethan, Ynez, and Sofia, who looked on the gathering with trepidation. Marti softly asked Ynez if they should also try to get some food. When Ynez didn't understand, Ethan translated the question.

Ynez's eyes grew wide, and she violently shook her head no. "We…wait," she said. "They…get angry," she whispered in Spanish, and Ethan translated for Marti.

"She said that the guards will get really angry with us if we try to go up there without being told," Ethan quietly explained, fear evident in his voice. "Ynez said that we have to be given permission to do anything: to eat, to use the bathroom, really everything. That is how it works around here. She said that she has seen them kill a woman just for going to the bathroom without asking first."

Since none of them had eaten all day, not even the breakfast that she attempted to get for them, Marti knew very well that they were all hungry. While she was trying to think of how she could possibly round up some food and water, a teenage girl walked over to them. She acknowledged Marti and Ethan with a small smile but then began speaking directly (but softly) to Ynez in Spanish. Apparently, they knew each other because they were speaking rapidly and with emotion. Marti guessed that the girl was probably sixteen or seventeen years old, but her mannerisms suggested someone older. Unlike many teenagers who are self-conscious when approaching strangers, this girl appeared confident, more like an adult. Marti guessed that her life experiences had aged her beyond her years, just like Ynez. Her appearance was also a contradiction; while dressed in worn, shabby clothes, she was beautiful. Neither her frayed blue jeans nor her gray flannel shirt that was worn and torn in several places could detract from her sparkling brown eyes framed with thick lashes. Her jet-black hair was plaited in a single thick braid that ran down the length of her back.

While she and Ynez spoke, it became obvious that they were trying to hide the extent of their conversation from detection. While their whispered voices had the usual inflections of emotions, they were being careful to keep their facial expressions and body language very neutral. After about thirty to forty seconds of conversation, the girl turned around and signaled to one of the cartel guards. Ethan whispered to Marti that they were going to be allowed to get into the food line. The girl then spoke to the group and then Ethan translated for Marti.

"She said to keep your eyes down, and do not look at the guards unless they speak to you. Do not speak to anyone else over there. Get your food and then come back here."

"Ask her if they are going to remove our ankle and wrist ties. We can barely walk and certainly can't hold anything in our hands."

Ethan translated her question. The girl nodded and signaled to the approaching cartel guard.

The guard arrived, first approaching Ethan. He squatted down and pulled out a large knife from the sheath clipped to his belt buckle. He pointed to Ethan's legs and gestured that he was going to cut the tie.

Marti looked at Ethan who was definitely scared of both the knife and the guard but was hiding it well. Ethan slowly extended his bound legs out in front of him, erased all emotion, and stared down at the ground. His past experience with violent gangs had oddly prepared him for this moment, Marti mused with a broken heart. Many people would be having a panic attack or crying now, she thought.

The guard gently grabbed Ethan's left ankle and began to saw the plastic tie around his ankles. After a few seconds, the tie was severed, and the guard pulled back the knife. Marti saw the instant relief on Ethan's face; he was free of the painful binding and from the large knife-wielding guard. The guard then turned to Marti and repeated the process.

Marti almost gasped out loud when the painful tie was cut. As the blood began to flow back into her feet, she knew that it would take days for the cuts and bruising to go away from around her ankles. Sadly, she thought, even if she could break free and run right now, she wasn't sure that her feet could support her. This was by design, of course.

While the guard was sawing her ankle tie in half, she stole a couple of glances at him. He too was young, probably in his early twenties. He was also fairly handsome, being dressed modestly in waist-high jeans and a regular T-shirt. Upon closer examination, Marti thought, he actually seemed a bit out of place, not being dressed in the normal cartel garb consisting of a tight-fitting underwear tank shirt and baggy jeans that are situated well below the buttocks. Additionally, he was not completely body-pierced and tattooed with cartel graffiti, unlike the rest of his peers in the gang. But what struck Marti most was how gentle he was being with them. The other guards literally took turns kicking and taunting them after shoving them all down onto the floor when they were brought in. But this guard, he was different. Marti was astounded when he briefly smiled at Sofia before he cut her tie.

When the guard got to Ynez, his face suddenly lost all expression. Marti then noticed an unspoken communication pass between them. Clearly, Ynez knew this guard. While they deliberately looked away from each other, Marti could tell that each desperately wanted to say something but didn't dare. After a few more seconds, it dawned on her: this must be Eduardo. By not reacting to Ynez, Eduardo was still protecting her.

When he finished cutting Ynez's ankle zip tie, he stood up. Taking on an authoritarian demeanor, he began ordering them loudly in Spanish. Pointing to the food line, he motioned for all of them to join the others for dinner. He made a show of kicking Ynez in the back (not too hard), presumably for the benefit of the armed guards observing them from across the room.

Marti's feet and ankles screamed in protest as she tried to stand on them. Her legs buckled momentarily, but she managed to catch herself on the rusty pipe behind her—not an easy task considering that her wrists were still bound together with the zip tie. She was not even sure that she could balance without any support. She just needed a moment for her body to pump enough blood back into her feet so that she could feel them again, and not just the pain. However, she was not granted that luxury. Another guard roughly pulled her up and away from the wall and shoved her toward the food line. He laughed when she fell hard to the ground, banging her knees on the cement floor. A swift kick to her back reminded her that he was still behind her. She braced herself for another blow because she still couldn't get up; however, it didn't arrive. She heard Eduardo's voice behind her, apparently yelling at the other guard to leave her alone. Silently she thanked God for sparing her from another attack. Eduardo picked her up, walked across the room, and set her down on her feet near the serving table. She could tell that he ordered Ynez to get food for both of them. He then gave her a quick wink and then left her. At that moment, Marti promised herself that if the moment presented itself, she would try to thank him. Looking around her, she then added another prayer to send help not just for herself but for everyone else who was being held captive here, including Eduardo.

CHAPTER 35

Michael ended the call with Cynthia, placed his cell phone down into the cup holder next to his seat, and then stole a quick glance at Trent. Trent's gun was still pointed at his head, so Michael returned his attention back to the road. They had been driving for a while now, away from the city. *Calm, Michael. Stay calm*, he thought to himself.

"Trent," Michael spoke in a low voice, "I believe that *I* should be the nervous one in this situation. However, *your* hands are the ones that are shaking." He took another glance at Trent and then again at the Glock 17 that was visibly trembling in Trent's unsteady hand. Even worse, Michael noted, was that Trent kept his finger on the trigger. While it certainly takes some force to pull the trigger, a severe bump in the road or a strong reaction to the wrong comment could provide the extra bit of assistance necessary to fire the weapon. "If you don't calm down," Michael tried to advise, "you are going to kill us both."

Trent's shrill laugh displayed the nervousness that he felt. He used his trembling free hand to wipe the sweat that was dripping down the sides of his face. His shirt was already soaked around the neckline, and he was trying to use a handkerchief to wipe off his hands while still holding the gun. "Just shut up and keep driving, Michael. We will be there soon."

Michael put together Trent's excessive sweating, dark circles under his eyes, and his trembling hands—it looked like Trent had picked up another bad habit: drugs. "Where, Trent? Where are we going? There is nothing out here." Michael gestured to the flat, open plains of grass extending for miles on either side of the road.

"You are going to meet some of my associates, Michael."

"Associates? Is that what you call them? I think I met a few of them already with Melissa back at the Garcia lodge."

Trent laughed again. "No, those thugs weren't my associates. Those were just some of the underlings who perform all of the manual labor. My associates have some important business to discuss with you."

"Well, I certainly hope that they are better dressed than the underlings. And smell better too."

"Very funny. I think that you will find them much more sophisticated. Actually," Trent added, "I think that you will find that they remind you of yourself."

Michael's eyes narrowed. "How so?"

"They are well-dressed, very smart, and they screw people over for money. Lots of it."

Michael briefly paused to let that insult ferment. Maybe it was partly true. Maybe he didn't actually care about many of his clients in the past, but he certainly made money for them and for his company. And, of course, he made himself very wealthy in the process. Not a crime, but no longer something that he was proud of. Before spending time with Marti and Dominic, he never would have thought twice about the personal lives of his clients; they were just customers. Now he decided, if he lived through this, he would make an effort to understand his clients as people and really consider their goals, even at the expense of his own. With his connections, perhaps he could help them in other ways outside of their investments. He already knew one connection he could use: Marti's clinic.

"People change, Trent. In case you haven't noticed, I am not the same person anymore. I haven't been that way for a few months now."

"Oh, no, Michael, you haven't changed, not permanently anyway," Trent sneered. "You will always be still the same self-centered bastard that I always knew. You are merely acting, playing the part of the 'newly-reformed nice guy' to impress Marti. Once you get tired of her, like you *always* do with your women, you will dump her cold, move onto the next bitch, and then return to all of your old habits."

Ouch. Michael winced at having his old callous habits thrown back in his face. But, interestingly, Michael knew the new truth in his heart. He had no intention of using and dumping Marti; his feelings for her were genuine. He was not sure how it happened, but he finally found the courage to trust someone again. God knows, he thought, it had been years since he found someone who not only inspired him to believe in human goodness again but who also inspired *him* to want to be good. It was amazing, but both Dominic and Marti gave him the hope to believe again in people and possibly also in Jesus.

With these thoughts in mind, Michael began to remember all that he and Trent had been through together. Each had pulled the other out of a dark place several times over the many years. With no real family to support them, they became family to each other. No matter what was happening, they always had each other even when they had no one else. Each had their vices: Michael used women and business success to smooth over the rough edges of his fragile grip on happiness, while Trent was into gambling. In the early days, Trent had been lucky and made quite a large sum. Trent enjoyed the lifestyle to the fullest, lavishing upon himself the most expensive clothes, vacations, and even a yacht. But when his luck ran out, Trent couldn't stop himself and quickly lost more than he had made. Michael had to bail him out quite a few times in the past and finally told him to get some professional help. Michael remembered some of the angry scenes with Trent in his office, the latest being about a year ago, explaining that he could not draw yet another advance on his salary. He also remembered giving Trent a personal loan at that meeting, a sum large enough to cover the mortgage on his condo and other living expenses for several months. However, after that meeting, their friendship changed; Trent became distant and stopped confiding in Michael. Whenever they were together, it was always cut short because Trent had an appointment or someplace he had to be. Thinking back on this, Michael wondered if this is when Trent had begun his association with the cartel. Michael reflected on all of this for a moment, deep sorrow welling up inside him for what has happened to his friend. He also felt tremendous guilt that his best friend had felt it necessary to turn to an evil organization instead of coming to him. On that note, how could Trent even tolerate to be in the same room with such people? he wondered. The list of their evil was endless: drugs, weapons, human smuggling, murder, rape, sex trafficking of women and children, money laundering, extortion. Not to mention the countless lives destroyed in the aftermath of their activities, including the thousands of families grieving the loss of loved ones from drug overdoses and cartel gang violence. Michael could only imagine the depths of Trent's despair when associating with that level of evil was deemed the best alternative. He also knew that Trent was not inherently bad, despite all that he was doing right now, including being somehow involved with the kidnapping of Marti, Ethan, and the girls. Somewhere deep within him, the old Trent, his best friend, was still there—Michael just had to reach him.

"What happened, Trent?" Michael gently asked, breaking their long silence. "This isn't you. What made you turn to a completely evil organization while turning against me and Melissa?"

"What happened?" Trent spat out, now using his gun-hand to wipe the sweat that was trickling down his face. "You happened! You made it very clear that you would no longer help me!"

"Wait, you mean with more money?" Michael asked.

"WHAT ELSE?" Trent shouted. "I was in real trouble, Michael. Much deeper than you even knew! I tried to tell you about it, but you just told me to get some counseling. I owed a lot of money to some pretty dangerous people—loan sharks—but you were only willing to give me enough to cover my living expenses!"

"People more dangerous than the cartel?" Michael responded.

Trent laughed. "No, I guess not, in hindsight, but since they threatened to kill me, I turned to the cartel to bail me out of trouble. You see, I owed money to multiple loan sharks, and they were all coming to collect."

"How much are you talking?"

"About seven million," Trent responded after a moment, diverting his eyes from Michael's.

Michael was speechless at this revelation from his friend. He could not imagine owing such a sum to mobsters while also being terrified for his life. How did it all go so terribly wrong for Trent? "So how did you first connect with the cartel?" he managed to calmly ask.

"Why do you care, Michael?" Trent asked.

"Because you are still my best friend, even with that gun pointed at me."

Trent laughed again. "Yeah, I'm your best friend, the one who cut the brake line in your car and also tried to poison you with your painkillers."

"You really did those things to me?" Michael asked, completely astonished.

"You would be surprised to know what all I have done, Michael," Trent answered with some sadness in his voice. "Even when we were still best friends," he added darkly and somewhat remorsefully. "You see, unlike you, I don't have many lines that I don't cross. Now that doesn't mean that I *enjoy* crossing them, mind you. It just means that I will cross them when it is necessary." Trent paused for a moment, reflecting on the past. "You would be very shocked to know what people will do when they are desperate, Michael. *I became very desperate.* The cartel agreed to pay my gambling debts in exchange for the use of the Garcia Lodge buildings, among other things."

Michael felt physically sick. He needed to somehow reach his best friend, so he was careful to keep his voice gentle when he spoke. "You mean the cartel was using our buildings for their…, uhm, business dealings?"

Trent laughed again. "You found the drugs and weapons, so you already know about that part. But, yes, I will tell you the gory truth so that you can hear it for yourself! Yes, we housed drugs and weapons in some of the buildings. In the other vacant buildings, we hosted nightly 'entertainment' for many very successful businessmen, politicians, and celebrities. Does that shock you, Michael?" Trent asked, smiling evilly. "Funny, we didn't even have electricity in some of the buildings, but it didn't matter! We made so much money from those evenings that we almost didn't need to do anything else! We had so many customers that we were running out of rooms for them! We had to put up curtains, split rooms in half—"

"Stop!" Michael interrupted, feeling like he was going to throw up. "Please don't tell me any more about…that."

"So the big, strong Michael Garcia can't handle this?" Trent responded, his voice oozing sarcasm.

"Trent, this isn't who you are! How could you stand by and let the cartel prostitute innocent women, girls, and boys? These people were kidnapped, stolen from their homes, their families! Remember that this isn't their choice—they were trafficked!"

Trent continued laughing. "You sound just like Melissa, and you know what happened to her!"

Michael was in complete disbelief, looking at his friend. Obviously, Trent no longer cared anything about Melissa's well-being. He then thought of Ynez and Sofia and felt a lump in his stomach. "Do you really feel *no* compassion for these victims? Some of them are children! Doesn't it make you angry or at least a little nauseous when you look into their innocent eyes, seeing their fear, their hopelessness, their abuse?"

"Grow up, Michael! We always give them something to help them get through the evenings, so it really isn't so bad for them."

"Drugs, you mean! You coldhearted bastard!"

"It really isn't so different than what you did with your women, Michael," Trent snorted, eyes narrowing menacingly. "You absolutely abused them, but you gave them lots of expensive gifts to 'soften the blow' when you dumped them!"

"That is not the same thing, and you know it!" Michael raged. "Don't you ever compare what I did to the evil you are doing now!" Michael screamed. Then his fury took over. He forgot that he was driving and grabbed Trent around the neck with his right hand. The movement of his body shifting to the right against the bottom of the steering wheel veered their car leftward, into the lane with oncoming traffic. Michael and Trent's faces were just inches apart, eyes filled with hate boring into each other's, when they heard the loud blasts of multiple car horns. As they were about to crash head-on with a large truck, Trent broke eye contact and managed to quickly grab the wheel with his free hand, steering them back into their lane. Michael turned some of his attention back onto the road but kept his right-handed grip on Trent's throat.

"If you want…*any* chance…of saving your friends and yourself…you will keep…your hands and eyes on the road," Trent managed to say, speaking through the tight grip that Michael had on his neck. He then placed the gun right at Michael's temple.

Michael inwardly screamed with frustrated rage but released Trent's neck. He then placed both hands back on the wheel and resumed his concentration on the road.

"That's a good boy, Michael," Trent drawled after a minute, still hoarse from the grip.

"What about Marti and Ethan?" Michael asked, managing to calm himself again.

"What about them?"

"What is the plan for them?"

Trent thought for a minute. "Well, the truth is that they could be killed at any time. But since they are not already dead, that means that the cartel has another use in mind for them—at the moment, of course."

Michael was afraid to ask, but he needed to know the truth. "What kind of 'use,' Trent?"

"Well, Ethan is young, so he will be in high demand," Trent answered matter-of-factly. "While he doesn't appeal to me personally, our customer demand is really high for teenagers and even younger children. The word has spread about our business, so we are getting many clients from all over right now."

Michael didn't think he could feel any sicker, but he was wrong. "Now Marti," Trent continued, "she has light-colored reddish hair and green eyes, so she may be considered 'exotic' down in South America. However, she may also be considered somewhat old, so they may just keep her alive for her medical skills. My guess is that both of them will be transported back across the border."

Michael briefly closed his eyes at the thought of this horrific future for Ethan and Marti. He had heard that the 'shelf life' for sex trafficking victims was fairly short—just a few years—with many ending up dead from countless rapes, sexually transmitted diseases, physical abuse, poor nutrition, depression, and drug overdoses. He was almost crazy with grief imagining their suffering somewhere outside of the United States and far away from help. *Is this really happening?* he asked himself. He didn't even care about what happened to him. He just needed for Marti, Ethan, and the girls to be safe. *Is it really possible that my best friend, Trent, could be capable of all of this?* he lamented. His thoughts further devolved into wondering if Trent had always been this evil but he just never realized it. After a few more minutes of anguish, Michael mentally shook himself and decided to focus on the immediate problem instead of continuing in his panic spiral over what might happen. He needed to be calm if he was going to find a way to save Marti, Ethan, and the girls. If only he could contact Dominic or FBI Agent Reynolds using the cellphone that they gave him…

Trent directed him off of the highway and onto some back roads. After a few more minutes of driving deeper into nowhere, Michael finally saw a few old buildings made of brick. From the outside, they looked like old factories or warehouses, but they appeared to have not been in use for some time, as the grounds were completely overgrown with weeds and the 'For Lease' signs out front were weather-worn. *Well, if you are going to kidnap people, among other crimes, this is probably a great place to locate your business*, Michael thought.

"Pull in over there," Trent ordered, interrupting Michael's thoughts. Michael drove around to the back of one of old warehouses and into the parking space indicated by Trent. Surprisingly, there were a few other cars in the parking lot, including a few expensive models. Very smart. The parking lot was well situated, as it was hidden from view from the main road. From just driving past these buildings, one would never know that anything was going on inside. Trent got out of the car first and kept the gun pointed at Michael as he got out of the car. Michael purposefully made a show of taking some time with his prosthetic limb so that he could sneak the cellphone from Reynolds into his pocket.

As they both started walking toward the warehouse door, Michael took in the whole scene. Looking at the cars in the lot, he shook his head, thinking what a dichotomy it was. A couple of new sleek BMWs, a shiny black Cadillac Escalade, and a new Mercedes-Benz S-Class all parked behind an old, decaying warehouse. As they arrived at the back entrance, Michael saw a large gray windowless van parked a few feet in front of the steps to the doors. He immediately thought of Marti, Ethan, and the girls and wondered if that is how they arrived here. He then wondered how many others had been transported to do God-knows-what in that vehicle of horrors.

Turning his mind back to the present, Michael examined the building. The back entrance appeared to be an old loading dock of some sort, with raised large steel double doors, an old staircase, and a wide side ramp leading down to the parking lot. Like the rest of the building, this entrance had seen its share of years and was badly in need of repair. Trent nudged him in the back with the gun to go up the crumbling stairs, so Michael complied, grabbing onto the rusty handrail with both hands to help him balance with his prosthetic limb. He had to go up one step at a time, placing both feet on the same step before moving onto the next. He heard Trent's laughter behind him when he had to adjust his footing to avoid the uneven places in the stairs where the weeds had grown through the large cracks. While struggling with this task, he marveled at his situation for just a moment: in literally just minutes, he was about to come face-to-face with a drug cartel—not exactly something that you do every day. Silently Michael pondered exactly who and what were waiting inside for him.

At the top of the stairs, Trent ordered Michael to slowly open one of the doors and step inside. They both entered the building, single file, with the gun pointed at Michael's back. It was a large empty concrete room that was most likely used to stockpile and station boxes or freight before being loaded onto the dock. Michael was grateful for the few windows positioned high above the floor that provided a bare minimum amount of light, otherwise they would be walking in total darkness. This was like a horror movie, Michael thought, as their footsteps announced their arrival, echoing loudly in the deafening silence. Just who or what would be out here, in the middle of nowhere, waiting for them? And how long would it be before anyone even located his body afterward?

After many steps through the damp room, Michael approached another set of large double doors and was about to open them, but Trent steered him to the right, into the long hallway that apparently lined up with the perimeter of the parking lot from which they just left. While mostly dark, there were a few bursts of late-afternoon sunlight coming through windows situated every few feet. The damp, pungent smell of the old carpet and the thick coat of dust on the walls spoke of how long the building had not been in use. After a short walk down the empty corridor, they came to a large open office. In sharp contrast with the rest of the building, the office was nicely furnished with a modern desk, laptop computer, new carpeting, fresh paint on the walls, and soft leather couches. The stink and grime from the hallway had been completely removed from this newly refurbished oasis in the filth. Quite a remarkable feat, Michael observed.

Trent gestured with the gun for Michael to enter the office and then take a seat in one of the leather chairs in front of the large picture window. The window was strategic, as it gave a good view of almost the entire back parking lot. It would not be easy to sneak into the building without being noticed. Trent walked up to the large desk and spoke to the young attractive receptionist, seemingly in her early twenties, informing her of their arrival. She was fashionably dressed in a tight-fitting navy-blue skirt and white blouse, and her dark hair was perfectly smoothed into a French twist. She got up from her seat, walked a few steps in her five-inch heels, and knocked on the adjoining door. After hearing a male voice answering "¡*Entre!*" she entered through the door. After a moment, she came back into the office. Smiling, she turned to Trent and asked him to please be seated.

"Please be comfortable for just a few minutes. Señor Alvarez will be with you shortly." She then walked over to the shiny gray granite counter lining the opposite side of the room and lifted up the top of one section, exposing a fully stocked minibar. "Can I get you a drink, Mr. Trent?"

"Sure, Juanita. How about whiskey over ice?" Juanita smiled as she carefully placed two ice cubes into the clear heavy crystal tumbler that she pulled out of the cabinet. After pouring the drink, she walked over to Trent and set it down on the coffee table, along with a cocktail napkin. Michael noticed a lingering glance shared between them and wondered if there was something going on between them.

Trent was obviously used to this place, as he fully relaxed into the soft leather couch, removing his windbreaker jacket and setting down the gun onto the chic glass coffee table in front of him. He let out an audible sigh as he took the first long sip of his drink. Apparently, Trent was very comfortable here and did not feel the need to keep the gun pointed at Michael in this place.

Of course, no drink or any kind of courtesies were shown to Michael, as he had fully expected. After all, he was not here on a social visit. As he looked around the room, he could not help but be impressed with this setup in the middle of nowhere. There were three flat-panel screens mounted on the wall behind Juanita that were showing the output of some security cameras. From what he could see, the cartel was very busy, packing and loading crates on one screen and engaged in various meetings on other screens. Since the building was empty and quiet, Michael wondered just where all of this activity was taking place. He then looked back at Juanita and thought how out of place she too seemed in this old abandoned building. She was very well-dressed, and he was impressed with her English, trying to decide if she was American or not, as he could detect a slight accent but not much.

After a few minutes, a handsome man in his early forties appeared through the door. He too was very well-dressed in black pants, a tailored linen shirt, and a matching sport coat. His trim and exquisitely groomed appearance indicated that he was a man of some means. Of all of his impressive features, his large dark eyes were the most compelling. They missed nothing, quickly scanning the room and assessing everything around him. While his smile gave the appearance that he was relaxed and pleasant, his eyes told a completely different story. This was a man with whom you would never be sure just where you stood, Michael observed. His smile increased as he approached Trent, holding out his arms for an embrace. Trent returned his smile, set down his drink, and stood up. The two hugged each other, and it was obvious that Trent cared for this man. "Trent, my friend, how are you?" the man inquired with a rich, deep voice.

"Doing fine, Luis! How about you?" Trent responded.

"Every day is a blessing," Luis answered. As with Juanita, Michael could only detect a slight accent with his English. "We work hard and then we also play hard. Am I right, my friend?" Luis and Trent shared a laugh together. Luis then indicated to Trent to sit back down on the couch, while Luis sat in the adjoining chair. "So I am gathering that this," he said while pointing to Michael, "is your boss, Mr. Garcia."

"Ex-boss, you mean," answered Trent. "I have only one boss now, and that is you, Luis."

Luis showed his appreciation with another smile. "Very good, Trent. It seems that everything is falling into place now."

"May I introduce you, Luis?"

"But of course, Trent."

Trent gestured to Michael. "Luis, this is the 'famous' Michael Garcia, president and CEO of Garcia Enterprises. Michael, this is Luis Rafael Alvarez, the CEO of our organization."

Luis smiled at Michael; however, the smile did not come close to reaching his cold eyes. Instead, they were focused, examining Michael, measuring him up from his appearance. "I would say that it is nice to meet you, Mr. Garcia, but I am sure that you recognize that these are, uh, challenging circumstances," Luis stated.

Michael smiled back at Luis, also a smile that only involved the lips but nothing else. "'Challenging' is one word to describe it," he answered.

Luis laughed. "I am sure that you have many others that you would gladly substitute for it, but we will leave it with 'challenging.' So you are probably wondering why you are here, Mr. Garcia."

"That thought did run across my mind."

Luis smiled and briefly looked down, adjusting the gold bracelet on his wrist. "It seems that we, that is you and I, are in a bit of a conundrum with respect to some of my property and operations housed in your buildings. You are here because we need to determine the next steps."

"You mean because the police and the FBI are, at this moment, confiscating all of your drugs and weapons stored in my facilities? That was a substantial inventory, Mr. Alvarez, just from the little bit that I saw, so this must be quite a disappointment to you. This must also put a rather large wrench in your prostitution operations too. You will have some unhappy clients to deal with, I imagine."

Luis's eyes narrowed with some controlled hostility behind them.

Michael's eyes were immediately diverted to the abrupt choking sound that Trent had made with his gulp of whiskey. From Trent's face of shock, it was apparent that he had not seen people speak to Luis in this manner before.

"By the way, Mr. Alvarez," Michael continued, "your English is excellent. I barely detect an accent. But, of course, this must come in handy when doing business in the United States."

Luis regained control of his growing anger and pasted a faux smile on his face. "I was educated abroad, in the UK and in other parts of Europe, finally obtaining my degrees from Harvard. My family believes that a well-rounded education is essential for the future of our business, Mr. Garcia. Or can I call you Michael?"

Michael kept his eyes narrowed as he answered, his voice dripping with sarcasm, "Oh, call me Michael, by all means. After all, we have apparently been 'close' business associates for some time now."

Luis laughed loudly at that. "A sense of humor is a useful asset, Michael. Yes, we have been business associates for almost three years now, thanks to Trent here."

Three years, Michael thought to himself. How could he not have known? He looked over at Trent, who was now smugly smiling at him in triumph over his glass of whiskey. Anger pulsed through Michael as he thought of how generous he had been with Trent in terms of job opportunities, lucrative salary and benefits, amazing exposure to the heads of multinational corporations, not to mention his close friendship. He always told Trent that their friendship was not based upon Trent's employment with Garcia Enterprises. If Trent were not happy with his job at Garcia Enterprises, he certainly could have had his pick of opportunities at many other companies. Michael would have gladly given him a stellar job reference and wished him well on his way. Somehow, all of this was just not enough. Trent had thrown all of it away in the worst possible betrayal, including embezzlement and money laundering, soiling the Garcia company name in drug, weapons, and sex trafficking, and two attempts on his life. He knew that he would certainly never trust Trent again. But how about Luis? he thought. Did Luis fully trust Trent? *Could an evil man really ever trust another evil man?* Even in the dark, twisted world of drug cartels, was there a kind of "honor among thieves" code of conduct in which Trent broke a cardinal rule by crossing a best friend as well his employer? he wondered. Maybe it was time to find out.

Michael looked back at Luis and smiled. "Yes, Trent is very resourceful. You will find him to be quite an asset to your 'organization.'" He paused while Luis smiled and nodded his head in agreement. "Speaking of your organization, what kinds of traits do you look for when seeking out new 'employees'?"

Luis seemed a little taken aback by that question but quickly recovered. "That is an interesting question coming from you. Are you considering a career change for yourself?"

Michael laughed. "No, Luis. I am just curious. I have never met anyone in, uhm, your line of work before, so I thought I would take this rare opportunity to ask some questions."

Luis studied Michael for a moment before answering. In his eyes, Michael could see Luis's vast intelligence mixing with touches of evil as he was contemplating his reply. "We are not much different in our hiring qualifications, Michael. We look for education, proficiencies in various operations, but mostly a proven track record of success."

"How about loyalty? Is that important to your organization?" Michael posed. He stole a quick glance at Trent, who was now glaring at him.

Luis laughed again. "It looks like you are making your friend uncomfortable, Michael. But, yes, loyalty is important to us, but not in the way that you mean."

"Enlighten me." Michael was truly curious now.

"Many of our 'employees' joined us in, let's just say, difficult circumstances. We recruit from different villages in Central and South America and even locally from cities in the United States, like your friend Trent. As a policy, employees that are not loyal to us do not typically stay with the organization very long."

You mean that they end up dead. Michael silently read between the lines. He thought of Ynez's boyfriend, Eduardo, and how he was "recruited" with no choice but to join the cartel. He then thought of the victims of their sex trafficking operation—women, young boys and girls. These must also be some of the "employees" that Luis was referring to, he thought with fury. His thoughts couldn't help but drift to Marti, Ethan, and the girls.

"However, we reward our employees very well. Isn't that true, Trent? It looks like you need it right now." Michael watched as Luis dug out a thin package from his sport coat and tossed it to Trent.

"Absolutely, Luis," Trent responded, almost like a trained seal. "There are many great perks with the job," he answered, setting down his whiskey glass and, with sweaty, trembling hands, opened the tiny package, pouring out white powder onto the glass table.

Cocaine. *Of course*, thought Michael. How low his ex-friend had sunk. Never in his life did he imagine he would watch Trent line up some cocaine, get down on his knees, and then snort it right off the table. This was much deeper for Michael than merely watching someone doing drugs; Trent was his best friend, and, for years, Michael had viewed him almost like a younger brother. This was too much to take. Michael felt sick and had to look away. However, his eyes drifted over to Luis, who was regarding Trent with an evil smile, almost like Satan enjoying the downfall of yet another soul. "So is this part of your employee 'loyalty' program?" Michael asked Luis.

Luis quickly glanced away from Trent, who was still occupied with cleaning up his nose, and smiled knowingly at Michael. His refusal to answer the question was all the clarification Michael needed. So, Michael observed, one element of Luis's employment strategy was to make junkies out of his employees. Amazing. If this is how they treat someone they supposedly care about, he didn't want to think about how they treat their enemies. Speaking of enemies, Michael thought, he was probably on that particular list. The knowledge that they were probably going to kill him very soon gave him a strange boldness, so he decided to ask another question that had always fascinated him. "So, Luis, does it bother you at all to do what you do? Smuggling drugs and weapons that end up killing thousands each year, rape, murder, kidnap, and especially the forced prostitution of young women and children? Just curious: Does any of this keep you up at night?"

Luis looked at Michael and laughed. "Michael, I am going to speak to you as a fellow businessman. I do what I do because I am filling a demand for my products and services. And believe me when I tell you that the demand is incredible. In fact, I cannot even come close to supplying enough for all of the demand." Luis's eyes narrowed as he continued, "You sit here filled with self-righteousness and judge me, so now I want you to feel 'patriotic' in knowing that the vast majority of the demand comes from your own countrymen. So you need to shift much of this blame you have placed onto me to them. After all, if there was no demand for my business, I would be out of a job."

"No matter whom you hurt in the process, right? It is just business," Michael retorted. "After all, a publisher may have to kill some trees for the books he sells. You may have to rape and murder some people for the drugs, weapons, and prostitution that you sell. Never mind the horrific and permanent impact on all of the people involved and their families."

"Maybe you should spend more time trying to figure out why such a high demand exists for my products and services, Michael. And it is not just from the lower echelons of society either. So much comes from your pillars of the community—powerful businessmen, celebrities, politicians. From where I am sitting, your countrymen must be pretty empty inside if they need drugs and an evening of entertainment with a young child to fill the void." Luis then turned his attention to his cell phone that he removed from his jacket pocket, clearly done with the conversation.

Sadly, much of what Luis said rang true. While Michael didn't necessarily agree with incarcerating people for a drug habit that was beyond their control, he certainly did for those purchasing the illegal weapons and especially the prostitution from sex trafficking. *Why is it*, he wondered, *that the criminal justice system did not harshly go after the* purchasers *of sex-trafficked prostitution?* It seemed that the only people arrested in these rings were the pimps and traffickers (the suppliers) but almost never the perverted individuals who purchased the services! Just thinking about the all of the corruption made Michael angry and sick. Luis was right: people had to be really empty inside to seek out this kind of stuff. *This has to be what Jesus is all about*, he thought, *filling the empty space with His love and forgiveness so that people would never even consider any of Luis's goods and services.*

Luis then called out to someone back in his office. As Michael was fluent in Spanish, he was able to understand what Trent could not. "It is ready. Bring everything with you—it is time to finalize this operation."

Finalize this operation? That can't be good, Michael reflected. He watched in horror as several men filed into the room, all carrying weapons of various sorts. A couple of men carried briefcases and portfolios of paperwork. He then watched Juanita calmly stand up and gather all of her belongings, including her laptop. Evidently, this had been well planned in advance. Trent was still oblivious on the couch, eyes closed, still enjoying the ride, apparently. He did not notice the men and their weapons, or the fact that they were now being pointing at him and Michael. One of the men reached over and picked up Trent's gun from the glass coffee table. The sound from that motion jarred Trent from his bliss, and he opened his eyes. Michael watched in silence as he witnessed Trent's emotions go from mellow joy to distorted confusion to finally shocking realization of betrayal. Michael knew that Trent would not be able to fully respond with clarity due to the drug-induced haze, but he couldn't help feeling a little sorry for him as Trent was struggling in his confusion. He watched as Trent clumsily stood up, then sat back down, obviously confused as to how to even respond. He was rendered completely speechless and then started to cry.

"Luis! Luis!" Trent finally managed to scream, tears pouring down his cheeks. "I did what you asked! I brought him here!"

Well, this certainly presents the answer regarding evil men and their trust, Michael thought with irony. He observed that Luis's demeanor had changed; apparently, the mask of civility had come off. This time, when Luis looked at Trent, it was with dark indifference, the same way one would view a moldy piece of food when cleaning out the refrigerator.

"Yes, Trent, and I thank you for that. Now you will finally shut up." Luis then gestured to the man closest to Trent. "Please search him and Mr. Garcia." When Luis was satisfied that neither Michael nor Trent was harboring any weapons, he directed the entire group to leave the room. Michael and Trent led the way down a different hallway, followed by the gunmen, and finally by Luis and Juanita. When they arrived at the large steel double doors, they were opened by two armed cartel members dressed in tight-fitting undershirts, baggy jeans, and lots of body tattoos. Now, thought Michael, they must be entering the actual operations of the cartel. Previously, he had been visiting with the executive management.

Nothing could have prepared Michael for the scene when he walked through the doors, at multiple gunpoints. First, there was the overwhelming smell of unwashed bodies mixing with the hot, musty dampness from the room. Next was the horror of seeing the large gathering of people, mostly young women and children, being ordered in Spanish at rifle-point by the numerous cartel thugs strategically placed in the room. Every so often, there was a loud shout and then a quick burst of violence to ensure that the orders were followed. There had to be over a hundred people in the room, babies crying and small children clinging to the nearest adultlike figure. Well, he thought, he had already seen the evidence of the drug and weapons trafficking back at the Garcia Lodge; here now was the human trafficking element. He was aghast at how many people were here, out in the middle of nowhere, suffering greatly, and no one appeared to know about it. Unlike the luxurious offices that he just left, the room was filthy and old, with little to no furniture except for an occasional hard-backed chair in the corners. There was a long metal table set up at the front of the room that looked like it held the remains of some food, but mealtime had apparently ended some time before.

Scanning the room, he could see lines of people slowly leaving the building through the far door that opened directly to the parking lot. The common themes were the dirty faces of the children and the attire of worn clothing. Everyone appeared to be carrying all of their belongings: bags, dirty backpacks, sleeping bags, and old pillows. Despite how feverishly he was looking, he could not locate Marti, Ethan, or the girls in the crowd of people; he had to calm himself down to keep from having a panic attack right in front of everyone. Within the lines of people, there appeared to be two distinct groups: those that were immediately leaving the building, and another group lined up to first receive some kind of pills. Those receiving the pills were dressed in very suggestive clothing and heavy makeup, he observed with revulsion. This group consisted of young boys and girls as well as women in their late teens/early twenties. Apparently, this group was being doped up, most likely with opioids, for another night of prostitution for the cartel. Michael frantically scanned this line and actually felt guilty for being relieved that he did not see Marti, Ethan, or the girls. Looking around the crowded room, Michael noticed that most of the people in the room were looking down, avoiding any eye contact with anyone, their despair written all over their faces. *So this is what it is like to be kidnapped, held indefinitely against your will,* he thought. His heart sank in his chest as he could actually feel the intense hopelessness radiating off of the people.

    Luis entered the room and asked one of the cartel thugs how long it would be to get everyone loaded onto the trucks. The thug informed that it would take about fifteen minutes at most. Michael watched as Luis looked at his expensive wristwatch to get a gauge on the time left. Luis then instructed the apparent leader of the cartel thugs to give the "evening workers" the priority for loading and transportation. This instruction was then passed down, and the lines of people out the door were adjusted. Michael had to admit that there was a high degree of efficiency in this exercise, considering the volume of unwilling people, including small children and babies.

    Michael was still trying to locate Marti, Ethan, and the girls when he heard some shouts coming from the door leading to the parking lot. Three cartel thugs were dragging a fourth thug into the room from the outside. It was apparent that the three thugs had severely beaten the fourth as his T-shirt was covered with the blood

HELP AMONG US

that was still dripping from his nose and mouth. Both of his eyes were bruised shut, and he was barely able to stand up. With one more kick to his back, he fell to the ground and did not move. Luis walked over and questioned the three about the man on the ground. From what Michael could overhear, the fourth thug had attempted multiple times to sneak back into the building instead of getting onto the truck with the others. Luis looked at the man on the ground with disgust. "Let him stay here with the others, then. He will get what he deserves," Luis answered. Michael was curious about this man because he was not covered with all of the normal body tattoos like the other cartel thugs. Why, thought Michael, would anyone try to sneak back into the building? It was a foregone conclusion that everyone left in the building was going to die in some fashion. Michael pondered this a bit longer while also scanning the room for his friends.

After most of the people had left the building, Michael finally had visibility to the back of the room. And then he saw them. His heart leaped for joy that Marti, Ethan, and the girls were still alive! "Thank you, God!" he whispered. Then, after the initial joy ebbed, he wondered why they were not joining the others in the lines leaving the building. Truthfully speaking, neither scenario was good. He was still trying to decide if remaining here was the worse choice when he heard Trent pleading for his life with Luis.

"But what about all of the money I owe you? Just give me more time, and I will make everything worth it to you."

"Trent, what about the significant amount of money that we have also lost because of your incompetence? You couldn't even handle a simple murder," Luis gestured over to Michael. "All of the drugs and weapons that were stored in the Garcia Lodge are now in the hands of your federal law enforcement. Tell me, Trent, you are in the investment business. Would you ever advise a client to throw *more* good money after bad into an investment that is collapsing? No, Trent, I am a businessman, and I have to carefully consider all of my decisions. Unfortunately, the order to kill you came from the top back in Mexico, and I happen to agree with it. In fact," Luis gestured widely to the remaining group of people left, "everyone left in this room will serve a purpose today by being a harsh example of the consequences for upsetting our organization." Michael's eyes widened with the realization that they were all going to die. Not that this was a complete surprise—he guessed it already—but to have it actually stated out loud cemented the prospect.

Trent, unfortunately, was having trouble accepting all of this. "But where are you going to store your merchandise and house your 'evenings of pleasure' with the wealthy businessmen who have traveled to get here? The Garcia Lodge has been very profitable for you in the past. I have other connections! I can find another place for you! Dammit, you need me!" Trent railed, sweat beads dripping down both sides of his face.

Luis just laughed and then his entourage joined in the laughter on cue. "Trent, *mi amigo*, did you really think that I was stupid enough to have just one source for all of my business in this wonderfully large city? I have multiple contacts and locations already working for me here in Chicago, so, really, I do not need you at all." At that, Luis signaled to his men that it was time to leave. "Farewell, Trent." He started to exit the door before his men but paused to add another thought. "Oh, I wouldn't attempt to open any of the doors in this building, as that will trigger the bomb to immediately go off."

There was a collective gasp in the room. "Bomb?" Trent screamed. "You placed a bomb in here?"

Michael quickly looked over at Marti and Ethan, who were looking back at him, in shock from the news.

"Yes," Luis calmly answered, notably bored with the conversation at this point. "We will detonate it from the car when we are far enough away from here, unless of course, you do it sooner. It saves bullets and removes evidence of our being here. After all"—Luis gestured to the remaining people left in the room—"we can't take everyone to the new location, so this is really the cleanest solution. But don't worry, Trent, you won't die alone. I believe you know a few more of the people here. I would like to say that it was a pleasure working with you, Trent, but, honestly, you were not really meant for this line of work. Your cocaine habit and general nervousness interfered with your ability to really do much for us. However, since I am a generous man by nature, I left a gun for you somewhere in this room with two bullets loaded in the clip. You can decide what to do with it after you find it. Maybe you can finally succeed in killing Michael this time and, if you have the courage, yourself before the bomb goes off. Well, adios, my friend." With that, Luis and his entourage turned and left. It was only a few seconds before they heard an audible beep coming from each of the two doors, indicating that the door detonation had just been turned on.

CHAPTER 36

Cynthia opened the door and let Gus in, filling him in on the news regarding Trent as they walked to the kitchen to join the others. "I do not have a good feeling about this, Gus. Something is telling me that Michael could be in real danger now." When they arrived, they saw Paul hanging up the phone in frustration.

"I still can't get Detective Jenkins, Reynolds, or Dominic on the phone. It keeps going to their voice mails. We need to get extra security around Michael as soon as possible."

Almost as if on cue, the phone rang. Maria answered, "Hello?" There was a momentary pause and then her eyes suddenly widened as she said, "Hang on, Dominic, while I put you on speakerphone. I have Cynthia, Dr. Sherman, and Gus here with me."

"Do you have any idea why Michael drove way the heck out of town right now?" Dominic said with urgency in his voice.

"What? He just dropped off Trent Wentworth at the racquetball tournament downtown. He told us not thirty minutes ago that he was on his way back here," Cynthia answered.

"Michael is with Trent?" Reynolds replied. "That is not good news as both the police and the feds have been trying to locate Trent all day. And, according to the GPS that we installed in the disposable cell phone we gave him, Michael appears to be at some kind of abandoned warehouse on the outskirts of the city. We have been tracking him for almost an hour and are nearly there now. Add to this the fact that we still haven't yet located Marti, Ethan, and the girls. Our suspicion is that this warehouse is a cartel hideout and they may also be there."

"This sounds really bad, Dominic, and I doubt that Michael's arrival at the warehouse is merely a coincidence," Paul said as his eyes met Maria's across the table. The deeply concerned look on her face matched his own.

"We don't believe in coincidences." Detective Jenkins added, "Which is why we have already called for backup."

"Oh, so you already have your suspicions about Trent," Cynthia stated, very relieved. "We have our own and think that he may have been involved with the attempt on Michael's life."

"We are way ahead of you on this," Reynolds chimed in. "Mr. Wentworth has been on our radar as his fingerprints were found all over the Lodge on many of the drug and weapons packages. We have also linked him to some illegal transactions made on behalf of Garcia Enterprises. Additionally, now that the Lodge is in possession of the feds, we figure that Trent is out of a job with the cartel and is likely to take revenge on Michael for ruining everything." There was a brief pause during which the voices coming over the phone could not be understood. "Sorry, everyone, but we have arrived near the warehouse and have to go check out the scene. We will call you when we know more." With that, Reynolds ended the call.

"How best can we help them?" Maria asked the other guardians in a soft voice.

"And how can we transport to where they are without knowing the address?" Paul asked.

"We need for Michael to pray," Gus answered. There was a silent moment when everyone looked at each other. "Once he prays, we can transport to his location."

"Do you think he will? I'm worried that we will be too late to help," Maria asked.

"It is up to Michael to finally put his trust in the Lord and pray for help. This is where it gets serious, folks. We can't do this for him. And remember, once we transport, we will have to remain hidden from all human vision because there is no possible explanation for our presence. Upon our arrival, we can channel and guide more help from heaven above."

"You mean we can call for angels, right?" Lexy asked.

"Exactly. But we are limited in what we can do until Michael prays for help."

With that, everyone closed their eyes, grabbed hands, and began fervently praying that Michael would finally turn to God for help.

Chapter 37

Once the warehouse door closed after Luis and his entourage, Trent began a frantic search for the gun at the front of the room. Michael wasted no time, running to Marti and Ethan, who were also rushing to get to him. They all grabbed each other and hugged, tears streaming down their faces. After the quick moment of happiness in finding them alive, Michael got a somber look on his face and quietly spoke, "I don't know what to say. I am so, so sorry for getting you both involved in all of this. Neither of you deserved any of this, and now it seems," he was choking on his words, "that we are going to meet our end here very soon."

Marti grabbed Michael's face with both hands, despite the painful plastic zip tie around her wrists. "I really don't care about any of that right now," she whispered urgently. "What I do care about is *you*. Are you prepared to die, Michael?"

Michael shook his head in confusion. "What are you talking about?"

"I am talking about your soul, Michael. Please, we only have a few minutes at most. Where do you want to be after death? This is what faith all boils down to, *choosing* to put your trust and love in Jesus even and especially when you are looking death in the face. Again, I ask you: Are you prepared to die?"

Michael's eyes filled with tears as the realization of what she was saying blazed through him. "No, Marti. Help me! I want to be in heaven with you, Ethan, my family, and Jesus, but I've done so many terrible things. I've hurt so many people. I don't deserve to be there."

Marti took his hand as she answered, "The good news is that you don't have to deserve God's forgiveness to receive it. None of us deserves it, Michael, or can even be 'good enough' to earn it. This is a gift, Michael. The best gift you have ever been given. Jesus freely chose to die in your place so that you and all of us can be saved."

"What do I say to be saved?"

Marti smiled as she spoke, "Repeat this prayer after me: Jesus, I am sorry. Please forgive me for all my sins. I believe that you died for me and were resurrected from the dead. I accept you as my Lord and Savior, and I choose to follow you for the rest of my life. Amen." Michael closed his eyes and prayed, repeating the words. He never meant anything more in his life. By the end of the prayer, he suddenly felt a strange, beautiful peace. He opened his eyes to find Marti smiling through her tears at him. He didn't even realize how much he had been crying because of the new joy he was feeling.

"This is crazy, Marti! Why are we smiling right now when we could be blown up at any second?" he asked her in utter amazement.

"We are experiencing the true peace and joy that *only* comes from Jesus. You cannot find this anywhere in the world, Michael, only in Jesus! This is why the apostles happily went to their deaths in order to spread the news about His resurrection and salvation. For believers, death is no longer something to fear when you know you will be with Jesus forever. And you are SAVED now, Michael! Praise God!"

Michael looked over at Ethan, who was also grinning at him. "Praise God!" Ethan whispered. "Welcome to God's family!"

Michael had been so engrossed with the last few minutes that he did not even notice that Ynez was sitting on the ground, cradling the head of the beaten fourth thug in her lap. She was crying but also smiling and gently placing a few kisses on his cheek. When Michael looked at the man's face, he too was crying and smiling. Michael finally put it together—this must be Eduardo. Marti confirmed it and then quickly told Michael how Eduardo had helped them earlier. Michael's heart swelled with admiration; Eduardo had chosen to die now with Ynez.

After only a few minutes, Trent found the gun duct-taped underneath one of the food buckets on the serving table. He checked the clip and verified that there were two bullets left for him. He paused for a moment and then let out a strange, evil-sounding laugh.

HELP AMONG US

He turned, gun in hand, to look at the remaining victims in the room and then smiled as he walked toward Michael, Marti, Ethan, the girls, and Eduardo. "Isn't it ironic, Michael?" he sneered. "Both of us appear to have been caught in our own traps. You are in this room now because you stupidly got your doctor girlfriend involved by raiding our storage facility at the Lodge, alerting the feds about it, and then attempting to help the two trafficked girls escape from the cartel. I am here because the Garcia Lodge can no longer be used, and now the cartel needs to cover their tracks." He briefly paused, reflecting, "Also, because I was not able to kill you, Michael, even after two tries." Michael inwardly flinched at that statement. Trent was now staring at the gun, almost mesmerized by it. His smile decayed to a frown, and he appeared grieved when he softly added, "Did you know that an inability to kill is considered a major sign of weakness in the cartel world? It forever marked me as a failure." Michael watched the tears that began to slide down Trent's face. "I was a failure to my parents too. No matter what I did, it was never good enough. All I ever wanted was to be the best at something," Trent stated. "But there was always someone in my way, someone who was always better than I was. For most of my adult life, that person was you, Michael."

"I never meant to make you feel that way, Trent," Michael responded, filled with sadness at Trent's confession. "Why did you never tell me?"

"Shut up!" Trent roared, waving the gun wildly. "I always lived in your shadow, Michael. Everyone always paid attention to you—never to me! You were *so* smart, *so* good-looking, *so* successful. You never bothered to notice or care how this affected me, so don't pretend to feel anything for me now! You only cared about yourself, which was why it didn't bother me to steal from your company all these years," Trent raved. Michael noticed that Trent's finger was *again* on the trigger while he gestured crazily with the gun. "You ruined my life, Michael! You and your stinking company can both go to hell!" Trent must have not realized how he held the gun because he screamed when it went off, blowing out one of the windows behind and above Michael.

Suddenly, there were shouts and banging on the warehouse door that opened directly to the parking lot. "This is the police! Stand back, put your weapons down. We are coming in!"

Michael recognized Detective Jenkins's voice and yelled "No! Don't open the door! It will trigger a bomb!" Everyone inside held their breath while they waited for the door to be broken down, terrified that the police did not understand what they were saying. After two minutes, which seemed like an eternity for the group inside, a rifle shoved its way through the blown-out window above them.

"Everyone, put your hands up where we can see them!" a loud voice from behind the window reverberated. "SWAT is coming in and will fire at anything that moves!"

This was the final straw for Trent, as he realized that there was a possibility of a successful rescue. "No! I decide how this goes down!" The group watched as Trent sunk further into madness. "Since you ruined my life, Michael, I will ruin what is left of yours!" Everyone watched in horror as Trent moved the gun from pointing at Michael to now being aimed at Marti.

The scene played out in slow motion for Michael. The split second that he saw the gun pointing at Marti's head, he jumped into action. He remembered what Dominic said about Jesus dying for him and also what Jesus said about love and giving one's life for one's friends. *Please, Jesus, I love her. Let me take her place*, he thought as he shoved her down onto the floor. He watched the bullet shoot through the air, and he moved his body into position to catch it, to block it from going into Marti. He felt the bullet rip through him as he fell to the floor.

As he lay on the ground for what seemed like long minutes, he became aware that the voices screaming his name grew softer, muted like a faraway echo. Strangely, the fierce pain in his chest finally subsided, and his breathing returned to normal. Sitting up, he checked his ribs and back and felt well enough to stand up. What he saw almost knocked him back to the ground. SWAT team members had poured through the high broken window and were helping people up the ladder to safety. Those on the ground had their weapons pointed at Trent. However, Trent no longer looked like the Trent he knew; there was a strange darkness emanating from him, engulfing him. The dark circles under his eyes had grown to completely cover most of his face. But the most disturbing thing of all were the menacing creatures surrounding Trent. Michael tried to count them: ten, eleven, but he couldn't see them clearly as they were all swirling together in a thick dark cloud. As the cloud circled around Trent, Michael could occasionally make out shapes that looked like heads and bodies. However, their most frightening feature were their sinister eyes that seemed to burn into Michael whenever one of them looked in his direction. These eyes held an ancient knowledge and already seemed to know him intimately. It was as if they were piercing his very soul and could see every evil thought and deed that Michael had ever committed. The longer he held the gaze of one of the creatures, the deeper the burning sensation cut into him. Michael had to finally close his eyes to break contact as the waves of burning, intense shame and nausea fiercely rose up within him. *How can Trent stand this?* he wondered. Michael had never been in the presence of pure evil before, so he was stunned by the scene playing out in front of him.

Michael watched as one of the SWAT team members yelled at Trent, ordering him to drop his weapon. Michael screamed to the SWAT officer that Trent was out of bullets, but no one could hear him in all of the chaos. Michael could sense that Trent was struggling with what to do next, that part of him wanted to comply with the officer and put down the gun. However, it was in that moment of Trent's indecision that Michael witnessed the creatures moving in closer to Trent, putting their mouths up to his ears and whispering to him in sharp hisses. Trent stared straight ahead, mesmerized by what the creatures were saying to him, and his face began to harden into an evil sneer. Michael screamed, "No, stop!" as he watched Trent move his arm and point his empty weapon at the officer. Michael dropped to his knees as he watched the bullets tear through Trent and knock him to the ground.

As Michael was scrambling to get to Trent's lifeless body, part of the darkness around Trent immediately shot out, violently picking Michael up by the neck and throwing him back and onto the floor.

The darkness then formed into a large wall and deliberately lingered right over Michael, the energy inside emitting a deafening roar like a freight train. From the middle of the wall, Michael could make out the shape of a large face. Suddenly, the creature's eyes opened, locking into Michael's gaze. They were hot and full of hate, piercing and burning deeper, deeper into Michael. Completely immobilized with searing, painful shame coursing throughout his body, Michael silently began to pray over and over again: *Please, Holy Spirit, please rescue me from this evil.* It barely took a minute of prayer, but Michael heard it before he could see it. The sound of a powerful wind tore through the room and released its full, explosive force on the darkness above Michael. The cloud creature shrieked in an earsplitting roar as it was blown apart and backward from the blast. "Trent is OURS!" the creature hissed loudly at Michael and then rejoined the others encircling Trent. Instantly Michael was freed from the pain and shame. As he lay on the ground recovering, the feeling of peace began to fill him again. This peace was beautiful, pure, unlike any other peace he had ever felt. Another feeling also began to fill him—love. He closed his eyes briefly to fully absorb these feelings and didn't want to let them go. *Thank you, God, for loving and rescuing me*, he prayed. Finally, he opened his eyes and sat up, suddenly remembering where he was. He looked over at Trent who was still on the ground, the dark cloud growing as it circled around him.

    After a minute, Trent appeared to recover as he sat up, checked himself, and looked over at Michael, apparently confused by what was happening. Michael called out to him but could only watch in horror as Trent took his first look at the creatures surrounding him. Trent's screams of terror filled the air as two of the many creatures viciously hoisted him up onto his feet, laughing with eerie delight at their work. Michael stood up and watched helplessly as the creatures completely engulfed Trent into the cloud, his body completely disappearing into the darkness. All Michael could hear were Trent's screams and the violent, shrilling laughter of the creatures as the cloud rose high into the air and then suddenly vanished.

    Michael was still trying to process the vanishing darkness and Trent when he heard a voice calling his name.

HELP AMONG US

"Michael! Are you all right, son?" Michael turned around and saw Gus approaching him.

"Gus?" Michael asked. "What are you doing here?"

He looked past Gus and saw Maria, Lexy, and Dr. Sherman also walking toward him. Okay, now he was really confused. He looked around the warehouse and could still see Marti, Ethan, and the girls being helped up the ladder to get outside. He also saw members of the SWAT team, FBI, police force, and what appeared to be a bomb squad working the area. Looking back at Gus, he repeated his question, "How did you all possibly get in here?"

"The answer to that question is a little complicated. The fastest way for me to help you understand is to have you look over there." Gus pointed to the newly vacated area near the back wall. There were two bodies lying on the ground; they resembled him and Trent. Two EMS responders were squatting over Michael's body, quickly preparing him to be placed onto a stretcher. Another responder was unfolding a body bag next to Trent's remains.

"Wait! Is that me?" Michael asked, running his hands over his face, chest, and arms, searching for any signs of injury but not finding any. Realization finally hit, and he looked back at Gus. "I am dead, right?"

Gus paused a second before speaking. "Well, technically no, but your soul has left your body. If you were dead, you would be getting processed in heaven right now. Since you are still down here on earth, that means that a final decision has not been made for you yet."

"So if I am out of my body, how is it that I can talk to you? No one else in the warehouse appears to see or hear me," Michael asked, still very confused. "Hold on! You are all outside of your bodies too?"

Gus smiled. "That is correct. We are your guardians, Michael. Sort of like what you think of as a guardian angel, but we are not angels. Our job is to help guide you in the right direction, to God, while you are alive on earth."

"But what happened to Trent? Who were those creatures surrounding him?"

Gus shook his head in sadness. "Trent is lost, my friend. He was under the influence of some very dark and dangerous demons. Now understand this, Michael: he *chose* to listen to them and made disastrous decisions. All attempts to help him find his way to God were not successful, and unfortunately, he did not make it to heaven." Gus then took a look at Michael, specifically at the bright glow from his inner light, and smiled. "But you should be feeling well right now, Michael."

"Yeah, you are right." Michael smiled back. "I have this amazing sense of joy and peace."

"Being filled with the Holy Spirit will do that."

"Yes, it rescued me from one of those demons. I called out, and it rescued me."

"God rescued you, you mean. The Holy Spirit, part of the Trinity, is our protector, comforter, teacher, and guide on earth." Gus smiled. "But before we continue this conversation any further, there are some people you should meet." Gus pulled out his transformer device and pressed a few buttons. Michael watched as Dr. Sherman, Mrs. Flaherty, and Jackie Flaherty were turned back into his family, Paul, Maria, and Lexy. Michael gasped in shock and started to drop to his knees, but his father, Paul, reached him and pulled him into an embrace. Michael didn't even realize that he was crying when his mother and Lexy joined them in a big family hug. Michael pulled back and looked at each one of them, his eyes feasting on the sight of his family.

"I can't believe it! You look exactly as you did the last time I saw you!" He laughed through his tears as he tugged at Lexy's long ponytail. "You are even wearing the clothes you were wearing!" He paused for a moment and then laughed. "Well," he said, looking right at Lexy, "that explains all of the animals in my penthouse!"

Maria grabbed Michael for another hug. "We missed you too, *mi Miguelito*!"

Looking back at Gus, Michael posed another question. "How was it that you all were with me when I was alive? And why?"

"There will be lots of time for these and all of your other questions later. First we need to get the final decision about your status." Gus pulled out another device that looked like a cell phone. He punched in a couple of numbers, turned away from the group, and began speaking into the phone. Just then, Cynthia appeared and walked toward the group.

"Hey, Cynthia!" Paul spoke, motioning her to join them. "How did your assignment go?"

"It has been successfully taken care of," Cynthia answered with a gleam in her eye. She smiled and gave Michael a hug. "Hi, Michael! It is good to see you reunited with your family."

Michael didn't think that he could take many more surprises. "Cynthia, you too?"

Cynthia grinned. "Yup! I was assigned to you quite a while ago." She motioned to his family. "These rookies joined me just a few earth-months ago," she continued in a more serious tone. "It is really a good thing that you prayed when you did, Michael. We barely got here in time to help. Unfortunately, we were too late to help prevent Trent from shooting you, but we were able to stop Luis from detonating the bomb. And speaking of that, Michael, that was incredibly brave and beautiful what you did. You should have heard the loud cheers of celebration from everyone in heaven when you gave your life to save Marti."

Before Michael could ask yet another question, Paul jumped in, "So, Cynthia, what happened? How did you stop Luis from detonating the bomb?"

"Let's just say that it is no longer possible to remotely detonate the bomb. The fire department is putting out the fire on what is left of their car right now."

"Solo accident?" Paul asked.

"Yes," Cynthia responded. "The angel made sure that no other vehicle was involved in the crash. It will look like Luis's driver was texting while driving and went off the road."

"Angels?" Michael asked. "They are real?"

Gus smiled as he rejoined the group. *So predictable. Same questions every time with humans*, he laughed to himself. "Yes, Michael, they are real." He put his hand up, blocking more questions from Michael. He looked at the group and paused before continuing. "I just spoke with Arrivals. It looks like Michael has been given quite a gift. The decision will be made by Michael himself."

"What decision?" Michael asked.

"The decision to come with us to heaven or to return back to earth. But you must decide right now."

Michael looked at the family that he missed so much. He then thought about Marti, Dominic, Ethan, and the girls; he loved them too. How could he possibly choose? "I am not sure that this is a gift since I want to be in both places. On earth, I finally found someone that I could love and marry. Now that I have Jesus in my life, I would like a chance to turn my life around and help others, starting with Ethan, Ynez, Sofia, Eduardo, and Melissa. However, in heaven, I have my family again. And I have never before felt such a depth of peace, joy, and love as I do here with you. It feels fantastic to have the weight of all of my problems lifted away."

"May I help you with this?" Paul asked. "All that you are feeling is from God, Michael. You can certainly feel these on earth, just not as strong. Outside of your human body, however, you can finally feel the full impact of His love without any human distractions getting in the way." He thought for another moment and then continued, "I want you to consider something for me. If you return to your life back on earth, everything here, including us, will be waiting for you. On earth, you have the chance to make a difference in the lives of other people and bring them to accept Jesus."

"It sounds like you are convincing me to go back," Michael said.

"I guess it does. I just know that I would have loved to have had more time to do the things that really matter—to serve Jesus by helping others."

"That is kind of how I feel too, Dad. I want to live better. I want to help others. Gus, how much of this will I remember when I go back?"

Gus smiled. "I was hoping that would be your decision. And as far as what you will remember, that is up to God."

"Well," Michael laughed, "it may not matter anyway. People will think that I am crazy if I told them."

"Then you will be in excellent company. Remember just how many of God's servants were not believed, including *His own Son*."

CHAPTER 38

The doors of the church finally opened, and Michael was free at last. It was the longest hour and a half of his life, he thought to himself. Especially the sermon—he thought it would never end. As he began collecting his belongings, Dominic walked up to him and slapped him hard on the back, projecting him a bit forward, as always.

"Great job, Michael!" Dominic exclaimed. "But you need to remember to relax a little bit before you begin. It started off like some kind of business presentation. But, once you got going, you moved everyone, including me!"

"Yes, Michael, great job!" Keisha exclaimed.

"Thanks," Michael stated, clearly relieved that the ordeal of delivering his first sermon was over. "I still have to get used to a different kind of delivery than I have at work and at press conferences. But I am working on that in my night classes at seminary school."

This is incredible, Michael reflected for a minute. If anyone had told him three years ago that he would be preaching a sermon in church, he would have laughed that person out of the room. But here he was, working toward his goal of becoming an associate pastor at his church. So much had happened in that last three years: he went through months of physical therapy (again!) for the nearly fatal gunshot wound that miraculously did not kill him; he married Marti and then adopted both Ethan and Sofia. They were now working on the paperwork to officially sponsor both Eduardo and Ynez in the United States legally. Both wanted to pursue careers in medicine, Eduardo as a doctor and Ynez as a nurse, so Marti and Michael were making this happen for them. He looked over at Marti, who was struggling a bit to get out of the pew. Being seven months pregnant with their twins was definitely slowing her down a bit. Their other two children, Ethan and Sofia, were running up to him, exclaiming their delight in having their dad deliver the sermon.

"Well done, Daddy!" Ethan shouted. "I think that they liked all the pictures of the comets, supernovas, and neighboring galaxies that we put together. Next time, we will include some surface photos of Jupiter and Mars to help bring home your point."

Sofia added her critique, the best that little girl could provide. "I love you, Papa!" Her English was improving every day. He picked her up, hugged Ethan, and waited for Marti to waddle down to meet them.

"Nice job, honey!" Marti exclaimed. "I guess we should go out and mingle with everyone outside. They are waiting to compliment the preacher man!"

"We will see how many people believe that I am completely nuts after that sermon," Michael laughed and grabbed her hand.

"Well, you are, but we still love you!" Marti laughed.

Together, they all walked out of the church. For the first time in his life, he felt complete. He had the joys of true friendship, family, purpose, and the love of God. Life truly was amazing if you just place your trust in Jesus.

*****

"Very good, Michael," said Gus out loud. Maria, Paul, and Lexy were watching the screen with Gus; they were just checking in to see how Michael was doing on earth.

"Looks like he is on track now to start helping others," Paul observed. "Thank you, Gus, for helping us to help Michael. It means more than you know."

Gus blushed. "It was my pleasure." He then switched the screen to show another human. "Looks like we have our work cut out for us with this one, so please open your guardian assignment books.

"Sorry, Gus, just a quick question before we start working again," Paul interrupted. "We have been asking many things about ourselves, but we want to know a little more about you. Down on earth, when you were a human, did you have any guardians?"

Gus paused and then laughed. "Quite a few, in fact. God love them!"

"Really?" Maria and Paul spoke at once.

Gus looked a bit sheepish with his reply, "My, uhm, early life was a bit on the wild side, you might say." Gus then answered his phone, which had been ringing. After a moment of conversation, he excused himself from the room for a moment.

Lou, their navigator, had stopped by to see how everyone was doing and had been listening to the conversation with interest. "You do know who Gus is, don't you?" he asked them.

Maria and Paul looked at each other in some confusion and then looked back at Lou. "Well, I guess we don't, since you put it that way!" laughed Paul. "From his inner light, I could tell that he has been around for quite a long time, but I never took the time to read that far back."

Lou smiled. "Our friend 'Gus' is also known by his longer name, Aurelius Augustinus. But you probably know him by his other earthly name, Saint Augustine."

Maria and Paul laughed with their amazement. "Seriously? Well, that certainly puts a new spin on the expression 'Saints preserve us!'" Paul responded.

Gus reentered the room. "Okay, okay. Enough about me! We have some work to do, if you don't mind."

With that, the group bowed their heads in prayer to the Lord, giving thanks and praise for His eternal goodness and love.

ABOUT THE AUTHOR

Ginia Falcón spent almost thirty years working in corporate America. She is now a functional nutrition lifestyle practitioner and a mind body eating coach. She enjoys cooking, fitness, meditating, reading, being in nature, and spending time with her family and friends.

Printed in the USA
CPSIA information can be obtained
at www.ICGtesting.com
CBHW030446021024
15219CB00027B/349

9 798887 314792